KING PAWN

ANITA RENAGHAN

Cover Design by Denise Collie www.deedesign.com

©2017 by Anita Renaghan

anitarenaghan.com

Kitchen Entertainment

ISBN-13: 978-0-9838700-7-4

Thank you to my family and friends who support me and help in editing my work, including Mom, Denise Collie, Jennie O'Malley, DD Call, Lia Caton, and Pam Gould.

DEDICATION

This book is for Paige Collie. Thank you for your encouragement and for telling me to write faster.

Chapter 1
Your Highness

Avalon knew Taggerty would be here any second, she had seen it in her dream, but the knowing hardly kept her calm. He had been gone for almost four months, and she tried to keep the anticipation from showing on her face. Avalon's heart rose in her chest as she remembered the curl of his dark hair, and how his knowing eyes took in a room, and how he'd taken her hand in his and kissed her fingers. She allowed herself to believe the romance for another short moment before letting in the disappointing truth. Taggerty hadn't kissed her fingers with love in his heart. Like everyone else, he thought she was a boy. He'd knelt in front of his newly crowned king with the rest of the King's Guard and the Council, and he'd kissed the king's ring to show his loyalty.

It had been eight months since her coronation, and for the last three months, Avalon had watched the dark horizon each night looking for a small sign of a campfire. She concentrated especially hard on the past three nights watching for any indication of Taggerty's return even though she had known it would be on this night. She had dreamed their meeting tonight at her birthday celebration. Avalon had never dreamt of something so seemingly insignificant, but she knew it had to come true. When she had a dream, it always came true. The first time she had seen the future in a dream, she had fallen down the stairs and broken her leg. The last time she had dreamt of Counselor Glenn's treason, and of him slicing her stomach open with his sword. Those were big events in her life, but for her to have such a random dream of her future, a dream of Taggerty's return, that was significant in itself. She had turned the dream over and over in her mind, but Taggerty was all she could see. She didn't know the outward substance of the message, but she knew it was meant for her.

Avalon was relieved that he had made it back safe from his outing. It meant that her first command as king, to banish her traitor uncle, was complete. It meant that he had left her Uncle Hawker out in the forest to fend for himself. It meant that Taggerty had survived the harsh winter in the wild and had found his way back to Fontanasia. It meant that Taggerty was back in her life, and it also meant torture because she couldn't tell him how she felt. She reached up instinctively and felt the cut of short hair on the back of her neck. She was a girl, but no one knew that. She was King Avalon Hall of Fontanasia.

Avalon felt the jealousy creep back in when she remembered that Taggerty would return this evening and seek out her sister, Princess Zaria, instead of his king. She had seen in her dream the way her sister had crossed to the entrance of the hall at the exact moment Taggerty had arrived, and the simple pleasure on both of their faces at meeting again after his long excursion. In Avalon's dream, it was apparent that Zaria knew Taggerty was back in Fontanasia. She too had been watching for him all evening.

The joy turned to angst again and Avalon looked away from the horizon and tried to stop her thoughts. She closed her eyes and breathed deeply, squashing her feelings. She had a duty to perform for her people. She was King Hall, and that was all that mattered.

She was in her bedroom in the king's suite, not yet ready to move into her father's room. As king, it was her room now as it had been her father's and her grandfather's before her. It had been less than a year since her father's death, and Avalon was still not able to accept that he was gone forever. She cleared her throat and straightened her indigo jacket. The motion caused her tiny, red jakkow lizard to scramble out of his case and race expectantly to the edge of the table. Avalon had received the jakkow as a gift from the Guides at her birthday exactly one year ago this day. Receiving him was the first in a series of events that had changed her entire life. She shook the thoughts from her head and tried to concentrate on the evening before her. She was dressed elegantly tonight, and her pet waited patiently as she stood straight and flattened her collar, but she did not put her hand to the table and let him crawl into her pocket.

"Not tonight, Jackie," Avalon said dismissively before walking out of her room and through the living space to the front of the suite. She cleared her throat, and the two members of the King's Guard posted at the open door stood taller. Wordlessly, they followed King Avalon down to the Hall of Kings. She paused outside the room while trumpets announced her arrival, and the entire room of guests bowed as she stepped into view at the top of the stairs. She saw her sister who had been waiting for her. Princess Zaria was the belle of the ball, and she had been on hand to greet all of the guests. Without meeting her eye, Avalon waited as her taller sister took her arm.

Avalon didn't need to take in her sister's attire. She knew that Zaria wore the most elegant dress and would turn the most heads this evening. They moved down the stairs gracefully, all royalty and pride. Avalon walked smugly through the crowd. She was fifteen years old and as king, all eyes were on her. When she reached the stone riser that held the king's throne, she released Zaria's arm and turned back to the guests. She signaled with her hand that they should rise. Then she turned her head to the conductor and raised her eyebrows, and the large band began to play.

Avalon felt a stab in her gut when she looked back at the empty throne, and a pang of guilt stung her heart when she thought about sitting in her father's place. She didn't cry every night anymore, but she still felt the empty ache left in the wake of her father's death. Avalon felt Zaria's discreet squeeze of the wrist. She needed to talk to her sister, but when her eyes met Zaria's, they both looked away quickly. Avalon had distanced herself from everyone since she had returned from Cormicks, and she felt alone in her plight. Avalon was the King of Fontanasia, and in that, she could relate to no one, not even her sister Zaria.

Being king was not a simple task. Avalon had to sit through all sorts of accounts on the people of Fontanasia, reports on any serious illnesses they would be watching in case of spreading disease, and she had to listen to reports of the food stores. She also had to come to the ball that Zaria had thrown for her birthday whether she wanted to or not, and she would be forced to meet all of the young women who would be paraded in front of her, their parents hoping that their daughter would be the next queen. Avalon tried to pretend that each of these girls was Zaria, which made it easier to be cordial when they bowed in presentation, but she was raised a boy from the day she was born and could find no redeeming qualities in the efforts girls made to try to get attention. The primping, preening, and fussing seemed all too fake for the treacherous world that had revealed itself to Avalon just before she was crowned king.

Avalon could see Counselor Robert's bald head bobbing above the crowd. His white dome tipped down often as he greeted the guests. He was warm and genuine, and every few minutes he would look toward Avalon. He had become a close advisor to Avalon since she had inherited the throne, and although no one could replace her father, Robert gave her the comfort of an old friend. She had known him all her life, and he had always been very sincere toward her.

"King Hall, happy birthday," Counselor Robert said in a bow when he finally made it to the dais. His decadently dressed wife curtsied deeply as Avalon winced at the greeting. Her father was King Hall, and she was sure that she would never get used to people addressing her as such.

"Counselor Robert," Avalon said with a nod.

"You remember my wife?"

"Mrs. Harwick," Zaria said as she dipped her head in recognition.

Avalon did not look into the eyes of the counselor's wife, instead looking up into her perfect, jet black hair and admiring the jeweled comb. It reminded her of the hair comb that Zaria had given her on her last birthday, the comb that had been their mother's. It was the only item Avalon had of her mother's because her father had forbidden any token for Avalon to keep. He had raised her with love, but he'd been strict, always worried that someone would uncover the fact that Avalon was a girl.

Counselor Robert handed a small box to Avalon and she opened it to find a polished, silver pin. Avalon rolled the box around and the shine revealed the carved detail in the wings.

"Thank you, it is a work of a steady and skilled hand, and I will be proud to wear it," Avalon said sincerely and handed it over to one of the servants who was attending. Zaria quietly excused herself as Avalon thanked Counselor Robert, and several others stepped forward to greet their king with birthday wishes. Avalon had been dreading the party, but she found herself thankful for the distraction, and she kept pace in conversation until she realized that Zaria had navigated to the entrance to greet Taggerty.

Avalon tried not to watch, but her eyes could not remain on the guests in front of her. He was across a small sea of people on the other side of the hall, but she thought that Taggerty seemed taller now. He smiled down at Zaria, and Avalon noticed for the first time Zaria's beautifully flowing yellow gown and the way her small tiara sparkled, but not any more than her eyes were sparkling.

Avalon felt the pang of jealousy, and just then Taggerty looked directly at her as though he knew she was watching him. His striking green eyes reached across the crowd and stabbed Avalon in her heart. His face had changed, she noticed. His jaw looked more square, his dimple more prominent. He looked more like a man than a boy to her. She felt her face flush, and she was immediately angry at herself for noticing him.

"Please, enjoy the evening," Avalon managed to say evenly to the small crowd that had gathered at the steps of the riser. They tipped their heads and moved on as Avalon's heart quickened.

She made her way discreetly back toward the entrance and came up slowly behind Taggerty. He was leaning toward Zaria, and Avalon overheard Zaria telling Taggerty, "I do not want to deceive the king this way."

Avalon saw Taggerty lean in close. "What else can we do? The time will come to tell King Avalon everything, but for now we must keep quiet. He may not understand."

Avalon swallowed her heart and swept into the private conversation.

"Quite a surprise to see you here," she said coldly to Taggerty.

Zaria stepped in quickly and took Avalon's arm, trying to contain the smile on her face. Avalon's blush turned to anger, and her face remained red.

"King Avalon," Zaria said formally to her younger sister. "May I introduce..."

"I know Taggerty," Avalon snapped, ignoring the shorter, muscular man who stood next to Taggerty. Any amount of joy in the group vanished.

"Avalon," Zaria pressed through gritted teeth.

But Avalon ignored Zaria, staring into Taggerty's face in anger. He looked around the room with his eyes, and Avalon knew that he was telling her to remain calm. She smiled coldly in case anyone was watching. "You are back from the king's work after four months gone, and yet you failed to report to me," Avalon accused cordially. Zaria looked around, but no one had been near enough to hear the anger in Avalon's voice.

"There was no time," Taggerty told her with his hands turned up. "We returned but two hours ago, and I wanted to look presentable..."

"And yet you had time to send word to my sister that you were back," Avalon hissed. She was now certain that Zaria had been watching the door for Taggerty's arrival, and that infuriated her. Avalon was king, and she should never take second bidding to Zaria ever again. And yet here she was, playing the jealous fool. She was a boy to her kingdom, she was king, but no matter how she tried to stifle herself, she was behaving like an imprudent girl. That fact struck Avalon and made her even angrier.

"Your Grace," the King's Guard next to Taggerty spoke up. Avalon's eyes ripped into him and he bowed deeply as Zaria wrung her hands. He cleared his throat. "Your Grace," he repeated, "we stank like pigs and did not want to present ourselves to you in such a state. Please forgive us." The man stood from his bow, and when he allowed his face to rise, Avalon could see thick, red and blond whiskers cut neatly around his pink cheeks. He was a few years older than Taggerty.

"Who is this?" Avalon asked Taggerty, but it was Zaria who spoke.

"Avalon, this is Kensington Woods," the princess said with a smile.

Avalon glanced at the man, but her attention remained on Taggerty. "We should not speak here, but I want to know about your journey." Avalon meant to meet with Taggerty now, to move him to the Council chamber and ask him a million questions. She felt she would grasp at any excuse to be alone in a room with him, but his lasting smile was gone, and Avalon could not know for certain why.

"All went well, Your Grace. I shall report to you at first light. Happy birthday." When Taggerty bowed curtly and turned away from Avalon, she almost shouted at him, but she couldn't. He had been away on a secret order that few others knew of, and she could not risk drawing attention to him or herself. She remembered back to the morning when she had awoken, sitting straight up in bed. She had dreamt these past few minutes as they were. She remembered how glad she was that Taggerty was returning, and how she had tried to contain herself for three days. She had spent these days coaching herself to keep her cool when this moment presented itself. And yet, unable to accept her jealousy, she'd been unable to control her temper and change the evening's outcome. She'd been a fool to think she could change the events as they were in her dream. She watched mute as Taggerty and Kensington left the hall.

"That was uncalled for. He's been gone for months and we have had less than five minutes together," Zaria chided. Avalon could see that Zaria was hurt. The princess, who had been toying with her own gaggle of men suitors for three years, was actually upset over Taggerty. Avalon wanted to burst in anger, but the hurt in her chest and the guilty lump in her throat prevented her from saying anything. Avalon could see Zaria inhale deeply to reset her smile. The princess turned away and slowly made her way through the crowd stopping to greet people here and there so no one would notice that she was going after Taggerty. Without watching, Avalon seethed, knowing just where her sister was headed.

King Avalon Hall spent the rest of the evening being introduced to the daughters from the prominent boroughs. When Counselor Robert suggested that the king should dance, Avalon rebuffed in quiet confidence that her father had thrown her last birthday party, and she wasn't in the dancing mood tonight. She'd said it on purpose because her father's death was still a conversation stopper.

Although her comment was true to her feelings, Avalon knew she wouldn't be able to use that excuse forever. Everyone in this room thought her father had died too soon of an illness that had closed the castle for weeks. After the quarantine, King Birch, his brother Prince Hawker, Counselor Glenn, and several servants had been declared dead. It was a ruse, a cover up of the treachery that had taken place. It was designed to keep her people happy and ignorant of the truths she knew. Their prince had killed their king and there could be more traitors in the castle.

"We are all still in mourning, Your Highness," a honey-deep voice said with regret.

The group turned to see Zaria being escorted by an old man in burgundy colored velvet robes. When they stopped next to Counselor Robert, Avalon could see that the man's attire had made him appear older than he was. His face looked young, but he moved slowly and deliberately too, and his confidence in self gave him the air of a wise, old man.

"There, Princess Zaria," he patted her hand as he removed it from his arm. "I am glad that I could convince you to stay for a while longer. You did such a wonderful job planning this exquisite party. You should enjoy the evening."

"Thank you, Archivist Creighton," Zaria answered ever so graciously. She exchanged smiles with Counselor Robert, but kept her eyes from meeting Avalon's.

"Please, you must call me Julius. Your father always called me Julius."

Avalon found that statement strange, because she had never heard of Julius Creighton and she was sure her father had never mentioned the man to her.

"King Hall," Counselor Robert announced, "may I present to you, Julius Creighton."

Creighton bowed, and when his eyes met Avalon's, she could feel their warmth radiate over her. She couldn't help but smile.

"A pleasure, my King," Creighton said. "Your father was a great loss. And with the loss of Counselor Glenn, I fear that there is much and more to make up for."

"I will try my best," Avalon said sharply.

"No, no, Your Grace. I don't mean you." Creighton coughed uncomfortably, and Avalon felt bad for her quick remark.

"Dear friend," Counselor Robert said to Creighton, "even after all of these months, we are all still short on words." They all nodded their heads but no one spoke so Julius Creighton continued.

"Your Highness, I wonder if I might talk to you about Counselor Glenn." He watched Avalon expectantly, and she was surprised, but she didn't know what to say. Counselor Glenn, and the entire Council for that matter, were subjects she had avoided since her father's death.

"This is not the time for business, Julius," Counselor Robert said. "Let the king have his birthday."

"Yes, yes. Happy birthday, Your Grace," Creighton said again as he bowed to Avalon. She smiled, but she could sense that Creighton wanted to say more, so she waited.

"Perhaps King Avalon would grant me an audience at Council?" Creighton asked with a warm smile on his face.

Counselor Robert interjected. "We have not scheduled a Council."

"Oh, fine, fine. When will you be scheduling a Council?" Creighton asked Counselor Robert, but Avalon felt the sting. There hadn't been an official Council meeting since her father had been king.

Counselor Robert blushed. "I have not requested a Council of the king. Much has happened this year and everything in Fontanasia has been running along smoothly."

Although he was trying to help the king, Avalon was hurt by Counselor Robert's statement. Avalon had seen the counselors a couple of times on a one on one basis, and she felt that she had been ruling as she must. Had everything really been running along without her? She was stunned and ashamed that she had taken the throne and yet had abandoned her post. "We will have our first Council together tomorrow, Counselor Robert," Avalon said directly. Counselor Robert looked pleasantly surprised.

"Of course, Your Highness." He tipped his head to the king.

"Now if you don't mind, I have guests to greet." Avalon smiled at Julius Creighton who smiled back warmly. She took Zaria's arm and turned away to move among the crowd. Zaria followed effortlessly but was not happy with Avalon's curt tone.

"That was unnecessary," Zaria told Avalon. "He is a harmless old man meeting the king for the first time, and you scared him off."

"His robes are old, but his face is not," Avalon said. "And it sounds like he has met a king before. It seems he was not at a loss for words in either case."

"You don't know who he is?" Zaria asked, amused. She looked at Avalon and patted her sister's hand. "Don't be jealous, Avalon. You like to comment that I know every man in Fontanasia, and alas, Julius Creighton is a man."

Avalon's cheeks reddened and she let go of Zaria's arm and clasped her hands behind her back. "I am not jealous," she hissed. It was a half lie. Avalon knew she was jealous, but not over Julius Creighton. She was thinking of Taggerty again. She looked down at her shoes and took a deep breath. All eyes were on the king tonight, and Avalon needed to remain in control. She had learned early in life that stereotypical women were outwardly emotional, so she bit her lip and forced a smile. "Will you be dancing with Julius Creighton tonight?"

Zaria laughed and squeezed Avalon's arm. "I love you, little brother," she said, breaking what ice she could. They both sighed and looked over the guests. "Avalon, you should relax." Zaria gestured with her eyes toward the throne but Avalon shook her head.

"I'm fine."

Avalon was dismissing her, but Zaria pushed on in a whisper. "You are the king, and if I have noticed that you have not sat upon the throne yet, then others have noticed too. It has been almost a year, and you have not held court nor Council."

Avalon cleared the pooling guilt from her throat. She had sat on that throne on her father's lap as a child. He had taught her everything about being a good king. He had passed her family's secrets and abilities down to her for the day she would be king. It had been ten months since the chair had become hers, and the kingdom of Fontanasia her responsibility, and that was decades earlier than she'd have ever thought possible. She swallowed hard and tried to think of a rebuke, but all Avalon could muster was, "I know."

The Malley Waltz started then, and Avalon felt relief. As much as her sister angered her, she needed Zaria. "Care to dance, Princess Zaria?" she asked with her gloved hand outstretched. The crowd parted as the royal pair stepped toward the bandstand. This was their song. They had practiced dancing for years while Myra George, their ever-present nanny and stand-in mother, hummed the Malley Waltz in the background. They had spun around and around, Avalon the short, stocky suitor to Zaria's thin, lively beauty. Tonight, they both looked away from each other, but their bodies moved effortlessly around the floor. Avalon was gaining height on Zaria who was an adult now and had stopped growing. Avalon was glad that she didn't have her sister's curves, and wondered in that moment if her own young body would remain so easy to hide under her baggy clothes.

"Myra and I missed you this morning for our private birthday celebration," Zaria said, cutting through their silence.

"I told Myra that the morning celebration is one tradition that will no longer stand," Avalon whispered with a curt smile. Ever since Avalon was seven years old, her nanny, Myra George, and Zaria had secretly dressed Avalon in Zaria's dresses on her birthday. She had looked in the mirror and felt out of place. She felt resentful of the tradition some years, and other years a small part of her was curious, wondering about a different future. But there was no other future now that she was king. Those possibilities had died with her father.

It was a full two minutes before Avalon nodded at the onlookers, and Counselor Robert and his wife took the floor, signaling to others that it was okay to join in the dance. Avalon wasn't focused on the dance though. She was remembering the last time she had seen her father alive and the pride yet concern in his eyes as she left for Cormicks. She was remembering the great warrior, Walthan, lying by the pool in the waning, blue elbagrass, and her feeling of utter helplessness as he died to save her life. She could sense the scar in her side where Counselor

Glenn had stabbed her. She tried to wash those memories away by fondly remembering the twinkle in Taggerty's salty, green eyes as he knelt and kissed the ring of his king. Most days, she could make sense of very little. Her first few months as king were like this dance with Zaria: practiced, perfected, and yet meaningless.

Then there was the throne. Avalon didn't have to look at it to notice its presence in the room. *It's just a chair*, she told herself. Zaria was right, though. She would have to sit on the throne to amplify footing in her position. She didn't know if her Uncle Hawker had any allies left in Fontanasia, and if there was a war coming, Avalon needed to be the king that her father had trained her to be.

Avalon misstepped and Zaria pulled on her sister's leading hand to keep their dance on course. In the past, Avalon would have been upset at Zaria because even though she was younger, she was the prince and would therefore have to lead. But leading the dance was the least of her worries. Avalon caught sight of the throne and tried to forget her father long enough to take her new place in front of this crowd. She had sat on the throne the day they had crowned her king, but she had avoided it since then. It was too soon. She needed her father's guidance for many more years, but it didn't change the fact that he was gone forever.

The Malley Waltz ended and Avalon bowed to Zaria's curtsey. Avalon's face was burning and her hand shook. When Zaria looked concerned, Avalon glanced at the dais and Zaria knew. She took Avalon's arm and escorted the king to the steps. With her lips barely moving, she whispered, "Deep breath. It's just for a moment." Avalon wondered how Zaria's typically self-centered personality could have turned so perceptive, but a lot of things had changed since their father's death. Avalon realized then that seeing her on the throne might be just as difficult for Zaria.

It was a large wooden throne that was beautifully carved, stained gray, and polished so that it looked like it was made out of soft stone. Some of the carvings reminded Avalon of the small box that the Guides had presented for her birthday, and she wondered if they'd had a hand in carving this chair. She knew each image by memory after years of looking at the throne, but now was not the time to study the carvings. She and Zaria took two steps up, and Avalon strode four long steps, turned, and sat. Zaria took the smaller chair next to Avalon, and they looked out upon their guests who continued to dance and enjoy the evening.

Avalon sat tall, her chin dipped low, surveying the crowd as her father had. She noticed the statues of the kings who had preceded her, at least the few her uncle hadn't smashed to bits. Those statues had been recommissioned, along with one of her father, and they would stand in this Hall of Kings again soon enough.

Avalon tried to pull herself out of the moment. She smiled over grit teeth, but the lump was returning, and she softly cleared her throat.

"Avalon," Zaria said quietly.

Avalon looked to her sister.

"What shall we have for supper tomorrow?" Zaria asked with a smile on her face.

Some of Avalon's pain subsided with the question. There would be a tomorrow, and perhaps then this moment wouldn't feel so overwhelming. A tear formed in Avalon's eye.

"I'm serious, Avalon. What shall we have to eat tomorrow? Tell me."

Avalon realized that she had been squeezing her hands into fists in her lap, and she slowly let her fingers go limp. "Should we make plans to dine together?" Avalon asked. Their family had always eaten dinner together, but since King Birch had died and their Uncle Hawker had betrayed them, they had only dined together a handful of times. Avalon spent much of her time alone, and Zaria had never pressed the issue.

"I think we should. We always used to."

Avalon found a smile and she relaxed. "You choose the menu, Zaria. I will meet you in the dining room for dinner tomorrow, and each night after that." She looked over the crowd and realized that she would have to sit at the head of the table tomorrow night, but she put the thought out of her head. Avalon was fifteen years old today, and she could hardly remember anything that she had accomplished in the past year. She was King of Fontanasia, yes, but she didn't consider that an achievement. She had been born to that task. Avalon had been hiding from everyone. She had been trying to block the memories of Cormicks and her father's death, but it was impossible.

"Thank you, sister," Avalon said. They shared a glance as Counselor Robert approached with his wife.

"Your Highness," he said with the tip of his head. "I will see you tomorrow at Council."

Avalon nodded her head realizing she was one day away from her first official King's Council.

"Princess Zaria," Counselor Robert said, "you throw a magnificent party."

"Thank you," Zaria answered graciously.

Several others took their leave after Counselor Robert, and when there was a break in the conversation, Avalon stood and turned toward Zaria. "Good night, Zaria. Will you be staying long?"

"I should think so," she answered playfully. "You know how I like a party."

Avalon nodded, and instead of stepping off the dais and returning through the crowd, she simply swept past Zaria and through the rear door that lead to the throne room. Guards posted at the door stood taller when Avalon moved past, but she hardly noticed them. She had taken a seat on the throne, but she could never take her father's place. Zaria had calmed her nerves and Avalon loved her for that, but she knew that the weight of her situation would always be her own. The job she had prepared for her entire life had trapped Avalon. She had lost both of her parents. She was an adult at fifteen years old, and she was a king in a girl's body. She returned to her room in the king's suite where she curled up in a ball on her bed, and cried herself to sleep.

Chapter 2
Battling Memories

Counting the months that he was imprisoned in the clean, unused castle dungeon, and then fifty-eight days on horseback, Prince Hawker Hall calculated that it had been about nine months since he'd tried to kill his nephew, Avalon. He couldn't be certain of that because on the journey since leaving Fontanasia, he was blindfolded during the day and sequestered to tent at night. He had fallen ill early in the journey and had to be tied sideways in his saddle, still blindfolded, still journeying ahead to where, he didn't know.

They rode endlessly through ice and snow until warmer weather approached. Then one day the soldiers saddled up and Hawker was left on the ground, bound hand and foot. Hawker had begged Taggerty to take him back to Fontanasia. He knew Taggerty, the young King's Guard. Taggerty was the one who Brick had taken under his wing to help with Hawker's plans to open the door to Cormicks. Yet Taggerty had come back from Cormicks alive with no word from Brick. Taggerty had stopped Hawker from killing Avalon. In the end, it was Taggerty who had stopped Hawker from taking the throne. Hawker intended to pay Taggerty back for his betrayal. And as for Brick, Hawker was disappointed in his failure to open the window between the cities, but Brick was a traitor to his king and a disappointment to Hawker, so he deserved whatever fate allowed.

He didn't recognize the other face, and he had not been able to discern a name or any personal information from either of the men. It was astounding to Hawker that for two months the men had moved him around the countryside and through the woods without speaking, not even to each other. Hawker didn't even catch a whisper late at night when he was tied up alone in his tent. They didn't share stories or plan the next day's journey. They didn't even complain about the bitter cold or the long days on horseback, or the insane mission their king had sent them on. They traveled in silence. They were well trained, militant even, and Hawker respected those traits even as he despised the men who showed such discipline. The only words he heard in over two months came from Taggerty.

"If you teach yourself to scrounge, you will find enough food and water here to live out your days. If we see you again, we will kill you."

The burly, red-bearded soldier prodded his horse and turned to leave without a word, leading Hawker's horse away with him.

"You can't leave me here. I won't last a week!" Hawker protested. Taggerty didn't answer, turning his horse to follow the other man. Hawker's voice was scratchy and it felt strange to talk. He had worked on them for the first two days of the trek, offering them money and positions on his council. He'd begged and threatened, and he'd been gagged for most of the past two months for his effort. He coughed again before yelling after the men. They reached the edge of the small clearing and then they disappeared in the trees.

To Hawker's dismay, it took him most of the day to get the knots loose enough to break free. He hastily swallowed a large gulp of water from the canteen they had left. He spilled some on his face, and then cursed himself for wasting the precious commodity. He rubbed his wrists and ankles where the rope had dug in and left scars, and then he walked into the wood where Taggerty had disappeared. It was there that Hawker had found the stream, and he realized that they had left him here on purpose so he would have fresh water to drink. They had left him enough jerky and dried fruit to last a few weeks, and Hawker found it hard to believe that these food stores were still available after two months of hard travel. It was early spring, and he could see vegetation popping up around him. He would survive, at least they had done their part in the matter. They had placed him in a spot where he had a chance, but they didn't know that Hawker knew anything about hunting or vegetation, so they might as well have left him there to starve to death.

Hawker found the small set of tools and knives that were left for him. He tossed the smallest knife over and over in his hand, feeling the weight of the blade and balance of the full tang of the knife. A small rodent approached the clearing, sniffing, scurrying, and stopping to sniff again. Hawker sat like stone and watched it for three minutes. He had pulled his arm back and released the knife before the rodent had sensed his presence, and the knife stabbed cleanly through the animal's torso. He stood tall and strode to the animal where it lay. He pulled the knife out and snapped the rodent's neck, all the while thinking of his nephew, Avalon Hall, the King of Fontanasia.

He had been exiled alone for a month now with the supplies an outdoorsman needed to survive, but he wasn't acclimated to the outdoors, and he abhorred camping.

Prince Hawker Hall was a bookworm, and his nephew knew that. Hawker relished the thought that Avalon didn't have the guts to kill him. Avalon should have run Hawker through when he'd had the chance, but Avalon didn't have the stomach for killing. It was a mistake, and Hawker hoped he could make the little rat pay for it some day. Still, to leave a man who knew nothing about the outdoors to his own devices, that was almost more cruel than outright murder. He could have starved to death or been poisoned. In the wilderness, there were hundreds of ways to die. Hawker smiled. Perhaps deep down his nephew harbored Hawker's own natural ability to torture.

As the weeks passed and he made his way in the wilderness, daily chores like cooking and washing his clothes in the stream made Hawker angry. He was supposed to be the king. He was supposed to be a ruler of man, not a peasant. Yet the longer he made his way on his own, the more powerful he felt. Hawker didn't need anyone to keep him alive. He was doing it himself. And if he could read the stars, he would be able to make his way back to Fontanasia and take his rightful place on the throne.

Avalon woke up startled like she could sense a presence in her room. She hadn't dreamed, and she didn't know why she felt the sensation that she was being watched. Her tiny jakkow lizard was sleeping on her chest, and he scrambled off of Avalon as she rose still fully dressed from the party. She crossed to the window and could tell by the moon that it was still early, not midway through the night, and it was too far from dawn to consider staying awake. She removed her coat and sash belt and was ready to dress for bed when there was a light knock at her door.

"Yes," she called more startled than angry. Avalon crossed quickly back to the bed and pulled on her robe as the door opened.

The night guard took a half step in and said, "I beg your pardon, King Avalon. It is Julius Creighton, and he says it is urgent. He won't leave. He said he would wait all night to see you if he had to."

Avalon looked at the guard. It was Thomas, and he was a trusted guard that she had known for a long time, but she could not read his expression. She wondered why he would let someone who was not family or friend into the suite at such a late hour. Still, she had just met Creighton this evening, and she was curious as to what he could want.

"Tell him that he can wait if he would like, but I will rise with the sun."

"Yes, Your Highness." He started to swing the door closed but Avalon stopped him.

"Thomas, why would you wake me for this request? Why do you think I would see this man in the middle of the night?"

"I don't know, sire, but your father always did," the guard said apologetically. "I mean, not often. Maybe a couple of times each year."

This was news to Avalon. Her father had told her to trust the Guides, and she knew that he had met with them on occasion, but he had never spoken of Julius Creighton.

"And how did he convince you to wake me?"

The guard's posture slumped a bit and Avalon knew by his gray shadow in the doorway that he was embarrassed. "Sire, he told me that he would wait, but he also said if you were upset when I woke you, you would be more upset if this conversation was delayed."

Avalon smiled. "By all means, I'd rather be a little angry now than very angry later."

The guard said, "Yes, King Avalon," but he would not turn to leave without a command from his King.

"I will be right out. Invite him to sit."

Avalon removed the robe and changed into pajama bottoms. She removed one of her top layers, but left on the bulky padded shirt that made her form look heavier and took the eye away from the thin curves of a young woman that were forming. She put her pajama top over the padding and tightened the sash of her robe around her. Once she was certain that she looked the part, Avalon practiced a yawn and moved to the outer room.

"King Avalon," Julius Creighton said with a slow bow. Even in the orange candlelight, Avalon could see very few wrinkles on Creighton's face, and she wondered if he had been injured in some way because he moved so slowly. It seemed as though he was practicing to be an old man.

"Please," Avalon said, her hand telling him to be seated. He took the smaller chair, the very spot that Avalon had spent hours sitting when she was listening to her father, playing verticks, and arguing with Zaria. Creighton sat down leaving Avalon to take her father's chair. Taking the seat bothered her a little, but Myra and Zaria had forced Avalon to sit here in the past ten months so it wasn't daunting like the throne had seemed. They had wanted her to begin living with the reality that she was the king. She was grateful for that now that she had an uninvited guest to contend with.

She looked at Julius Creighton with his shoulders hunched down and his hands tucked inside the sleeves of his robe like a monk. She realized that although he had asked for this meeting, he was waiting for her to speak.

"How old are you?" she asked him directly, studying his face in the dim light for a lie.

"Why do you not take the king's bedroom?" Creighton shot back in such a deep, soft tone that Avalon did not feel insulted. She could understand how this man had charmed Zaria and Counselor Robert. Creighton was studying her face, and she was sure by the slight movement of her cheeks that he had noticed her discomfort. The thought made her think of her Uncle Hawker and how he would twitch his nose sometimes, or how his cheeks would start to curl up and he would catch himself and relax his face back to a serene blank slate. Avalon was trying to hide her emotion as Hawker had all of his life, and she hated that she might be anything like him.

"Very well," Creighton answered. He was condescending but not insulting. Although he was here at the king's pleasure because she had agreed to the meeting, Avalon felt that she was most certainly here at his bidding. She could not make him out. "I am thirty-two years old," he admitted.

Avalon was very surprised that he was so young. "Are you ill?" she asked.

"No," Creighton chuckled. "Like father, like son. King Birch, rest his soul, he asked me the same thing when I first approached him ten years ago." Avalon was surprised again, that her father had taken private council with Julius Creighton for ten years without her knowledge.

"So you have been meeting with my father for ten years?" Avalon asked.

"No, no," Creighton chuckled in a slow, deep voice. "I approached your father about becoming the librarian in the archives. You see, I'm something of a prodigy because of my memory, and when you're young and know too much, people just think you are a know-it-all, so it's difficult getting them to listen to you or take you seriously."

He was telling his story, but Avalon wondered if he was really insinuating about her age because she was a very young king.

"I learned early to model my behavior, my gestures and words, and even my attire on that of my grandfather. People take me more seriously because they think I am a much older man. Your father was kind to me and he assigned me to the archives very willingly. I have spent the past ten years reading everything downstairs, and I have made new records of reference on all matters. It was but four years ago that I started meeting your father from time to time to answer some, shall we say, interesting questions."

Avalon felt closer to her father in this moment. She took pleasure feeling that if he had secret meetings with Creighton as she did now, it somehow drew them closer, even in death.

"I was glad to meet you at your birthday party this evening. Did I remember to wish you happy birthday?" Creighton asked pleasantly. Avalon nodded, although she was sure he remembered doing just that. His forgetful manner was part of his act. "I'm glad to see you are coming out of the loss of your father. I'm very sorry that your Uncle Hawker died, too."

Avalon was startled at how forward Creighton was being. Was he a prodigy with no manners, or was he fishing for some answers? She saw the slight smile on his lips and knew the answer.

"You spent a lot of time with my Uncle Hawker?" Avalon asked, distancing herself from the emotion of her father's memory for the moment.

"Yes, I did. Prince Hawker spent a great deal of time in the archives, and although I usually worked from the library on the main level, I was able to spend a great deal of time with him over the years. He was interested in all manner of subjects." Creighton paused, staring at Avalon, and she realized that he wanted her to ask more questions.

"And what subjects was Hawker interested in?"

"I think you should come down to the archives and see for yourself." Creighton put his hands on the arm of his chair and scooted to the front edge, making sure to use the chair arms for support to stand up, but Avalon was quite sure this was part of the act. He turned sideways and extended an arm to the door.

"What, now?" Avalon asked.

"I can wait for you to dress, Your Highness. But yes, it's easier to speak freely among the books when there is no one else around."

Creighton seemed genuine, and her father had trusted him, but Avalon trusted no one. "I am glad that my father trusted you, and that you were able to get to know my uncle, but I think I will visit you at a better time. Goodnight," Avalon said conclusively. She stood and turned to go back to her bedroom but his words stopped her in her tracks.

"One of Prince Hawker's favorite subjects was botany. Specifically, he has been studying plants that can be eaten in the wilderness. He has studied how to pick them and cultivate them." Creighton spoke expectantly. "He'd been quite taken with the subject. I assume he was working on a project for King Birch. Something for Fontanasia's agriculture perhaps?"

"I don't really know," Avalon said truthfully.

"I see," Creighton responded. He turned toward Avalon and studied her face fully.

"And you didn't know about his foray into banpiel?"

"What is that?" Avalon asked. She didn't like the fact that Creighton was looking at her like he was trying to decide if he could trust her. When he smiled, she knew he had made up his mind.

"No, I see you don't know at all. Banpiel is arsenic, King Avalon. It has no taste, but just a small amount of it can kill a grown man."

His tone was instructional, and he waited for Avalon to connect the dots. "What do you know?" she asked cautiously.

"I know that King Birch died during dinner, and that Prince Hawker was the only other person at the table with him."

Avalon was going to lie and stick with the official story that they had both died from a mysterious illness, but she remembered that Creighton was a prodigy of sorts, and she decided to find out what else he knew.

"That is true, but my father could have choked or had a heart attack."

"Following King Birch's death, the castle was put on lockdown by Counselor Glenn, and your Uncle Hawker was put in the dungeon."

"Where did you hear this lie?" Avalon asked unconvincingly.

"Funny thing about the archives. They are forgotten and no one bothers to search them during a lock down." Creighton's back straightened up just then and Avalon was reminded of her uncle's reedy frame. "I have heard all sorts of things, King Avalon. I can see that you had nothing to do with your father's death and that I can trust you, but you in turn must trust me."

"You really thought that I had something to do with my father's death?" Avalon asked incredulously.

"You were next in line for the throne, so I had to suspect that you and Hawker were working together. But you were missing for several weeks, and when you returned everything was set straight." Creighton took a couple of steps forward and looked straight into Avalon's eyes. "And Hawker was dead." He said that last part matter of fact, but Avalon knew by the look on his face that Julius Creighton was asking her a direct question. She did not answer.

"I see." Creighton shook his head and placed his hand over his eyes for a moment. "We are wasting time, King Avalon. I will wait for you."

"You will?" Avalon was stunned. She wasn't quite keeping up with Creighton.

"You will want to see what your uncle was studying before his announced death. It was a book about the Anthracites."

Avalon was rocked back on her heels remembering the mountainous charcoal beasts that had tried to crush her and everyone else on her recon mission to Cormicks.

"The Anthracites?" Avalon asked innocently, but the game was over.

"Your Highness," Creighton said slowly and with regret, "your father trusted me, and I understand that it will take time for you to do the same, but you should see this book."

"Then bring it to me," Avalon said.

"I would, but it is very old. I don't think that it should be moved. And this subject is not for prying eyes."

"I will keep it safe. Bring it to me." Avalon was not used to asking twice, and her words cut the air.

"As you command, King Hall." Creighton slowly bowed. He turned toward the door and walked methodically like an old man, and Avalon couldn't help herself.

"It's the middle of the night and no one is watching," she reminded him.

Creighton turned back and smiled. "And so it is. Matter of habit, I suppose." Creighton straightened his spine and made a grunting sound before sighing. He pulled his shoulders back and walked purposefully from the suite.

She thought it would take Creighton at least thirty minutes to retrieve the volume from the archives and return, but Avalon had just enough time to call for an early breakfast when the young, old man returned. Thomas opened the door from the hall and announced, "Julius Creighton has returned, Your Highness." He did not wait for her answer though, and Creighton walked into the suite and placed the book on the low table where she was sitting.

The book was very old, and Avalon had never seen anything like it. She had been down to the archives a lot when she was a child adventuring about the castle, but she had never actually pulled a book from the shelf. This book was bound with a worn black cover, and as she leaned over it, Creighton opened the cover gently with just the tip of his finger. The book fell open, and Avalon was staring at the black drawing of an Anthracite. Her face went white.

"This is an Anthracite," Creighton said pointing at the picture but looking at Avalon's face. "They are the beasts of Cormicks, and losing control of them is partly how we came to be in Fontanasia." Avalon tried to speak, but she could not make a sound. The Anthracites had been terrifying, ripping the ground and shaking the world as they stomped toward her and tried to crush the group. She had seen these giant black rocks chase Taggerty, and it was still very unsettling to think about. Avalon knew that magic tricks were just that, tricks played by the magician to fool the onlookers, but she had witnessed true magic, and the Anthracites were an anomaly that she couldn't explain.

It took her a moment to realize that Creighton had said 'Cormicks' instead of 'Hawkerness', and this frightened her too. He was a man her father had trusted, who worked side by side in research with her traitor uncle, and who knew much and more about a subject that didn't exist to anyone but the kings and a very few Guides and King's Guard.

Creighton continued, still looking at Avalon's face. "Hawker was studying them, and you too should read this book. Turn the pages slowly like this," he said, turning the first page over with just his fingertips. Avalon saw five black hills on the countryside, and she understood that there were five Anthracites. She had only seen three, and knowing that there were more did not sit well with her. Avalon swallowed in her drying throat.

"What was that you said?" Creighton asked politely, and Avalon met his eyes.

"Nothing," she croaked. "Thank you for bringing this book to me," she added as dismissively as she could.

Creighton nodded neutrally, but he knew that she had seen the Anthracites. "I have read this book, and it looks like these Anthracites are fifty feet high and will crush anything in their path. That frightens me," he confessed. Creighton stood slowly and walked to the window to look down over Fontanasia. "Imagine," he said just above a whisper, "just one of those Anthracites crushing the Fingers and climbing up to smash this very window."

Still in her robe, Avalon walked to the window, looking down on Fontanasia in the moonlight. She could see a trace of the Fingers running down from the castle to the open plains beyond. Small fires were lit this late into the night as the early workers rose to start a new day. The sky would be gray soon, and she would wake Gamon and make for the small plateau where she still practiced the sword each morning.

Avalon squinted into the blackness and wondered what the window to Cormicks looked like tonight. It was a small, stone-lined pond, yet it held the power to allow armies to cross between Cormicks and Fontanasia. She remembered looking at her reflection in the pond and the feeling of crossing over. It felt like nothing really aside from her own frightful anticipation of its magic. Avalon looked up to the half moon, a few of it's bright diamond-like spots glittering in the black sky. There had been ten black moons since she had become king. That meant there had been ten chances for the Monarch to lead his army through the window, and he had not. Had they found the place that would lead them to Fontanasia? Did they know that the elbagrass was poisonous except by the light of the full moon? These questions compounded after her meeting with Julius Creighton and they made Avalon's head ache. She hadn't even tried to go back to bed when he'd left her chambers.

Avalon had studied the old book for a while before hiding it in her room for safekeeping. Creighton's eerie speculation of the Anthracites smashing through the Fingers crept up her back and made her shiver. She hated not knowing the future, and she hated feeling helpless even more.

Avalon reached the door to her suite and barked, "Tell Gamon, ten minutes!" She didn't see either guard in the dark, but she heard footsteps rush away to wake the head of the King's Guard. She threw off her robe and crossed to her sink basin. Avalon only had a couple hours of sleep, but she was charged by panic and indecision. She splashed cold water on her face and inhaled deeply, trying to lighten the weight of the past few hours. She dressed and pulled on her sword belt, grabbing the hilt of her sword. She needed to swing it. She needed to stab and block and stab again to forget her fate.

For fourteen years, she had worked toward becoming king, and she had dreamt of nothing else. She had followed her father's careful instruction, hid the fact that she was a girl, and prepared for the day her father passed on. She thought that would be many years from now, but he had been poisoned by his own brother, and Avalon was bound to fulfill her duty. The timing was unfair. She had just met Taggerty and was for the first time questioning her future. She had always fiercely protected her secret, going so far as to wear only long sleeves and padded coats, but recently she found herself wishing she would be found out. She would lose the throne, but she would gain the chance to tell Taggerty that she was a girl, and that she had feelings for him.

Avalon shook her head to clear her mind of the impossible daydream. She needed the cold morning air and the beauty of the sunrise to rein her in. She was the king, and there was nothing else worth worrying about. Taggerty was simply her first crush and that was all. She could not hope to hold the attention of a young man who thought she was a boy. She needed to pull her thoughts together and figure out the best way to protect Fontanasia from the Monarch of Cormicks.

Gamon was already downstairs when Avalon arrived, and she smiled at him. "I didn't think you could get ready so fast. You're taking your new job as the head of my guard seriously."

"I am at my King's command, you know that," Gamon answered respectfully.

With four guards in tow, they made their way down through the Fingers on horseback. The only people on the street before dawn were the shopkeepers who were setting up for the day. They all bowed in reverence as she passed by, and some said, "Bless you, King Avalon." She clenched her teeth and nodded at them trying to stay her breath.

Her people had treated her well. Still, no one came too close to her, which was fine with Avalon. The people had heard that the castle had been closed off because of a sickness that had taken King Birch, Counselor Glenn, Walthan, and Hawker. They'd buried the king with all the pomp and circumstance deserved of him, and they buried Counselor Glenn in turn. Walthan's coffin was placed with honor near King Birch's, guarding his king forever. There were stone tombs being carved for both men to be placed at their graves. Hawker was buried near his brother to keep the ruse alive, but his coffin was empty.

They'd had a funeral pyre for the rest of the bodies that were actually three elderly Guides who had recently passed of natural causes, but word was spread that the pyre included the warrior Brick and six servants. Rumors fed from the castle to the town about the soldiers who had died standing guard for their king, and the staff who had been quarantined and then died. Unaware of the ruse, the people whispered in the Fingers, grateful that the sickness had been contained. The King's Guard had already been sworn to silence when they were commissioned, but Gamon made sure to remind the few who knew anything different of their oath and of their duty.

Avalon silently dismounted in their usual clearing and stretched. The guard tied the horses and Avalon and Gamon swung their swords lightly to loosen their limbs. Their combat practice was the same as when Avalon was a prince except instead of taking charge, Gamon bowed low and waited for Avalon to command the start. That was different, and the fact that they used real swords now and not wooden practice swords. They volleyed for a short time, swords clanging together, each of them dancing the dance, and Avalon was more vigorous than usual as her mind was on Taggerty's return last evening. Part of her wanted to be the perfect king toward Taggerty, business-like yet aloof and impartial to his personal life. Another part of her was angry, remembering her dream and how Taggerty had returned and gone straight to Zaria. It was like the point of a needle pushing sharply into Avalon's chest. She thrust in anger and Gamon easily knocked her sword aside.

"King Hall," Gamon said, reminding Avalon to focus on the task in front of her.

"You can call me Avalon. You are still my instructor and the head of my guard."

"Yes, my King." Gamon answered.

Avalon sighed and reset her stance. "Again," she commanded him.

Gamon tapped Avalon's sword lightly before coming at her hard. She was able to deflect his offensive and retaliate with a parry of her own. Avalon thought she was getting the upper hand until Gamon started speaking with ease while they fought. "I would like to talk to you about my position, Your Highness."

"There is no discussion. I trust you, and I need you to lead the guard. You saw what happened with Hawker. I don't know who else I can trust." Avalon was losing her breath and she moved sideways to dodge Gamon's thrust.

"I don't know what I saw, Your Highness, and I'm not asking. I am loyal and I'm honored that you trust me, but there are many good men who can handle this job better than I can. I may be a warrior, but I am no leader like Walthan and Brick were."

Avalon was angered by Gamon's words, and she went at him with a fury, her sword swinging forward with a vengeance. "Walthan was a great man, and no one can fill his shoes. But are you telling me that knowing what you know about the attempt on my life, that you are comfortable with just anyone protecting me? I don't expect you to be Walthan." Avalon's attack took Gamon off guard. It was beyond practice. Her face was red with anger, and she swung her sword with full force.

Her mind was far away though, back at the edge of the elbagrass, Walthan's dead eyes staring into nowhere. He was the greatest warrior of Fontanasia, and her personal guard on the secret trip to Cormicks, and he was dead. The helplessness returned to Avalon and she swallowed back the emotion. Gritting her teeth, she willed her heart into stone, but instead it exploded into raging fire. Her anger caused her to swing with more force than she ever had before. With the sword in her hand, lashing out her emotion stroke after stroke, she did not feel like a young man. Avalon felt like an adult.

In her anger, Avalon had forgotten her defenses. She threw caution to the wind, pushing Gamon back and matching each of his attempts to retreat sideways. She swatted and landed a cutting blow to his ribs. Gamon's protective padding ripped open and they both froze. It was the first time Avalon had ever gotten inside on Gamon. She was stunned by her success, and he was stunned by her fury. They stared at each other for a moment before Gamon's smile cut the tension.

"You don't seem to need anyone's help in your defense," he said as he wiped the sweat from his brow and took to one knee, bowing his head.

"Stop that, Gamon," Avalon protested. She had never been bothered when people knelt for her father. It had been appropriate because he was the king. For her, she could accept it when the strangers bowed for their king, but Avalon still didn't know how to behave with those in her inner circle. She had grown up with most of them, but the moment her father died, they had all put her at arm's length.

"Rise," she finally said in monotone, and Gamon stood and sheathed his sword. Avalon walked in a small circle flexing her muscles and cooling down from the exercise. She needed time to get her mind straight. She was glad that she had finally fought well enough to get the best of Gamon, but she didn't like the fact that it had come at such a cost to her mentally. She couldn't fault Gamon for not taking his position as seriously as he should. He didn't know about Cormicks or the Runners. He didn't know that they would surely come through the elbagrass one day and try to crush Fontanasia. He needed to know, if he was going to protect her. She needed him to see Cormicks. Avalon was confident that once Gamon saw what they were up against, he would not step down.

"Did you cut yourself, Gamon?" a familiar voice asked. Avalon didn't turn around. She knew Taggerty's voice, and as much as she had watched the horizon for him every day that he was gone, she wasn't ready to see him this morning.

"King Hall got the best of me," Gamon said with pride in his voice.

"Not you, Gamon. You aren't taking it easy on the king, are you?"

When Avalon turned around, she held her breath and looked straight at Taggerty, but he did not meet her eye. Instead he bowed his head.

"Taggerty," Avalon said, and he stood straight. She noticed that he had brought two other guards with him.

"My King," Gamon bowed. "I will take my leave of you and get ready for Council. I leave you in Taggerty's capable hands." She didn't want to be left alone with Taggerty, but Avalon nodded and Gamon turned to leave.

"King Avalon, did you hold back at all?" Taggerty asked with his hand moving to the hilt of his sword.

"You are but five minutes late," Avalon announced as she sheathed hers.

"Better late than never," he said just above a whisper, and Avalon flushed red. She knew that he couldn't have meant anything by that remark, but the hairs on her neck stood up with his easy manner and close proximity. She was still angry with him for not reporting to her straight upon his return, and Avalon needed to hold on to that anger if she was going to remain aloof about him and Zaria. She moved to her horse and tried to busy herself with removing her protective vest, but Taggerty followed closely and helped untie the straps. He handed the gear to one of the guard who packed it away.

"Gamon!" Avalon called. "Wait, we will all ride up together."

"Yes, Your Highness," Gamon reined up on his horse and waited at the head of the path as the rest of the group mounted their horses.

"My King?" Taggerty asked. "I believe that we have some business."

"We do, but if it could wait the night, it can surely wait until after breakfast." It's not what Avalon wanted to say, and she didn't look at him as she bucked her horse forward.

They rode down the side of the low rise that Avalon had been training on since she was young. It used to be Avalon and Gamon and one or two of the guard, but now she was with Gamon and Taggerty and six of the guard, and she wondered what her people might think as they approached the brick walls that rose out of the valley. Walthan had devised and built the walls, and their rise had separated the boroughs of the city. They were nicknamed the Fingers because they climbed up the mountain rise, giving the impression of five fingers grabbing the side of the mountain, ready to rip it from the earth. The thought reminded Avalon of the Anthracites in Cormicks, and how the giant charcoal beasts had risen out of what had looked like a dormant mountain rise and tried to crush her reconnaissance party.

There hadn't been another recon mission to Cormicks since they had returned, and only a few of the Guides had gone into the elbagrass to retrieve Walthan's remains by the light of the next full moon. There were Guides watching the window even now, taking shifts by the month to make sure no one crossed over to attack Fontanasia. Avalon was scared, and if it were up to her, she would have the entire army waiting around the pool to guard the window between the two worlds. But no one had come through yet, and if Brick had told him enough about how to get across, the Monarch must not have been able to find the field of blue elbagrass.

Taggerty wanted Avalon to send him and one of the Guides to Cormicks for an update. He had pressed for that before he had left to vanquish Hawker, and he would ask again, but she couldn't allow it. When she was in the prison below Cormicks, Walthan had told Avalon that they had to break out or they would never be rescued. "If we are rescued, then the Monarch will believe Brick, and he will know that there are more like us. He won't wait for an attack, he will go looking." Avalon remembered Walthan's words and shuddered, looking over her shoulder and down at the plains beyond the wall. She half expected to see the Monarch's savage army of Runners there, charging an attack on Fontanasia. She could not send another recon to Cormicks now that the Monarch was on their scent. No matter what Taggerty asked of her, Avalon could not chance someone leading the Runners back to Fontanasia, even if by accident. She had to hope the thick grove of trees that shaded the elbagrass would be enough to keep her city safe.

Taggerty pushed his horse forward in pace with hers and cleared his throat pulling Avalon back to the street. She looked into his expectant eyes and strong face and tried to return his smile.

"How have you been sleeping?" he asked.

"Okay," she said dismissively. He waited as though he knew the real answer, and Avalon relented. "Not well at all," she admitted. "When I close my eyes, it's all right there in front of me. Walthan, the trip, I can't seem to leave it behind."

"I know." Taggerty leaned over in his saddle toward Avalon, and she thought he would touch her back, but instead he stroked Avalon's horse. "Are you dreaming?"

"No," Avalon admitted. Taggerty knew Avalon's family secret. He knew if she dreamed, her dream would come true. That happened to all of the Hall kings and many of their family members over the centuries. She had dreamt of Taggerty's return and it had happened just as she had seen it. She dreamed that Counselor Glenn would stab her, and he had. Avalon liked the black void of her sleeping hours. It was the only refuge she had from her waking stress.

"It will pass," Taggerty told her. Avalon heard this often from Myra George, and she nodded her head and tried to be present as they made their way up the last block to the castle.

There were more storeowners out now, and the city had started to awaken to a new day. She waved her hand at a pack of boys who ran up on the group and were trying to catch the king's eye. This was the only part of the Fingers that she recognized. She hadn't explored all of the boroughs since she was little. The only time she had been alone in the city was during the Festival of Fontanasia the year before, and she had gotten lost wandering down street after street. That was the day she met Taggerty, and he had led her back to the castle.

It was ironic that she loved her city and the people in it when she was so separated from them. The thought made her push her shoulders forward a little to hide her chest, and although she wore bulky padded clothes, she was suddenly self-conscious. She wondered if they would still accept her if they knew her secret. Walthan had accepted her, and the thought of him dying in the waning, blue elbagrass choked the breath from her lungs again. Avalon stared down at the mane on her horse and tried to steel her mind.

Chapter 3
Taming the Council

Avalon was waiting alone in the King's Council chamber making herself comfortable in the space while she waited for Taggerty to arrive and give his report. He'd wanted to tell her about his trip when they returned that morning, but Avalon felt vulnerable, and any footing she had gained during her training with Gamon had been brushed aside by her memories. She had waited for months for him to return, so she felt justified in making him wait two more hours. It was one of the perks of being the king, everyone was on your time.

She looked at her old chair, the one to the right of the king's chair. She remembered her first official Council only months ago when she'd turned fourteen. Her father had been so proud that day because his heir had turned of an age to rule, but Avalon was not supposed to sit the king's chair for decades. She had spent very little time in this room since her first Council. Avalon tried to harden hers mind. She walked to the king's chair and sat down, rubbing her hands over the polished wood. There was a small divot in the arm of the chair where she had seen her father rub his thumb, and she realized that it had been made a groove over generations. Avalon placed her thumb in the space and turned it in circles, but before she could get lost in her emotions, there was a double tap on the door and Taggerty and Gamon entered followed by the red headed man who was with Taggerty at the party. Avalon tried to remember his name, but she couldn't.

"King Hall," Gamon announced as he entered and bowed. Avalon noticed Taggerty and his comrade bow in sync, and she gestured quickly with her hand that they should stand.

"Well?" she asked Taggerty when she realized they would not speak before their king.

Taggerty looked straight at her as he always did. "All is well, Your Highness. After riding in circles for two months, Hawker has been delivered to the elements. He was blindfolded or in a tent the entire time, and we did not let him see the sun nor moon. There is no way he knows where we have left him, and no chance he could find his way back."

"Who is this?" Avalon asked Taggerty. Her eyes pointed at the stout man who stood next to him.

Taggerty's eyes flashed concern. "King Avalon, this is Kensington. I introduced you last night at the ball."

The red-haired man stepped back with one foot and performed a gentleman's bow, but Avalon could tell that genteel was not in his blood.

"And why is he here? This is private business."

"I thought you might have questions about the trip, and since Kensington accompanied me, I brought him so that my report could be most thorough." Avalon could tell that Taggerty was growing impatient with her. Out of respect, most people bowed or looked down when addressing their king, but now his eyes cut directly into hers.

"How can you be sure that Hawker won't find his way back?" Avalon asked in reflex. She knew that Taggerty would not let her down, but her Uncle Hawker had been so cunning as to poison her father and almost take her own life. She had a hard time believing he would go quietly. And yet even as a swordsman and archer herself, Avalon knew she would have a hard time surviving in the wild.

"I don't think I would even be able to make it back here on foot after an ordeal like that. You will never see Hawker again." Originally Taggerty had asked for permission to dispose of Hawker, to kill him and bury him where no one would ever look, but Avalon had instructed that Hawker be kept alive. He was to be given a small amount of ration and some simple tools to live out his life in the wilderness. Taggerty had argued against it, but Avalon stood her ground. She was finding it impossible to separate her loving uncle of fourteen years and the man who had held a sword to her chest.

Avalon swallowed hard. She had given the order knowing in the back of her mind that his pampered body would succumb to the elements sooner than later, and if Hawker died in the wilderness, his death was on his own hands.

"Kensington," she said, her eyes still on Taggerty. "What state was Hawker in when you left him?"

"Your Highness?" Kensington stuttered.

"What I mean to say is, was he alive?"

Insulted by Avalon's insinuation, Taggerty shifted his weight and grit his teeth.

"He was tired, but he had his wits about him, Your Highness," Kensington answered, his eyes on the floor in front of Avalon.

"Thank you, Kensington. You are dismissed." Taggerty and Kensington turned to leave.

"Not you, Taggerty," Avalon commanded. "Gamon, please leave us."

Gamon followed Kensington out, and Avalon waited until the doors were closed before she spoke, but Taggerty cut her off.

"You dismissed Kensington rather quickly. He is a loyal and noble man. You should learn to trust him."

"He is no nobleman," Avalon retorted. "He's very rough around the edges. Where did you find him?"

"I didn't *find* him. He's of the King's Guard and we became fast friends when I joined. He was a strong companion on this journey."

"You should have taken Connor."

Taggerty tried to retain his sigh. "We went over this, King Avalon. Connor is but a boy."

"Connor and I are the same age," Avalon retorted.

"You are not anything like him, King Avalon. You grew up with Connor and he is loyal, but Hawker was very talkative, and he taunted us when he could. Connor would have beaten Prince Hawker for insubordination by the second day. I trust Kensington, and I had to tell him everything. I don't know that Connor is grown enough to keep a secret that big."

Avalon had no doubt that her uncle had done his best to goad Taggerty. "Well then, I guess there are three men I can trust now," Avalon replied with only a hint of sarcasm.

"So you have told Gamon everything?" Taggerty challenged.

"Gamon knows about Hawker, and he has helped me piece together the events that followed my father's death."

"And he knows about Brick's betrayal? Will he help me find out if there are any other traitors in the Guard?"

"Well, no. I haven't told him about Brick." Avalon saw the look of masked disappointment on Taggerty's face. She was surprised he was restraining his words as he, Zaria, and Myra were the only three who treated her equally. "Speak freely, Taggerty."

He was quiet for a moment, regaining his temper. He took a long breath and sighed before continuing. "I need Gamon to know that Brick was a traitor. I need help if I am going to properly ferret out anyone else who was supporting Prince Hawker. I know you don't like to think that way, Your Highness, but we have to assume that he had help until we prove it untrue. And King Avalon, I beg of you, you must prepare for the Runners to come across the window."

Avalon's face reddened. "We will watch and wait. It has been ten turns of the moon and no one has come."

"But the few Guides who keep watch is not an army at the ready," Taggerty begged.

"The men are preparing. Gamon has been running extra drills with the guard, and he has reinstated Walthan's borough protection protocol, so the men of the town are starting to do drills too. It will be a miracle if the rumors don't start." Avalon was referring to when she was a young prince and Walthan had made the townsmen do defensive drills after the Fingers had been raised. Fontanasia had been peaceful for many generations, and with no evident enemy, most people were lax in their drills. When Walthan didn't let up, rumors raged over time that there was imminent doom on the horizon, and King Birch had to put a stop to the drills to keep the city calm.

"That's not enough," Taggerty said. "I need to go back to Cormicks to find out what they know."

"No!" Avalon barked. "If they haven't come through yet, they don't know how to find us. I will not send men to their death without cause. We need to sit tight."

"Sit tight?" Taggerty accused. "That's all you're going to do? Sit on your hands and wait to be raided by the Runners? We need to arm the men and cross over. We need to take the offensive."

"We can't do that!" Avalon yelled, slapping her palm into the arm of the wood chair. She bit her lip and tried to regain her composure. "This is a secret that your family has been keeping for hundreds of years and you are willing to expose it within months of learning of it?" Avalon accused.

"It's not a secret," Taggerty snapped back. "No one knows what is happening in Cormicks, not like we do. But there are still stories that people tell, stories handed down from generations..."

"Fairy tales!" Avalon barked.

Taggerty was ready to raise his voice and argue with Avalon, but he realized that the Hall family had been keeping this secret just as long as the Guides. He didn't take the bait but calmed himself with a deep breath.

"Taggerty, I'm sorry," she said looking directly at his face, which was a mistake if she was going to prove her point. When she looked into his salty, green eyes, all thought left her mind but the daydreams where he took her chin in his hand and leaned down to kiss her. Avalon had never thought of being kissed before, but meeting Taggerty had changed everything. She looked back down at her feet so she could focus.

"For hundreds of years this secret has been guarded from everyone, especially those on the other side of the window." Chills ran up her spine as she spoke. "The Monarch, the Runners, they didn't know we existed. They thought that when they raided our castle at Hawkerness and murdered our people all those years ago, that they killed everyone. They didn't know that anyone got away. My family, the Guides, those who made it out and founded Fontanasia didn't exist to the Runners. They haven't found us in over two hundred years."

"But now, they know we exist, and that traitor, Brick, told them everything," Taggerty spat. Avalon knew that his anger was not for her this time, and she felt the same sickening hatred for Brick. Still, the bile rose in her throat when she remembered his death and how the everred spiders had pulled his bloody remains into the ground.

"They didn't find us all those years because they weren't looking for us. Now they know we are here."

Avalon shook her head. "We don't know that. We don't know what Brick told them, and they haven't come here since we escaped almost a year ago. We don't know if they even realize how to get here, Taggerty. The last thing we need to do is go back and show them the way. If they are looking for us, and I am sure they are, the Monarch will have Runners all over the countryside. If we go over and emerge from those woods, it's like showing them where Fontanasia is."

"So, we sit and wait for the people who crushed our ancestors to come and crush us?"

Avalon played her finger around the wood divot and tried to think of what her father would do or say, but she couldn't find his words, so hers would have to do. "Taggerty, I would not allow Hawker to be hanged or run through, because I know the cost of blood on my hands." She hadn't been talking about Walthan's death, but the words stung both of them just the same. Taggerty knew that if he had stopped Brick sooner, then Walthan would be alive today.

Avalon crossed to the tall slit of window and looked down from the mountain that Fontanasia was built upon, but she could only see her memories. She was angry that she could not avenge her father's death. Doing nothing, sitting tight, meant that her father had also died for nothing. She was surprised to find a tear in her eye, and she let it fall alone down her cheek. She had learned how to do that when she could, to let the grief have its moment when no one was watching. Taggerty couldn't see her face, but she would have to control her voice to keep her tears concealed.

"My hands aren't tied. This is my decision." She wasn't put off by Taggerty's opinion, and she had kept the sarcasm out of her voice. Her father had told her many times that as king she would have to learn to cover her own opinions until she questioned her counselors. She would make the final decision, but she needed to hear all sides to be fully informed. She had only her view, and the others might enlighten her.

"As you say, Your Grace," Taggerty said softly. No matter what his feelings were, he would obey his king. His tone told her that he was backing down, and Avalon wondered if Taggerty could sense that she had been crying.

Keeping her back to him, she said, "You want peace, don't you?"

"Yes, I want peace. Of course I do. But I beg you, send a team into Cormicks so we can get ahead of the Monarch. Make this a priority."

"It is a priority, but I need to fix things with the Council first so that everyone can prepare for this threat united as one. I need to take some time and just learn how to..." her words faded out because she was going to say 'how to be king', but that was wrong. She knew how to be king if she would let herself. She had been rehearsing for this roll since she was minutes old and her father had mistaken her tiny baby body wrapped in blue for a boy. Why was she afraid of taking her rightful place now? Her father had prepared her all her life, and his death would be for naught if she floundered. Avalon discreetly wiped her cheek with her fingertips and looked at Taggerty's stony expression.

"Your Highness, you are far away and safe back at home in your castle, but don't forget the intensity of the situation." His tone was level, but his hands were clenched and that immediately put Avalon on the defensive.

"And don't you forget those boys who attacked me in the street. I don't have the leisure of rushing in. I need to clean my house so that we attack united, and I don't have to look over my shoulder."

"And I will help you, King Avalon. I'm only trying to be your friend." Taggerty's tone was sincere but his words upset Avalon.

"Friend?" Avalon spat bitterly. "You want to be my friend? What a king needs is advisors and good counsel, not friends."

Taggerty's face railed with anger. "Please, excuse me," he snapped. He bowed his head and swept out of the room without being dismissed, and Avalon was immediately sorry. She didn't want to be his friend though. She felt more than that, but it was impossible. She would need to settle for his friendship or they would continue to argue and she would lose him altogether.

"You are the future of the king," she said out loud to the closing doors, quoting the Guide's prophecy given to Taggerty when he was a baby. But again, maybe Taggerty had already realized his destiny when he had saved her life. Maybe the prophecy had already been fulfilled, and he was the future of the king because she was still alive. It might be that simple, she thought, shaking her head in protest.

As soon as Taggerty left the Council room, there was a quick knock and Counselor Robert entered with a proud smile on his face. He walked halfway to Avalon, stopped to bow where the sun shone through the window and gleamed off his balding head, and then approached.

"King Avalon, today is a momentous day."

Avalon smiled as warmly as she could and gestured toward the seat that she knew Counselor Robert would be taking. As he moved to his seat, Avalon tried to shake off the lingering emotions left by her conversation with Taggerty. "I am looking forward to our work and planning what is best for the people of Fontanasia."

"I couldn't have said it any better myself," Counselor Robert beamed.

Counselor Robert had been at her father's side for her entire life, and unlike Counselor Glenn, he had always been kind to Avalon. She found him a calming and genuine presence, and she was glad to have him here. She felt her burden lifting a bit knowing that he would help guide her through the politics and details presented in Council today.

"May I be so bold as to offer some advice before the other counselors arrive?" Robert asked.

"Of course," Avalon granted, glad for the respite.

"It is impossible to please everyone, so you must weigh all sides, and make your decision without hesitation," he said gently. "We are like a family in here, and where there is camaraderie, there is also conflict. Your father has taught you well, and I know we will continue to thrive under your guidance." Counselor Robert was nodding, the smile not leaving his face.

"Thank you." Avalon was truly grateful for the older man's advice. She felt a heavy political weight knowing that she was answering to a few men for the livelihoods of many. It was sound advice not to try to please everyone.

The door opened and Gamon entered with the remaining counselors filing in behind him. Unsure of what to do next, Gamon closed the door and stood in the back of the room. Avalon wasn't certain of the protocol since Walthan didn't sit on the Council, but she wanted Gamon here for protection.

Counselor Nelson stepped forward first with his easy smile. She smiled back at him. "King Avalon," he said as he bowed deeply and moved off to his seat.

Counselor Igway was next, his short, round figure swaying his robes like a metronome as he stepped forward. "King Avalon," he said through his nose. Avalon didn't take offense to his trite mannerism because that is how Igway spoke to everyone. He was from the Downs which was the borough closest to the plains at the bottom of the mountain, and it flooded during bad storms. Avalon traveled through the Downs each morning that she practiced her sword, and she knew the people there were straight faced and all business, getting on with life as it was dealt them.

Counselor Jennings was next. He approached slowly and bowed with reverence. "King Avalon, I have brought you a delicacy from the Reaches," he said as though his borough was a hundred miles away. He placed a box on the small table.

"Thank you, Counselor Jennings. I'm sure I will enjoy your gift." Avalon remembered that Counselor Jennings was known to be serious at all times, but not without a sense of humor. The Reaches was the closest to the Helon Sea, and the people in that borough had created wooden floors to float on the water. They had pulled sea creatures from the waters and ate them, although not many others had taken to eating the food. Avalon could tell by the odor that he had brought her some of this delicacy.

The last in line was Counselor Dekarecol. He stood just taller than Avalon with an average build and many age lines on his face, but he still retained his dark brown hair. Dekarecol bowed cordially and smiled through his thin brown beard. It was said that Counselor Dekarecol brightened any room he walked in to, and Avalon felt that was true as his lingering energy gave her the confidence to start her first official counsel as king. "King Avalon, I look forward to providing you with my best counsel." Avalon smiled back as Dekarecol spun to take his seat, his robe swirling behind him.

Avalon was unsure what to say, but she had planned to start with what she remembered to be the longest and most boring topic so that she could use the time to solidify her bearings. Counselor Glenn was the head of her father's Council, and with his passing Avalon turned to the person she trusted the most. "Counselor Robert, I would like to start with an account of the food stores."

Counselor Nelson cleared his throat and stood, but his eyes did not meet Avalon's, and he knew he was talking out of turn. "Your Highness, perhaps the king would be so generous as to offer some clarification for the Council before we move forward."

Avalon's stunned silence gave Counselor Nelson the confidence to continue. "The Council has a question about what happened to Prince Hawker. Counselor Glenn confided in some of us, and we know Hawker was imprisoned..." Nelson's voice trailed off and Avalon looked to Counselor Robert, but he didn't stop the conversation.

"My uncle is dead," Avalon stated, moving her stomach muscles around with the ache that returned with the thought of Hawker. Avalon looked at Counselor Nelson suspiciously. He had never been so forthright with her father. Was he in line with Hawker? She couldn't believe that he was, but the truth was, she trusted no one, and so she lied now to everyone.

"I don't mean to upset you, Your Highness. It's just that your father died, and Hawker was locked up, and then Counselor Glenn was killed. We are your trusted Council. We are your servants, and we would like some answers so that we can give you the proper guidance."

Counselor Robert cleared his throat leaving Counselor Nelson to take his seat. Avalon thought that she might be able to side-step the conversation, but Robert continued, "Since Counselor Nelson brought it up, I would like to know the truth. Is Prince Hawker locked up somewhere still? If Prince Hawker had anything to do with your father's death, then he deserves to be hanged." Avalon's eyes widened and she slid her thumb into the worn spot on her wood dais.

"He deserves to burn for what he did," Counselor Igway rumbled with conviction, and Avalon's stomach turned. Avalon had witnessed murder first hand in Cormicks, and she doubted any of these men had seen death first hand in peaceful Fontanasia. She hated Counselor Glenn and her Uncle Hawker, but she could not celebrate anyone's death. Now that the Council was questioning her, she wondered if Counselor Glenn had pulled them all into his plans to take over Fontanasia after her father had been killed.

Counselor Dekarecol stood and waited for the other counselors to settle down. He looked at Avalon and then at each of the men in turn. "I can't say that Counselor Glenn entrusted me with his secrets, but I don't think we should be calling for anyone's blood. We are a peaceful people devoted to our king and to the people of Fontanasia, and we don't want to act in haste." Avalon was glad that Dekarecol had spoken up, but she couldn't help being suspicious of him. If the rest wanted Hawker dead and he didn't, did that mean he was working with Hawker? Avalon was confused and had lost control of her first Council within the first minute.

The king lifted her hand and slammed her palm on the arm of her chair. Gamon took two steps closer but stopped, seeing that Avalon was upset but not in danger. Avalon stood, and the rest of the counselors sat and watched her closely. "My uncle is dead," she clarified, her voice cutting the room like a knife. "My father and Counselor Glenn are also dead. I was ill during this time. I don't know what transpired between my Uncle Hawker and Counselor Glenn, but I assure you, they are both deceased. And Dekarecol is right. We are a peaceful people. I understand completely where your emotion stems from, but it sickens me that after a time of disease and death, you could even think of calling for blood." Avalon had never seen her father lose control of the Council, and her spirits waned. Men who she hoped were trusted counselors could no longer be trusted.

There was a knock on the large wooden door, and Gamon was so enthralled in the Council discussion that he jumped when he heard the sound. He looked at Avalon who gave a barely noticeable nod, and Gamon opened the door. Avalon was relieved for the distraction, but she was not prepared for what was to come.

Standing in the center of the archway was Julius Creighton, hands folded, magenta robe barely shifting under his movement. He walked slowly into the room like a solitary old man. He smiled at Gamon who closed the door behind him. Avalon took note of each counselor's expression, but none were smiling as though he might be expecting a visitor. This concerned Avalon. Creighton didn't know anything definitive, but if he were here to expose what he knew about Cormicks, then she would have a lot of questions to answer.

Creighton finally made it to the center of the room and bowed slowly, his practiced age a perfect performance. He didn't look up at Avalon, but held his short bow in place until Avalon spoke first.

"Archivist Creighton, what could be so important that you would find the need to disturb my Council?" Avalon asked. Creighton slowly regained an upright posture.

"King Avalon," Creighton started slowly as though he was about to give a lecture on history.

After spending some time with Creighton only a few hours earlier and learning the truth of why he acted an aged man, Avalon was still surprised at how he could make his voice sound weathered, as though he had been around since time itself. Still, she understood the need to disguise her voice as a boy to play her own part.

"I like to think that I was helpful to your father in many aspects. I helped him design some of the water upgrades that he had installed in the castle when you were just a baby." Creighton smiled, and Avalon realized impossibly that he would have been Taggerty's age when those upgrades were made. "We also regularly reviewed the accounting of supplies for each borough. I have helped each of these counselors with borough logistics. I was at King Birch's service as I am at your service."

"I thank you for your dedication," Avalon said.

"Yes," Creighton said as he hunched his shoulders like a turtle and nodded. "King Avalon, I would like to offer my service to you in a greater capacity. I am from Counselor Glenn's borough, as it would be, and so it only seems natural."

"You want a seat on my Council?" Avalon asked incredulously before she could stop herself. To his credit, Creighton's face lit up with surprise, but Avalon was certain that he had manipulated this short conversation as a means to an end. In this moment, she was sure that she was Creighton's pawn.

"Well, Your Highness. I could never suppose that I could fill Counselor Glenn's shoes, but if that is the capacity that you would like me to serve. I am at your command."

Avalon was visibly shocked. She had spent over an hour with Creighton the previous night, and he had not even hinted at his interest in the Council. "I thank you again for your service to my father, but I just met you last night at my birthday celebration. I couldn't presume to know what your interest can be in this Council."

Creighton chuckled cordially. "My King, I couldn't expect you to know everyone in Fontanasia, and I am sorry that our paths could not cross before last evening. I assure you that my interest in the Council extends to my caring about those in my borough and the people of Fontanasia, and I will serve at the capacity that suits you best."

Avalon didn't know what to think, but she didn't see anyone else stepping forward to take the empty Council seat. If Creighton was working with Hawker, then she would be giving him a voice in her inner circle, but she needed to believe that he was trying to help her after what he had shown her last night.

Counselor Robert stood and saved Avalon from making the decision alone. "King Avalon, if I may be so bold as to suggest it, Julius Creighton is more than qualified to serve on the Council." Counselor Robert continued when Avalon didn't stop him. "As he suggested, he is involved in our day to day operation, and he has looked over our numbers for several years, giving advice when he could."

"Your Highness," Counselor Nelson concurred, "that is all true."

Avalon nodded slowly trying to find a reason to deny the request, but it all made sense. "I see no reason to deny your request, especially with Counselor Robert and Counselor Nelson weighing in on your behalf in the matter. I will consider it, and I will make my decision known at the Festival of Fontanasia."

Julius Creighton tipped his head up and looked into Avalon's black eyes. He smiled, and Avalon thought she could see a chuckle. She had appeased Creighton and the Council by saying she would consider it, but the festival was almost two months away, so she had kept her prerogative as king and final decision maker.

"Thank you, Your Highness," Creighton said humbly. "I seem to always be searching for the right words to convey my apology. Perhaps my faithful service to this Council will prove to you how serious I am about the future of Fontanasia." Creighton hadn't apologized for anything specific, and he was talking in code, Avalon was sure of that, but she was just glad that he hadn't exposed what he knew about Cormicks.

"The future of Fontanasia is my only concern. It seems we will both need to trust each other if we are going to work together in this new capacity," Avalon told him with an outward smile.

Julius Creighton opened his hands and tipped his head forward. "I am at your disposal."

"You are dismissed," Avalon said in a controlled tone.

He turned and walked slowly to the door. Gamon knocked twice and the guards outside the room swung the heavy, wood door open. As Julius Creighton's magenta robes disappeared, Avalon exhaled. She hadn't realized that she was unsteadily holding her breath for the entire meeting. She would have to relax if she was going to make it through the next few hours. She rubbed her thumb in the notch on the chair, a reminder of her forefathers before her. Although, her father and his fathers had never been a fifteen year old girl-king with the Monarch of Cormicks on the hunt for their head.

Chapter 4
The Archives

Council went for three hours, and Avalon was exhausted when she returned to her suite. Lunch was ready in the dining room, but after the sleepless night and her first official Council as king, Avalon needed privacy. She asked for a plate to be brought up and retreated to her suite. It felt impossible to focus on the day-to-day ruling of Fontanasia knowing that Cormicks was a threat, and it exhausted her to keep up pretenses. She sat down with a loud sigh and her tiny, red jakkow lizard crawled up onto her shoulder. She picked up the box that Jackie slept in at night and looked closely at the woodcarving. It had made little sense to her when the Guides had presented the finely crafted box, but now when she looked at the carvings on it, she could see the two moons for what they were. One was her moon, the one that shown over Fontanasia, large and white with diamond light sparkling in places. The other was the dim, yellow moon over Cormicks.

There was a knock at the door and lunch was brought in and placed on the side table. The servant pulled a chair to the table and made a makeshift place setting for the king before withdrawing from the room and closing Avalon in alone. The food smelled wonderful and Avalon's mouth watered, but the sword that her Uncle Hawker had given her on her fourteenth birthday caught her attention. She pulled it from the mount on the wall and drew the sword from its holster, wondering if she would lead Fontanasia into a war that kings before her had been able to avoid.

She noticed the words on the blade near the hilt. *The sun may rule, but it is the moon that guides to our true destiny.* These were the words that Hawker had written for her. These were the words he intended for her to know, and Avalon knew them well. Avalon thought for the hundredth time that she could have stopped Hawker if she had read the signs right. She remembered overhearing Counselor Glenn talking to Hawker in the basement. She knew now that it was Hawker with the upper hand and Counselor Glenn trying to convince him to come forward about Cormicks. Of course, Counselor Glenn couldn't have known Hawker's real plan. Prince Hawker, with his false allegiance and brotherly love all of those years, counseling Avalon until she became of age to take the throne. If she had only seen, her father might still be alive.

Avalon gripped the handle, moving the sword and slicing the air in front of her. She had considered having the sword melted down to nothing, but she realized that it needed to stay at her side so that she could feel her enemy was within reach. She hoped that she could eventually get comfortable in her position, but if she did, she needed a reminder to never trust anyone ever again. Avalon took a deep breath. She needed to trust and to confide in her sister, but maybe it would be easier to keep her distance since Zaria didn't know the whole truth and would only be frightened if she did. And then there was Taggerty to consider. He had saved her life more than once and he had sworn his allegiance, but if Zaria and Taggerty were together, that was all the more reason to keep them both at arm's length.

There was a light knock on the door and then it opened. Myra George looked in and when she saw Avalon sitting on the bed with sad eyes and her sword in hand, Myra slipped in and quickly closed the door behind her.

"I didn't say you could enter," Avalon teased.

"Pish posh," Myra retorted, stopping her stride. She was loyal to a fault, and although Avalon had obviously been playing with her, Myra was second-guessing her entering without permission from her king. Myra bunched her apron for a moment in a nervous tick and then continued forward. She pulled up a chair and sat opposite Avalon, pointing at the sword.

"This is the gift from your Uncle Hawker," Myra said softly.

"He's not my uncle," Avalon whispered. It was difficult to say.

Myra read the inscription. "I never realized he was a poet. I didn't know he had a creative bone in his body," she said with all the disrespect she could muster.

"He didn't." Avalon pulled the sword back from Myra and sheathed it, tossing it behind her onto the bed. Myra sat in silence waiting for Avalon to open up. "It's just, I can't stop thinking about how he was my uncle, but he tried to kill me. I think about all the time I spent with Hawker, and none of it was true. It's like nothing is real."

"It was real, Avalon. Prince Hawker might not have ended up who you thought he was, but your time is your time, and your experiences are yours alone. So you see, that time was real, and the emotions of love and respect were real because that is what you felt. It doesn't matter what Hawker felt. You could not have known."

Avalon tried to unravel Myra's meaning, but she was not convinced. She had confessed to Myra that Hawker had tried to kill her, and now she slowly told Myra about seeing Hawker with Counselor Glenn, and Hawker lighting the mouse on fire. She remembered how the mouse had shrieked in agony as it ran past while Avalon crouched out of site behind a pile of steel slag.

Avalon was surprised at Myra's cool acceptance of Hawker's treachery. Myra bit her lower lip like she was trying to decide on something, but she had remained completely calm. She rose and crossed to the washbasin wetting a cloth. "Here, King Avalon. Use this to wipe your face. It will refresh you." Myra had addressed Avalon as king with purpose. She intended to remind Avalon that she was the strongest hand in the land, that she had the strongest voice, and that she had the might to rule as she would.

Avalon wiped her face, the cool rag cleaning her skin. She ran the cloth over the back of her neck and then handed it back to Myra. Her back had straightened with Myra's encouragement, but she still felt lost.

Myra continued to speak as she returned the cloth to the washbasin. "When Hawker was only seven years old, the servants found him burning the tail of a cat while the cat was alive." She grit her teeth and sat next to Avalon on the bed. "The entire cat would have surely been burned to death if Hawker had not been interrupted. Your grandfather, the king, was furious, but Hawker's mother convinced him that it would never happen again. One month after the cat incident, on Hawker's eighth birthday, a stable hand was badly burned in a fire trying to save a horse. Birch learned that Hawker had been present in the stables watching the men douse the fire. The horse was so badly burned that they were forced to put it down. It took months for the stable hand to heel. Birch didn't tell his father the truth because Hawker was his brother and he didn't want to get him in trouble. And none of the hands wanted to tell the king that his son had lit the fire."

"I never heard about that before," Avalon said, eyes wide open and appalled.

"Oh, people talk plenty. They just don't talk to you." Myra smiled knowingly, but Avalon was a bit offended by the comment. Why shouldn't they talk to her? She was their king.

Myra wiped her hands dry and returned to sit next to Avalon. "As the years passed, Hawker was not caught torturing animals again. I think his mother put a stop to it, or she kept it hidden. He started to enjoy the bowels of the castle more than fresh air, and he kept to himself. His skin became very pale and his demeanor changed for the better," she said with a flourish.

"How could anyone do that?" Avalon asked.

"The thing is Avalon, Hawker was your uncle, but he was also that bad person who burned animals. He had the capacity for outward kindness, and the cold hearted ability to turn on his own family." She placed her hand on Avalon's knee. "The moments you saw as out of character were, in fact, part of Hawker's true character. It was part of who he was. It is sad and very deceptive, but that doesn't mean you shouldn't trust anyone because of the actions of one person."

Avalon leaned back and looked at Myra. She hadn't told Myra what she had been thinking, but Myra had guessed. It was an issue of trust, and Avalon would not change her mind in one day, but Myra's words might convince her to try.

"Why should I be surprised anyway? I have been keeping a secret my whole life. Hawker wasn't who he seemed to be, and neither am I."

Myra smiled and ran her hand over the back of Avalon's head. She had been caressing Avalon like this since she was a baby, and Avalon still found it soothing. "I know you have your own things to deal with," Myra told her. "I know that you are hiding something, but you are nothing like Hawker. He was the exception, you are not."

"Do you think that my father made me his son because he suspected Hawker?"

Myra smiled at Avalon. "No, child, no one suspected Prince Hawker of being capable of what he has done. I never trusted Prince Hawker either, but even I didn't suspect him of being capable of such treachery."

Myra stood and walked to the side table where the servant had placed Avalon's lunch. She pulled the chair away from the table and snapped the napkin open. "Have lunch, my King."

Avalon felt better after she ate lunch. Still, it shamed her that she spent more time thinking about her Uncle Hawker than she did her father. Avalon was obsessed with Hawker in a way. She couldn't believe how Hawker had fooled her. He had fooled everyone, even his own brother. Her father should have suspected something was wrong, but it was too painful to think of her father now.

When she left the suite, four of the King's Guard followed her. Avalon was starting to grow tired of always having to announce her movements. Her father never did. She understood their vigilance, though. Her father was dead and the King's Guard was not going to lose another king.

She rounded the corner before the Hall of Kings and was ready to make her way down the steps to the archives, when she noticed Zaria outside on the terrace. Avalon almost changed her direction to meet with her sister, until she realized that Zaria was with Taggerty.

Avalon was close enough to hear Taggerty say, "Kensington, please escort the princess back to her quarters when she is ready." Then Taggerty spotted Avalon, and before she could turn back to the staircase, he was closing in on her. Avalon didn't look in his direction, so he walked directly in her path. She tried to smile but was gritting her teeth, and it left a serious look on her face.

"What's wrong?" Taggerty asked.

"Nothing," Avalon replied, trying to smile. Avalon moved to the stairs with Taggerty and the guard in tow. "I am headed to the archives to do a bit of research."

"We can have some books from the archives brought to you, Your Grace."

Avalon stopped on the first landing and looked directly into Taggerty's eyes. "Gamon has not caged me yet," she said with a forced smile. She didn't want to be rude to Taggerty, but it stung to see him with Zaria out on the terrace enjoying the midday sun.

Taggerty looked back at two of the guardsmen. "To the archives," he said. They stepped around the king and started down the next flight of stairs, shielding her front and back. Taggerty smiled at Avalon and held his hand out showing her the way, and it reminded her of the day they had met. He'd had the same twinkle in his eye then, like he was toying with her but also like he was taking care of her. Avalon's mixture of excitement and resentment made her want to punch him in the face, but instead she moved down the stairs with Taggerty and the last two guardsmen in tow. Avalon waited patiently at the door while one of the guards did a sweep of the archives. She tapped her foot trying to be patient with them, but it wasn't easy.

"They are just doing their job," Taggerty said, but she kept her back to him.

The door swung open and Avalon stepped in. One guard stood near the librarian's desk, but the other guards remained outside. Uninvited, Taggerty followed her in. Avalon noticed the robed man seated behind the desk. He had his head turned to the ground, and Avalon could see that he was trying to bow as low as he could, but his old body would not let him. "Be at ease," she said to the wizened elderly man. Then she turned to the guardsman near the desk. "I will be fine in here," she said to him. He didn't leave right away though. Avalon caught the glance he made over her shoulder to Taggerty. He hesitated and then tipped his head in a bow, removing himself from the room.

Avalon tried to ignore what had just happened, but she couldn't. She turned to Taggerty and said under her breath. "They are supposed to listen to me. I am the king."

"Yes, Your Highness, but sometimes we are blinded by those who would deceive us and we need an extra eye," he whispered back. He wasn't wrong, and Avalon chose not to have an argument in front of the librarian. She turned toward the desk where the old man looked up at her expectantly.

"King Avalon," the librarian's tone was raspy, adding to his apparent age. "You just missed Counselor Nelson."

"Did I?" Avalon asked. "Do you have many visitors here?"

The old man thought about that for a moment. "No, not really. We take care of the books in the library upstairs. That is where most people go. I don't spend much time down here, but Counselor Nelson needed my help."

Avalon liked Counselor Nelson, he'd always been kind to her, but no one was beyond suspicion these days. "What did he need help with?" she asked.

"He was asking if Counselor Glenn had been doing any research. He also asked about Prince Hawker, bless his soul," the librarian said in earnest as he placed his hand over his heart. Avalon tried not to read anything into the old man's gesture. He had been a faithful servant to the Hall family, that was all.

Avalon nodded and tried not to let her mind linger on Hawker, turning away and slowly making her way through the stacks. The old man rose, his chair silently sliding back through its worn path in the stone. He followed several feet behind Taggerty as Avalon walked up and down a few of the rows. She wasn't sure what she was looking for, but Avalon knew that Julius Creighton had wanted to show her something of Hawker's last night, and she wanted to see it without him. Then Avalon jumped back, startled when she came around a stack of books and almost walked into Julius Creighton. Her hand was over her heart and she squealed. It was as though her thoughts alone had brought Creighton here, and it made her spine tingle. She was embarrassed by her reaction when she saw Taggerty had already drawn a knife from somewhere and was standing between her and Creighton.

"Your Highness," Creighton said with a molasses bow. "I thought I might find you here. Please, follow me this way. The volume I was telling you about is right over here." He looked directly into Avalon's eyes and nodded slightly before dismissing the librarian.

Creighton seemed not to notice the knife as he turned ever so slowly and made his way to a side table. Avalon looked at Taggerty who pushed the small knife back into his sleeve.

"I'm so glad to see you are interested in the value of the archives, King Avalon. You can learn invaluable things from reading." Creighton's tone was neutral, but Avalon knew he was addressing the fact that she would not come to the archives the night before. Creighton approached a corner table where there were several books open at different intervals. He turned slowly and smiled, and Avalon could see that he was looking past them to see if they had been followed. One of the guard now stood twenty feet away at the end of the stack, but there was no one else.

"Should we speak alone, King Avalon?" Creighton asked. Avalon felt that they were alone, and then she was surprised when she realized he was asking about dismissing Taggerty.

"You may speak freely in front of Taggerty. He can be trusted," she told Creighton.

"You sound certain," Creighton answered with a smile. "No offense, young Taggerty."

"None taken," Taggerty sighed.

"Of course, of course," Creighton said slowly. "But King Avalon, it is truly best we speak alone."

"I said that Taggerty could be trusted. He has saved my life more than once."

"More than once?" Creighton repeated slowly as his brow furrowed. He rubbed his chin and looked between Avalon and Taggerty. "As you say, King Avalon." Creighton turned to the table and pulled a drawer Avalon hadn't noticed. "You will want to read this book also, King Avalon. This is the diary of the first King of Fontanasia, a document brought over by himself when the Runners invaded Hawkerness and killed all of the people there." Creighton handed the worn leather book over to Avalon. "It is interesting reading. The first King Hall of Fontanasia was a scientist, and well before he was king, he kept notes on the Runners society, and noted how the Runners were violent even to each other. He was not very close with his cousin, the King of Hawkerness, but he did note that some of the family feared being invaded by the Runners." With a paralyzing fear of invasion that mirrored her ancestors, Avalon ran her hand over the worn cover of the book, and tucked it into her robe.

Zaria was all smiles at dinner, and Avalon was reminded that her sister's regained happiness was brought on by Taggerty's return. Avalon took bites of her food while Zaria chattered on about her next intimate private party. Avalon swallowed back her resentment with each bite. Zaria was beautiful, kind, and a woman. Of course Taggerty was interested in her sister. Still, it was difficult to listen to

Zaria gush over Taggerty and how he always came around and made sure she got enough fresh air each day.

"You really should come to the party next week," Zaria said, catching Avalon's eye.

"You're joking," Avalon told her with a grunt.

"Well you can't stay closed up in the suite all of the time."

"I'm not!" Avalon protested. She put a bite of food in her mouth so she wouldn't have to say anymore.

"You're right, Avalon. You aren't holed up anymore. You have gotten back to work, and that is good. But you can't live on work alone." Zaria moved her food around her plate.

"Come to the party, please do, Avalon," Zaria begged.

"Why, so I can meet one of your young lady friends and get married and start a family?" Avalon said sarcastically. She was all too aware that everyone in the castle had a match for her now that she was king. It was exasperating.

"Well, no," Zaria said slowly. She knew she had hit a nerve. "You can come as my cousin," Zaria said with satisfaction. "I will dress you in a gown and put on some makeup and no one will know who you are."

"Our cousins will know when you show up with a cousin who never existed before," Avalon retorted. They ate in silence as Avalon thought about the invitation. She had never given Zaria's idea a moment's thought in the past, but a party might be a way she could see Taggerty relaxed and having fun instead of talking about Fontanasia and his thoughts on the guard. She wondered how he might look at her all dressed up and pretty for a night. Not that she thought she would be pretty, but Taggerty seemed to notice most girls at any rate.

"Taggerty and Kensington will be there, so you will know someone," Zaria was saying.

"Yes, but they won't know me," Avalon protested. "And if they do recognize me, that would be even worse."

Avalon tried to sound thoughtful instead of resentful, "Zaria, I don't think that Taggerty is someone you should really be spending time with." Avalon could feel her face burning in blush, and she hoped Zaria would not notice. She covered her face with her goblet and pretended to drink for a moment.

"Taggerty?" Zaria laughed. "He is very handsome. You have to come to the party. You could be so pretty, Avalon. You have very beautiful eyes. I could tell that Taggerty was noticing them the night of your birthday."

Avalon cleared her throat and tried to dismiss her sister. "Beautiful? Is that any way to describe a king?"

"Avalon, come to the party," Zaria begged again. Just then there was a knock at the door and Taggerty and Kensington entered. Avalon noticed how Zaria's cheeks flushed at the sight of him.

"No," Avalon said to Zaria.

Taggerty stopped to close the door and Kensington bowed to Avalon and Zaria. "I hope we are not too early for our walk," Kensington said.

"Not at all," Zaria answered in a shrill voice. "We were just finishing up. Come Avalon, we must take in the evening air." Avalon was surprised at her sister's invitation, and then Taggerty was at her side and bowing, and Avalon could not bring herself to decline the offer.

"Princess Zaria," Kensington said with a bow, offering his hand and helping Zaria from her chair. The pair wandered out the door, and Avalon stood to follow with Taggerty in tow.

They strolled through the castle and out to the small lawn that overlooked the Helon Sea. The sun was setting and the sky was a beautiful mixture of pastels. They leaned on the short wall that edged the garden. Kensington complemented Zaria on her complexion in the pink light, and Avalon rolled her eyes and turned to stroll around the yard. Taggerty followed and Avalon came to a bench and sat, but Taggerty remained standing. They didn't speak, and Avalon could feel her ears burning in the silence.

Zaria and Kensington were now out of earshot, and Avalon saw Zaria reach out and tap Kensington's arm with a giggle a few times. It made Avalon angry that Zaria would flirt with Taggerty's friend, and right in front of him.

"You don't approve?" Taggerty asked, looking over at Zaria and Kensington.

"Doesn't that bother you?" Avalon replied. It made her distressed that Taggerty didn't even seem to notice Zaria's behavior.

"Why would it?" Taggerty asked.

Avalon wanted to say a million things, but she held her tongue. She didn't want to insult Taggerty or her sister, but the whole situation was making her more and more angry. "It's just, Zaria is so fickle."

Taggerty laughed loudly. "She used to be. I think she is happy now."

Avalon opened her mouth to speak, but Zaria cut her off. "Taggerty, come here and settle a bet between Kensington and myself."

"Excuse me, King Avalon," Taggerty said, and he quickly walked over to Zaria. Avalon swallowed hard and squashed her hope. She saw Taggerty laughing with Zaria, leaning down toward her and sharing a smile. Maybe the Guides were right. Maybe Taggerty was the future of the king because he would marry Zaria and become the father of the next king. Avalon stood, and without the others noticing, she slipped back into the castle.

Chapter 5
A King's Place

He was a bookworm, at least that is what Avalon and everyone else thought, and it was true. But no one knew what Hawker had been studying for over ten years. His life seemed boring to them, and when anyone would ask what he was reading, he would drone on about a bland topic until they lost interest. He would of course never share what he was really working on. Hawker had been studying plants and animals, knots and snares, stars and navigation by stars. He had been studying survival, knife and sword skills, and he had been studying the road to Cormicks.

Prince Hawker never had a beard before, but his face was now covered in several months of soft hair. He had been rubbing his hands on his face since he'd started with the stubble, and he didn't recognize himself the first time he'd found standing water and used it to see his reflection. He no longer looked like royalty. His nails were black with dirt and his robes were worn and fraying. He had stared at his reflection for a long time, his skin gaunt and close to the bone, his hair long and unkempt. He would have thought he was a dying man but for his eyes. He had stared into his eyes for a long time, and there he saw the fire of hatred and anger that kept him moving forward.

He had remained for over a month in the place where the two soldiers had left him, foraging for plants and small animals to eat, and using the stream nearby. He had always been lean, but his body had lost some weight, and he could now see all of his muscles. Hawker first thought that they had left him with a fighting chance to live, but he had never been a hunter and no one knew he could survive, so they truly had left him for dead. It made him angry to think that his nephew could be so cold-hearted. Avalon should have run Hawker through when he'd had the chance, that would have been more humane than leaving someone with no skill in the woods to fend for himself.

It had taken him three days to light a fire, and he'd almost gone mad shivering at night. He'd read the books and practiced a few times in the castle, but Hawker always had the items he needed at hand in the castle. He'd never had to find dry wood and clean away an area for himself. He'd always had a flint handy and didn't have to rub wood on wood endlessly, the sticks ripping his palms raw. He'd never truly had to accomplish the task with his life in the balance before. In the castle there was always a torch burning within arms reach. As he rubbed the sticks together, all of his book smarts could not keep the maddening despair from creeping in. If he didn't start a fire, he would not live.

He had mastered the task in the following weeks. He had also found a sharp rock and fashioned a spear, but he was not able to make a bow. He had tried in the following months, but that was a craft he did not have the patience to master.

Hawker Hall watched the stars on this sweaty, summer night. He'd been studying the stars for over a year, and he could read all of the stars over Fontanasia, but he had trouble with the sky in this place, which meant he was more than thirty days from Fontanasia because that is how far the books marked the night sky. Hawker had sat at night with his back to the fire looking up at the stars and trying to get his bearings. He thought he could recognize a few stars, but they were far off from where they should be in the sky. In the end, he decided to head south. He assumed that Avalon would have put him as far away from both Fontanasia and Cormicks as possible, so he would have to be far east of Fontanasia. He reasoned that he must be somewhere north of the Helon Sea that bordered Fontanasia, and he walked south for months looking for the water or the star of Avalon, but he found neither.

It was summer, and dawn on the morning of the Festival of Fontanasia. This year she would play her part, but Avalon had not spent much time thinking about the festival this year, which was ironic to her since it was all she had spent her time preparing for last year.

She was up late reading the journal of the first king of Fontanasia, and she should be tired, but she felt full of energy. She walked her horse down through the boroughs and watched the shop keeps hop about as they got ready for the big day to come. Avalon hardly noticed the King's Guard who followed her. Her mind was lost in the pages she had been reading the night before. The journal had belonged to her great-grandfather many times removed who had founded Fontanasia over two hundred years earlier, but there was no history on ruling Hawkerness in the pages she read. This was the journal of a scientist. She was amazed at the detail he kept on his time spent studying the elbagrass, the first time he saw a deer eat the alleya leaf, and the connection he made his first time finding the window and crossing over.

He had trusted the Guides because they spent as much time in the woods as he did. They had watched him over the years, and shared food with him. When he had found the window, he eventually told the Guides about it, and they decided to send men across to investigate the new world. As Avalon read, she could see why the Guides had become so trusted by the first king, and by every king there after.

Avalon felt like she understood her ancestor and his growing solitude as he studied his discovery. In the past few months, she had spent many days and nights locked in her room. Myra and Zaria thought she was depressed, but Avalon was desperate to get herself to dream the future. They thought that she couldn't face the future, but Avalon wanted the future to show itself so she would know what direction she should move in. Days before, there had been a huge thunderstorm, and through the window Avalon had seen a bird lost in the wind, flapping its wings as hard as it could, but it was still moving backwards. Avalon's heart sank. She was that bird, using up all of her energy trying to plan her next move, but still moving backwards.

As much as she wanted to dream, Avalon knew that she would not be able to blindly follow any vision of the future. She had always fallen into the meaning of her dreams so easily, but her first dream had mislead her to Counselor Glenn when it should have shown her that Hawker was the true evil. He father had told her that she needed to recognize the dream, but not believe what she saw either, and yet he'd believed his dream when he saw a baby boy in the blankets.

When she returned from her outing, Avalon walked through the suite to her bedroom, absent-mindedly loosening her sleeves so she could wash up. She was five strides into the room before she noticed anything was amiss. Her room hadn't been ornately decorated like Zaria's was, because Avalon liked to keep her space uncluttered. Still, her tables were clear of everything, and her ornately carved trunk was gone. Avalon swung around to the bed table to see if Jackie was there, and then she sucked in her breath when she noticed Myra George sitting in a chair against the wall. Myra was the only true friend that Avalon had left in the world, and this morning she wore a look of quiet concern.

"Myra!" Avalon said. "You startled me."

"What kind of warrior have you become if your old servant can sneak up on you so easily?" Her words were light, but Avalon could tell that there was something wrong. When Avalon saw that Myra had been holding Jackie, she was certain that something was amiss. Myra thought the little, red lizard was cute to look at, but she never volunteered to touch it, and she always shied away when Avalon would try to hand it over. Avalon crossed the room and Myra held out her hand. The tiny jakkow lizard ran up Avalon's arm and into her pocket where he nestled into a ball.

The lizard made the tiny purring noise that he had started when they had returned from Cormicks. The trip had frightened them both for different reasons. Jackie had been terrified when, on the other side of the window, he had turned into a huge red lizard larger than the size of three horses combined. Avalon held her own horrors in the death she had seen, and in the giant rock creatures that had tried to crush them all.

"Wake up, Jackie," Avalon said, pinching her pocket. "Come on, Jackie, you can't sleep forever," Avalon said not wanting to address Myra's visit. Myra chuckled and slapped her hands on her knees to stand, and Avalon knew there was no avoiding a conversation.

"What's going on Myra? Where are my things?" Avalon asked. It wasn't a question though. She knew what was happening, but she still wasn't ready.

"I told the staff that you wanted to move to the king's chamber today."

"But I didn't, and I don't," Avalon protested.

"But you must," Myra said softly.

"You had no right!" Avalon shouted. Myra seemed to be waiting for this because she only bowed her head.

"You are correct, Your Grace. I had no right. I understand that this is a difficult time, but you have been king for almost a year. If you can't make small decisions for yourself, then how are you going to be ready to make the big ones for Fontanasia?"

Avalon swung her fist in the air. "It's not a small decision!" Avalon yelled, but this time from despair instead of anger. "That was my father's room, Myra." Avalon's shoulders slumped, and Myra stood to hug Avalon.

"It was your father and your mother's room, Avalon. You and your sister were born in that room, and your father before that. It is a room fit for a king, and it has always been the king's room." Myra rubbed Avalon's back softly, feeling her lungs taking in the air as she stifled her tears. "This room was for the prince. That room is for the king."

Avalon broke away from Myra and she slid her feet toward the bed. She let herself fall on the soft feather mattress. To avoid being crushed, Jackie slipped out of Avalon's pocket and scampered to the foot of the bed, but he didn't go back to sleep. He curled up and watched Avalon as a dog might watch its owner.

Myra sat on the bed next to Avalon and touched her shoulder gently, letting Avalon take the time she needed to accept her future. Nothing more was said between the two until Avalon stood up, wiping her face and her nose in her handkerchief.

"The staff is slipping, they forgot to move my sword." Avalon walked to her dresser. She pulled the hilt from the sheath far enough to see the inscription. She wondered where Hawker had found those words, or if he had made them up on his own. She hadn't thought of asking him when they were both princes and he had given the sword as a gift.

Myra cleared her throat. "I wasn't sure you still wanted that, under the circumstances."

Avalon nodded in understanding. "I can't seem to part with it." This sword was given to Avalon as a gift from the man who had killed her father. That made her feel guilty, but it was the truth. "It's a lie, this sword, but then so am I."

"Stop saying that," Myra rebuked. Then she remembered herself and her face reddened, but she would not take it back. Avalon was king, but she was also a child to Myra, a child who needed a parent.

Myra silently scolded herself. She had lost King Birch and she missed him dearly, but other than the loss of her lifelong friend, her life was still the same. She was still the keeper of the Hall family, and she would always assist the king. But Avalon's life had changed drastically. She had lost her father and her uncle. She was the king now, and Fontanasia was looking to her. Myra could not imagine the immense pressure that Avalon must be feeling, but she could no longer postpone the future. Today Avalon would take a huge step, a step closer to filling the shoes that she was born to wear.

"Pish posh," Myra said in a softer tone. "You are not a lie. You are King S. Avalon Hall of Fontanasia, and it doesn't get more real than that." She smiled at Avalon and tipped her head sternly toward the door, and Avalon conceded. The young king scooped up Jackie in one hand and the sword in the other, and she strode out the door of the room that had been hers for fifteen years. She crossed the hall to the king's chamber with confidence. Myra watched Avalon for a moment, and then she closed the door and waited silently in the hallway.

Avalon took one turn around the room feeling strange that her things should be in it, but before she could get too sentimental, she went back to the large wood door and swung it open with both hands. As she had expected, Myra was standing silently in the hallway.

"Well, don't just stand there. I will need to dress," Avalon announced.

"Yes, Your Highness," Myra said with pleasure. She had expected Avalon to sulk for a while, and the child's resilience surprised her. Avalon crossed to look out the window as Myra moved about the room readying things for the king.

"This is the same window your father was looking out on the day you were born. I watched him as he stood there and contemplated your future." Myra kept laying out Avalon's attire as she talked. She wanted to give Avalon a link to her past, but she didn't want to stir up any overwhelming emotion.

"That was fifteen years ago," Avalon answered in a faraway voice. "How is this even the same sky that I was under one year ago?" Myra didn't answer, but Avalon wasn't expecting one. She took a deep breath in and steeled her resolve. Myra was right. Avalon had to move forward and step into the shoes she was meant to fill. "I'm going to bathe quickly so leave me to it." Avalon placed the sword on the side table and moved to the washing room. She had a kingdom to run, and she could not allow something like where she would rest her head at night to distract her any longer.

Taggerty stormed in during dinner with Kensington on his heels. The doors would have slammed full against the walls if the guard outside hadn't stopped them.

"Your Grace," Kensington said and they both knelt. It seemed strange to Avalon because she had never seen anyone kneel in this room her entire life. This was the dining room, and no one had ever approached her father during dinner unless they had already been invited as guests to the meal.

"What is it?" Avalon asked.

"Princess Zaria," Taggerty said turning his attention to Zaria. Avalon ignored the pang of jealousy. She had to come to terms with remaining friends with Taggerty. "I am so sorry to interrupt your dinner. If I might, will you allow me to have a word with the king?"

Zaria smiled at Taggerty and stood. "I was finished anyway," she said, although she'd only had two bites of her soup and hadn't even been served the meat yet. "I will leave you to your business. Perhaps, though, I could first ask for an escort to my room? I just haven't been feeling safe since my father's death." Avalon could hear the sincerity in Zaria's words, but she was surprised. Zaria had expressed much concern for Avalon's safety in the past months, but none for her own well-being.

"Please excuse me, my lady," Taggerty said regretfully. "I must speak with the king. Would you accept young Kensington here as a suitable substitute?" Kensington was full-bearded and in his mid twenties, at least six years older and six inches shorter than Taggerty, and Taggerty was calling him young. He was more pompous than ever, Avalon thought.

"Yes, he will escort her," Avalon snapped at Taggerty. Then she inhaled and smiled. "What do you need? I'm in the middle of dinner."

Kensington stretched out his arm and Zaria gently looped her hand on his forearm. He had manners for a soldier. Avalon was surprised to see Zaria accept his close escort, although they were probably friends now that Taggerty and Zaria were together. The two strolled out and the guards closed the door behind the princess, leaving Avalon fully aware that she was alone with Taggerty.

"You cannot do this, King Hall," Taggerty demanded.

"But I like my soup," Avalon retorted, taking a spoonful.

"You cannot go to Cormicks," Taggerty said in anger and louder than he'd intended.

"Lower your voice," Avalon bellowed like her father would have. Taggerty straightened up, and Avalon knew she had hit a nerve in him. She took a calming breath, but her temper was hardly steadied. "I'm not going to Cormicks," she said and tried to smile.

"You want me to believe that you have summoned a meeting with the Guides for any other purpose?" he said accusingly. Avalon was surprised that Taggerty knew about her request so quickly, but the Guides had probably reported to him at once, trying to figure out what was on Avalon's mind.

Avalon rang a bell and two servants swept into the room. They cleared the soup and placed two plates on the table before silently slipping out. Avalon picked up her knife and cut into the steak taking a large bite. She was trying her best to have a conversation with him without noticing her emotions. She was practiced at this from her years pretending to be prince, and now she was king. It was becoming easier with everyone but Taggerty.

People bowed when she walked past, and she looked straight at everyone so she could avoid their eyes because no one wanted direct eye contact with the king. It seemed that no one would look directly at the king unless they were addressing her directly. Taggerty did look at her though, straight into her, and Avalon smiled at him as she chewed the salty meat. She didn't know why she smiled, only that it would in some way make him angry, and she somehow wanted him angry. Taggerty smiled back through grit teeth, moved to Zaria's plate and picked up a bread roll. He stuffed it into his mouth, and standing behind the chair, he ate the entire roll in one bite. Avalon tried not to notice the daring glitter in his green eyes or the perfect curve of his chin. She hesitated to swallow because she needed to look at Taggerty for as long as it took to see him as a brother. She lost her smile and swallowed the large bite, chasing it down with water.

"You are planning to go to the elbagrass. You cannot do that. I saw what you saw, Avalon. If you want someone to go, send me."

"I'm planning..." Avalon started, but Taggerty rudely cut her off.

"You summoned the Guides. Did you think that would go unnoticed?"

"You're spying on me now?"

"I'm protecting you," he pleaded.

"I am the king. Don't forget that."

"How could I forget that?" Taggerty said bitterly and then caught himself.

Avalon pushed food around her plate. "I will forget the tone you have taken with me here, but this is none of your business."

Taggerty looked as though he'd been punched in the face. His eyes fluttered down and then back into Avalon's eyes, and she could see regret there. "We collected Walthan's remains on the first moon after we went to Cormicks," Taggerty said in a whisper. "This is my business."

Avalon regretted raising her voice at him, but she was stung by this reference to Walthan. The greatest warrior ever known was buried without his purest reward, the honor that he deserved for saving the life of a king. "I am not going to Cormicks, Taggerty. I need to plan, that is all. I need advice. My father taught me that there are certain people I can trust, and I need their counsel."

Taggerty sank into Zaria's chair and fidgeted with her knife on the table. "Send me to Cormicks. Let me and some well trained soldiers end this once and for all."

Avalon shook her head. So it wasn't that Taggerty didn't want to chance going into Cormicks, he just didn't want her going. "Taggerty, there is nothing there. The Guides have been keeping watch for ten months and not one person has come across. This secret is safe. I have to believe that. Leave the door closed, Taggerty. The Monarch doesn't know the secret or we would have seen something by now." Avalon's voice sounded calm, but she was full of uncertainty. Avalon lived in fear, and she spent hours in her mind each day plotting how to defend Fontanasia.

"Just one expedition, King Avalon. We can't sit here and wait. It's impossible," Taggerty pressed.

"We have waited all of these years. Even if the find the elbagrass, it might take them years to make any progress to the window."

"That is why we must crush them right now. They may not have even found the elbagrass. We may still have time to strike in surprise." He was too eager to take the offensive, and Avalon was getting more confused as to the best course of action, but inaction had served her forefathers.

"What do you know, Taggerty? You are not a king," she said sharply and immediately regretted the words. Taggerty rubbed his hand over his eyes and down his chin. Without looking at her, he stood and left the room.

"I'm sorry," she whispered as the door closed. She promised herself then that if her words only continued to hurt him, she would vow to never speak again.

Through the official invitation delivered by Taggerty, Avalon had been invited to visit with the Guides. They had come to the castle to treat with kings in the past, and they had climbed through the secret passage to meet with her before. Today she was invited to their village to eat with them and share stories, and this was an honor. It would have been a greater honor if she hadn't asked for the meeting herself.

She had seen Taggerty with Zaria three times in the past two days, and she was short with him when he had delivered the small gift and invitation. Avalon felt bad for her behavior, but she was the king, and she didn't have time to concern herself with other people's feelings.

"King Avalon," Taggerty said with a bow when he met her at the suite door. Avalon strode past him, and he stepped up next to her as the guards fell in behind them. Taggerty walked with Avalon down through the courtyard outside the front of the castle. He tried to start a conversation twice, but Avalon's one word answers strangled the exchange and left them to walk in silence. They came upon a small locked door built into the wall that ran along the outside of the city. Avalon had been through this door one other time on the morning she had gone to Cormicks. The King's Guard who crowded the arch saw the king approaching and they quickly unlocked the thick, steel door. Avalon stepped through the deep archway that went through the outer wall. She gulped back her sadness as she remembered Walthan and how he had barely fit through the opening.

Taggerty stopped to say something to the guard, and Avalon heard the large steel door clang shut. She started down the small, dirt path and could only hear the rustle of one person behind her. It was Taggerty, she knew, but she didn't look back. She was half way down the hill before she saw the expanse of stone and grass huts under the towering trees that grew at the bottom of the mountainside. She had been in this village upon returning from Cormicks, and with her mind much more focused this time, she walked slowly to take it all in. She smelled barbecue, and Jackie peeked his head out of her pocket to see. Avalon had devised small sounds and taught Jackie to heed her command on these sounds. She gently patted his head and hissed like a snake to get him back into her pocket.

A large group of Guides of all ages approached Avalon as she reached the edge of the village, and they enveloped her and Taggerty. Whereas Taggerty would never allow a crowd of her own people this close to Avalon, he was relaxed as she greeted the Guides.

"You're a celebrity," she said to Taggerty who was smiling and touching the heads of all of the children who pressed in on him.

"He is a hero," one of the Guides said. This was Taggerty's uncle whom Avalon had traveled to Cormicks with, and he smiled at her now as she recognized him, but she did not know how to respond because she still did not know his name. It was strange to Avalon, that she did not know any of the names of the entire Guide tribe. It seemed impossible. Five of them had gathered at her fourteenth birthday and given her the pet jakkow lizard, and yet she had no idea who they were. She nodded her head in recognition, embarrassed that she didn't know who she was responding to.

"Uncle Chylyn," Taggerty said with a pat on his uncle's shoulder.

"He has fulfilled his prophecy and is favored by the king. The children love him for it," Chylyn said to Avalon. He was not boisterous about his nephew, but Avalon could see the pride in his eyes.

"And now that he has fulfilled his duty, what will become of Taggerty?"

"That is up to you, King Avalon, but if you will keep him, he will always protect the king." Avalon felt a warm seed in the pit of her stomach. That he could have been shunned for being an albino as a child, only to be brought to a position of respect with the Guides, was in itself a tribute to the years he had worked to fulfilling his prophecy.

They were led to a large stone structure garbed in huge white fabric that rippled gently in the wind. They ate a light lunch, and Avalon enjoyed listening to the Guides talk with each other. Those seated with her spoke the common language of Fontanasia, but she heard some small children saying words she had never heard before. The bulk of the crowd left after lunch, and they were led to retire in a smaller stone house. Chylyn held his hand out and Avalon and Taggerty took the low seats across from him. Six other men in long, thin robes joined them.

They were served a sweet tea, and Avalon waited for one of the hosts to speak first. She enjoyed her drink, and she looked to Taggerty, but he remained silent, looking each of the Guides in the face, and not showing the subservience to these leaders that the other Guides had. Avalon assumed that was because he was not raised among them, and although they were his origins and had trained him in some ways, he was a Fontanasian at heart.

Avalon felt Jackie move in her pocket. She had forgotten about her tiny pet, and she beckoned him out with the click of her tongue. The Guide's faces all lit up as they watched the jakkow lizard scramble up onto Avalon's shoulder.

"Phfssss," Avalon breathed, and Jackie scrambled down her leg and across the small divide to the Guides. They each took their turn letting Jackie inspect them before rewarding him with a treat.

"I must thank you again for the gift you presented me last year on my birthday. Jackie has been a wonderful pet, and he has been most resourceful on the other side of the window."

They all nodded their heads in turn, but Avalon's words brought them back to the business at hand.

"King Avalon, it is an honor to have you visit," the gray haired Guide said formally, his direct tone calling the meeting to order.

"The honor is mine. I did not expect all of this," she said a little sheepishly, knowing that she was the one who had called the meeting. No one else spoke. All eyes rested on Avalon, and she realized they were waiting for her to tell them why she had asked for a meeting. She cleared her throat. "We have been one people for over two hundred years. We have a common cause and that is for the survival and well being of our peoples." They each nodded as Avalon met their eyes. "I have not sent an army to Cormicks, nor am I planning to go there myself right now." Avalon looked at Taggerty when she said this.

"You have seen Cormicks," the man most central to the group stated. Avalon recognized him as one of the men who had brought her Jackie on her birthday a year earlier.

Avalon nodded slowly. "I have."

"All of the men here have seen Cormicks," he told her. "We are the only nine people alive to have been there. We are the only nine people alive who understand the true danger of what lies beyond the outer wall."

Avalon looked around and studied their faces, but none of them showed any distinct emotion except Taggerty. His eyes were hard focused and his hands were clenched.

"Is this meeting about forming a strategy?" Taggerty asked hopefully.

Avalon saw Chylyn's brow ripple for a moment, and the man in front of her smiled.

"We invited the king here for a visit. We can talk about something else if you wish, King Avalon. We do not intend to tell you what you should do, and we will continue to watch the elbagrass for any trespassers." He said this kindly, and Avalon nodded in appreciation. Julius Creighton and some of her own counselors reveled in telling her what to do, but the Guides would not make her their pawn.

Chylyn spoke. "Aside from the old forgotten tales passed down from generations, there is one other who may have known about Cormicks for what it truly is." This sounded like a threat and Avalon's ears prickled.

"Who?" she asked.

"Your Uncle Hawker."

His name rang through her head and it took a lot for Avalon to control her emotions. They were all watching her, and Avalon turned to Taggerty. Had he told them that she had let her uncle go? Maybe he didn't need to. The Guides seemed to know things before anyone else. Taggerty didn't move but his hands relaxed. She controlled the urge to say anything because she didn't want to lie, and she didn't want to confess her secret either.

"It was the city of his namesake," Chylyn backtracked. "And your father saw Cormicks, which leads us to believe that Prince Hawker did as well."

"Our main concern," the center Guide cut in, "is whether Hawker knew his way to Cormicks, and if he shared that information with anyone other than Brick."

Avalon clenched her teeth. She had wondered this same thing night after night. She worried about betrayal within the Council, and she was suspicious of everyone. "I don't believe that my grandfather ever allowed Hawker to see Cormicks as my father did. Hawker was a learned man, but he was not an outdoorsman. He wouldn't even ride a horse."

They all nodded slowly. She wished she could command them to tell her what they wanted, but her father had always told her to respect the Guides and to trust their council. Her inexperience with their culture made her second-guess herself.

Gray hair leaned forward. "King Avalon, what are your plans?"

Avalon took a deep breath. She knew that Taggerty wanted to cross over and attack Cormicks. She wondered if the peaceful men in front of her felt the same way. "You have graciously invited me here today, and I would like to ask your council before making plans. Do you think as Taggerty does that I should send soldiers to the window?"

Gray hair shook his head. "No, not at this time."

Chylyn leaned forward and spoke softly. "But you should be ready to close the fist."

Avalon leaned back in her low seat and caught her breath. He was using Walthan's words from when he'd had the Fingers built. Her father had told her that Walthan had said the walls were meant to close like a fist on any enemies who might attack. Avalon imagined the walls of her city moving like the Anthracites had, pulling out of the ground and crushing her enemy. Jackie sensed Avalon's discomfort and scampered back to her hand.

"King Avalon," the leader addressed her. "From the nine of us in this room who have seen the elbagrass, I now have thirty of my people who have been there."

"I owe you a debt of gratitude for what you are doing," she said.

He nodded. "We are glad to serve, but we serve our people as well. We have carried on some of the old arts not only to perpetuate our heritage, but also to protect our own existence. We are glad that you have planned to stay at the window and watch instead of crossing over."

It was Avalon's turn to nod. "I am glad that we have taken the same stance." Avalon bit her tongue. Deep down she wanted to send an army through to crush the Runners and kill the Monarch. It was the only way she would ever feel safe again.

Chylyn leaned forward. "King Avalon, we don't want to introduce any more of our people to the window. We have always trained and remembered our history, but very few of us have carried this secret, just as your father and his fathers did. You should know that we will spare the thirty men who have been to the elbagrass, but no more. We have been preparing, and we are ready to leave this place. If the Monarch finds the window and the Runners come, our men will defend from this side of the window to keep them from this city. They will sacrifice their lives, if need be, to give our people the time it takes to leave this place for a new home."

Chapter 6
Taggerty's Request

It was dusk when Taggerty escorted Avalon back to the castle. She could still feel the shock of the Guide's words. They would pack up and leave if war came to Fontanasia. They fled Cormicks, and it only made sense for them to flee Fontanasia. Still, Avalon did not have that option. Her people were not nomadic. They had been here for over two hundred years, and Walthan had helped to make this place a fortress. They would stand and fight if the time came.

"I never got the chance to ask how you managed to stay alive in Cormicks for those two weeks," Avalon said to Taggerty as they reached her suite. She held her hand out and invited him in. She walked to the sitting area and took her father's chair, and Taggerty sat opposite. Jackie climbed out of Avalon's pocket and down her leg to scamper across to Taggerty. Avalon looked toward Zaria's room but didn't see any light coming from within.

"Well, I ran away from those Anthracites like a lunatic on fire," Taggerty said with a chuckle, but his eyes betrayed his cavalier attitude, and she could see that he remembered the abject fear of the moment. "They were more interested in the fire itself, so when I dropped what I was holding, I was able to skirt around some rocks and break free. They must not see regular objects too clearly. Then I found a place to hide out. I was freezing, but I found Jackie and we kept each other warm." Taggerty was cupping Jackie in his hand and using his thumb to pet the jakkow. "You did good," he said to Jackie. "I went back two days later and scrounged up a couple of blankets in the rubble, and that is when Chylyn found me. And then we waited to see if anyone else made it back."

And no one had, Avalon knew. Betrayed by Brick, Avalon and Walthan had been captured and beaten. If it weren't for Taggerty's rescue, she would be dead. "And then what?" she asked. She watched his curly hair move a little as he spoke and enjoyed the animation that showed on his face.

"And then nothing. We ate berries with the paiche birds and waited for the full moon. It was pretty miserable."

"And you came back for us," Avalon said. She recognized her innate want to keep talking in this moment and to carry the conversation past where it was meant to go. It was the unconscious tactic that Avalon had noticed of the girls in the king's presence. They were girls who were hoping to catch the king's fancy. Avalon shook the thought from her mind.

"Of course," Taggerty said quickly and then paused. "My uncle didn't want to stay because it was important that they didn't think there were more of us."

"He was right, but you convinced him to change his mind?"

Taggerty chuckled. "Well, it was actually easy to convince him when I mentioned my destiny as proclaimed by the Guide. I reasoned with him that since you were the future king, perhaps I was meant to save you on that trip, and that was what the prophecy meant." Taggerty had his sly smile back, and Avalon sat back and enjoyed the moment.

"I suppose I know the rest," Avalon said with a smile of her own, shedding the day's stress, but the moment didn't last. If she admitted it, she was terrified of the Monarch and the Runners. She wished it were her father sitting in this chair discussing Cormicks. Avalon longed for her father. She had thought about him for almost a full year, trying to bring back every conversation they'd had, scolding herself for not holding on to every word that he'd said. She wished she had recognized while they were happening that the moments spent with her father were the best of times.

"And while I was doing that, what of you and Walthan?" Taggerty asked. Avalon shuddered and Taggerty sat forward quickly. "I don't mean to ask if it's too difficult to bear."

"It's all right," Avalon said with a tight smile. She shook off the memories. "I need to tell you what Walthan said, every word of it. You understand the Fingers and how they are designed to work?"

"Of course," Taggerty answered. "We should have Gamon here though if we are to talk about defending the city."

Avalon smiled. "I'm sure that is all you two speak of, so if you learn anything new in my words, I trust you will impart them to Gamon." Walthan had conveyed to Avalon that it is important to take action, but sitting still is the most important but difficult of endeavors. Walthan had also told Avalon that the most important thing to her father, and to her grandfather, was that the people of Fontanasia live in peace and not in fear. The fear of the Runners at Hawkerness had been lost with the passing of generations, and that is why the secret of Cormicks was so important. She and Walthan had spent hours talking in the dirt and rock cell, and Avalon felt a pang of regret as she imparted their conversations to Taggerty.

"But what of conquering the Runners so that we may truly live in peace?" Taggerty asked.

"Walthan didn't get to spend time with the Monarch, but I saw his court and his council. His people will fight for him, but he keeps such a tight control. I don't know if they would truly attack without the head of the snake." They had discussed this in the cell, escaping and killing the Monarch before returning to Fontanasia, and coming back with an army before the Runners could regroup and a new leader could take hold. "Walthan said that the problem with crossing over with any large force is the lack of alleya leaf."

Taggerty nodded thoughtfully and his eyebrows creased. She could tell that he hadn't thought of that before, and she watched his eyes as his mind moved through the problem before him. The alleya leaf would always grow in the light of the full moon, but it was never a consistent amount. The last time a large amount of people had come across was when her people had fled the murderous hands of the Runners.

"I hadn't thought of that," Taggerty finally admitted. He was about to say something when the door opened and Zaria came in followed by Kensington. Zaria had been giggling and she turned toward Kensington, her flowery dress billowing with her spin.

"Your Highness," Kensington said in a clip, causing Zaria to twist back around to face the room. Taggerty rose quickly and crossed to the pair, and Avalon was left with her disappointment. She could have talked to Taggerty all night if they hadn't been interrupted. It was difficult to talk about Walthan and Cormicks and the enemy, but it was necessary.

"Avalon," Zaria said in a chirpy voice. She crossed and perched on the arm of Avalon's chair, just as she had done with their father.

"Dinner went late?" Avalon asked.

"I invited some of our cousins this evening. I hope you don't mind."

"Of course not," Avalon said, missing the reddening blush on Zaria's cheeks.

Avalon stepped out into the heat of summer. She was thinking that it was cold this time in Cormicks as she stepped up to the carriage that would take her to the king's platform at the Festival of Fontanasia. She rode through the boroughs looking at the stalls of food, garments, and jewelry. They passed through the gate at the bottom of the Fingers and the people cheered. The prairie expanse was filled with goods for sale, men drinking ale, and women chasing children about. Avalon waved as she passed and then took to the platform in front of the temporary fighting grounds that had been gated off from the crowd. Horns announced the king, and a cheer erupted from the crowd. Her people looked to her, Avalon thought, just as the Runners looked to their Monarch.

Avalon allowed a tear to fall during the tribute for her father. She didn't hide this time, realizing that even a son might show emotion when honoring his dead father. The choreographed battle in honor of Walthan and Brick was next, and Avalon felt only remorse.

The entire Council was present on the platform behind Avalon and Zaria, and Gamon and the King's Guard formed a barrier on the back of the platform between the Council and the people. Taggerty and Kensington stood guard at the front of the platform looking away from Avalon and Zaria. This was the same festival that the people had always enjoyed, but it was an entire new festival to Avalon. She had always been concerned with the battles, the warrior's moves and how she could emulate them. But today the men fighting in front of her were like children at play; children who only understood the home that their parents kept them in with no real sense of the outside world.

"More to drink, Your Highness?" Gamon asked as he stood at Avalon's elbow. She shook her head no. "It's not quite the same anymore, is it?" he asked as though he was reading her thoughts.

"No, it's not," Avalon admitted.

"We should talk," Gamon said. He had reluctantly taken position as the head of the King's Guard, and after a year, Avalon knew that he was ready to step down. He had told her several times that while he was a good sword instructor, he did not revel in strategy to defend the city. Avalon had been avoiding the subject, and she did not respond. She was already planning to replace Gamon with Taggerty soon.

"It is time," Counselor Robert said when the archers had completed their trial. Avalon stood and presented the winner with the silver pin in the shape of an arrow. Everyone cheered, and Avalon remained standing to make the announcement she had promised months earlier. She had made her decision, and Julius Creighton would join her King's Council.

"Today, I appoint Julius Creighton of Gates Hill to my Council. Counselor Creighton served my father as librarian, and he has counseled me in the past year. I know that Gates Hill looks to Julius as a leader, and so it is my duty to make official what he has already undertaken in an unofficial capacity." Avalon turned to Counselor Glenn's family who was seated with the other families of the counselors. She met the eye of Glenn's widow but the children looked to the ground. Avalon moved to the side of the platform so she would not need to yell. "Your father's shoes will be hard to fill. Counselor Creighton will do his best to honor your family by serving to the best of his ability."

Avalon sucked back the regret that was forming in her throat. They were still mourning as she was, Avalon could tell. She turned back to where Julius Creighton was on the platform. He stood in the hot sunlight and looked entirely the old man that he was pretending to be. Avalon took the circle pin that had been held out to her and stepped up to Creighton.

"As you wish," Avalon whispered as she pinned the circle on Creighton's robe. She still felt as though he had tricked his way onto the Council, but her other counselors had convinced her over time that he was the best man for the job.

"As you command, King Avalon," Creighton said looking directly into Avalon's eyes. "You have your mother's eyes," he said, catching her off guard.

"Welcome to the King's Council," Avalon said loudly as she patted him too hard on the back. She knew that it didn't hurt, but he took a half step forward as though the pat from the king had thrown his old frame off balance. A cheer went up from the crowd.

"Now that I am officially your counselor, I would like to give my first bit of advice," he said just above the roar of the crowd.

"By all means. The day is yours," Avalon said graciously. The crowd had died down, and Avalon could see Creighton's eyes dart about. She leaned forward instinctively, knowing he did not want others to hear.

"Please come down to the archive, Your Highness. I need to show you something. It is very important." Avalon nodded and turned from Creighton to take her seat. She soon forgot the pleading tone in his voice as she watched the rest of the competition. He had given her books of great value and she had been studying their contents. Avalon knew that if it were so important, Creighton would bring the books to her.

Avalon surprised the people by making the King's Guard stop at one of the cook stands on the way back to the castle.

To the great pleasure of the vendor and his family, King Avalon ate meat and vegetables that were grilled on a stick. Avalon enjoyed watching the man with his family working around him. She was glad to see them happy and healthy, and she dismissed the pang that their happiness brought.

Avalon returned to the castle and drank three glasses of cool tea as she reflected on the day. She was grown up now and was done with games. She wondered if her father had felt the same way. He'd always smiled and laughed at the festival and seemed as though he was enjoying himself. Avalon had smiled and tried to laugh for the competitors more than the people. She wanted them to know that their preparations pleased their king. She might need their swords before long.

Avalon sat at the table and pulled the verticks blocks out. She stacked them up end to end until they looked like a dried out tree and then knocked them over with her hand. As the blocks rattled to the table, Avalon had a revelation. She stacked them up again, seeing in front of her the field of elbagrass, and the verticks as platforms for her men to perch on, looking over the field of deadly grass, and waiting for the enemy. Could she build towers in the grass too so that they had immediate site of the pool of water within?

"Thomas!" Avalon called. The guard opened the door of the suite in an instant, his hand at the ready and on the hilt of his sword. "I'm fine, Thomas. I need to see Taggerty. Can you find him for me?"

"Of course, Your Highness. I believe he is dining with Princess Zaria this evening." Avalon didn't care to know that, but she nodded and Thomas turned to go. It took longer than expected for Thomas to return with Taggerty. He entered and walked directly to Avalon.

"Look!" Avalon said, not wanting to hear about his dinner with Zaria. She had stacked the verticks back up and she pointed at it.

Taggerty smiled. "You want to play verticks?" he asked.

"No," Avalon said sheepishly. "I want to build towers around the field of elbagrass so that we can defend against an invasion." Taggerty looked at the verticks closely, but his mind was miles away at the edge of the blue field.

"Are you ready to attack Cormicks?" he asked doubtfully.

Avalon shook her head. "No. I want to build towers in the grass if possible, right up to the window. I want a thousand arrows on these towers to rain down on our enemy. I want to plan a defense and then decide how many men it would take to keep position there. I still don't know if we should tell the city what is happening, and the men have families who will miss them if they are gone for a long time."

"I will work on this," Taggerty said evenly, but she could see the excitement in his eyes. Any forward motion was fine with him, as long as he didn't have to sit on his hands and wait.

Avalon noticed that his hair was not in place and that one side of his shirt was sticking out below his jacket. "Did I interrupt your dinner with Zaria?" she asked.

Taggerty looked up in surprise. "I was not with Princess Zaria this evening. The festival got the best of me and Thomas caught me napping." Taggerty's lips tightened, and she could see that he wanted to say more.

"I'm sorry to have woken you," Avalon said.

"It's all right. I don't sleep for very long usually. When I close my eyes at night, I remember the bodies that I helped Walthan chop up in the woods. You're lucky you don't dream." Avalon remembered too well, and she hadn't done the deed. "It was necessary, and I would do it again. We had to get you to safety, King Avalon. But it haunts me, and I don't want anyone to ever have to go through that." He said that as though he had already lived one hundred years.

"I know," she said. "That is partly what keeps me here and not going into Cormicks. That is even more reason to wait it out."

Taggerty nodded. "And I'm the one who always wants to go on the offensive. That is ironic." They both stared at the verticks before Avalon knocked them down with the sweep of her hand.

"I want you to know that if I ever seriously consider going to Cormicks and waging war, I will think long and hard about the men I would be sending there. I don't dream at night, but they will have nightmares."

There was the flicker of understanding in Taggerty's eyes. He could see now that Avalon didn't have the luxury of running into the fray. What she wanted done, she commanded others to do. He had to live with his own nightmares. The king would have to live with much more.

Avalon had thought about her discussion with Taggerty for two days before she saw him again. She heard the familiar two knocks before the door to her suite opened.

"Is Zaria here?" Taggerty asked as he straightened his jacket.

"No, I thought she was dining with you."

"Not tonight," he said with pursed lips. "Can we take a walk together? There is something that I would like to discuss." Avalon controlled her emotions. He didn't want to take a walk with Avalon, the girl who had fallen in love with him. He didn't want to stroll along and hold her hand and tell her how he felt about her. He wanted to take a walk with King Avalon, older brother to the girl that he was really interested in.

"Of course, Taggerty. I have time for you."

They left the suite and went up to the parapets above the Fingers. They walked at a slow pace, Taggerty's hands clasped behind his back, Avalon's thumbs tucked into her belt and her head held high. Avalon loved the view from here. It was a true view of Fontanasia and all of her people. She tried to concentrate on that view, but it was no use.

She noticed Taggerty's head was bowed and he studied the ground nervously. It was a pose he had not taken since the day she had first seen him. He would bow for his king, but his head never remained lowered. He was too proud. Yet today he couldn't seem to look at her. She woke up from her daydream, the one where he wanted to be alone with her. Avalon cleared her throat and tried not to take in the heartbreak that was surely coming.

"You wanted to discuss something?" Avalon began. Her throat constricted as it often did while in his presence. She hated herself for the tears that were trying to come. She was a fool to believe that she held any future with Taggerty.

"Yes, Your Highness." Taggerty looked around, and when he was satisfied that the guards were far enough away, he continued. "I wanted to discuss Princess Zaria."

"Of course you do," Avalon blurted. She thought that she should say something else to cover her impatience, but speaking made her lips tremble so she waited for Taggerty to respond.

"Your sister won't remain single forever." Taggerty stopped walking as he spoke, but Avalon kept moving. She stepped to the edge and looked out over the stone wall, but she saw nothing.

"Yes," she said above a whisper.

"She is of an age, Your Highness. You may be too young to realize, but she is of an age to marry." It was Taggerty's turn to clear his throat.

"Yes," Avalon pushed through her teeth. She inhaled a deep breath and remembered that she was king of all she saw. She pushed her feelings back where they belonged, back where they needed to remain. "I'm not sure what my father would think," she said involuntarily.

"Your father is not here," Taggerty said, and immediately regretted it. He saw that nothing had been easy between them since he had returned. "King Avalon?" he asked. "Do you remember the trek back from Cormicks? Do you remember the stars and the pitch black and the conversation we had?" She could see that he had stepped up next to her and he was looking at her, but Avalon kept her eyes on the city below. "I miss that night. We didn't know each other then, but we could talk. Now we know each other well, and we can't seem to finish a conversation."

Avalon chuckled and wanted to tell Taggerty that he knew little of her, but she would be wrong and she knew it. He might not know her gender, but he seemed to understand a lot about her.

"As I remember, we seemed to argue a lot on that trip."

"We were honest, and we were friends." His tone was soft and he had turned toward her, but Avalon dared not look into his bright, salty green eyes.

"You can't be honest with me?" she asked.

"You were a prince then." Taggerty hesitated and moved in front of Avalon. She could avoid his gaze no longer. "You are a king now," he said softly and she swore for a moment that he meant something else entirely. Avalon turned away and looked back out over Fontanasia, ruining the moment that she was not allowed to have. "How old was your mother when your parents married?" Taggerty asked.

Zaria was already older than many of her cousins who had been married. "I never got to know my mother," Avalon lamented.

"At least your mother loved you in the moments that you had together, and she is dead and you don't have to wonder about her every day." It was a harsh thing to say, and Taggerty regretted that immediately. "I'm sorry, King Avalon. I shouldn't have said that."

"It's okay," Avalon said, still not facing Taggerty. Maybe he was right. Her mother was gone and buried and yet she had heard from Myra and her father how much her mother would have loved her and how proud she would be now. Taggerty's mother was alive, and he had to wonder why she had allowed another family to raise him. It was self-torture, but Avalon understood that it was unavoidable. She was surprised to find such depth in the heart of a man who acted cavalier most of the time.

"Why did you want to speak to me about my sister? There is something you wanted to ask me?" Avalon's mood darkened as she braced herself for the words to come.

"There are suitors for Princess Zaria, many who I am sure would like to win her heart and her hand in marriage. But if there was someone who could make her happy, someone who was not of high birth, wouldn't her happiness count for more than pedigree could offer?"

"Of course I want my sister to be happy, but everything must be taken into consideration. She and I will discuss this when the time comes." Avalon was drowning and she couldn't have this discussion any longer. She spun on her heel and walked back inside. She needed to lock herself in her room and pull the blankets over her head. She needed time to think and not feel. Taggerty was on her heels, and she was suddenly angry with him, but she didn't want to start another fight. "I give you my leave," she said without looking back at him.

"Thank you for listening to me, Your Grace," Taggerty said as his footsteps fell back. "And the time has come to hear what I said," he said loudly, his words echoing down the brick corridor. Avalon flinched but she didn't slow her pace.

Chapter 7
Permission

There was a knock at her study door, and it startled Avalon. She had spent some time in this room, but no one ever sought her out here. She stood and leaned over the desk, pretending to be in the middle of work instead of lost in daydream. "Enter," she called, and the door swung open. Counselor Nelson walked in followed by the ever-slowing Counselor Creighton.

"Your Highness," they both said, tipping their heads forward. Avalon could hear Creighton's low grunt as he entered.

"You are slipping," she told him.

"My apologies, Your Highness. I just wasn't expecting to see so much of your father's influence here." He was being tactful, but Avalon was beyond mere courtesy.

"You mean to say that you didn't expect to see it exactly as my father left it." She smiled curtly to let him know that she wasn't angry.

"Leave us," Avalon said, and the guard pulled the door closed again. "Please, sit."

"Thank you, King Avalon," Counselor Nelson said, making sure that Creighton had a seat before taking his own. Avalon saw the irony of the older man giving the younger man a chair, and she shook her head.

"You are here to offer counsel?" Avalon asked, knowing that there must be news of great importance for Counselor Nelson to bother her.

Counselor Nelson looked at Creighton and then cleared his throat. "King Avalon," he said respectfully, "I have been talking to Counselor Creighton about some things that have been on my mind." Avalon tensed. He was stalling, not sure of how to pose his question. She looked to Creighton but his face was passive and he turned his head to face Counselor Nelson. He would not help his colleague, and he didn't want to be the one speaking here. He was a genius, and Avalon understood his strategy. She was not going to like what she was about to hear.

"Go on," she instructed.

Counselor Nelson cleared his nervous throat again. "King Avalon, I was privy to several conversations that took place between Prince Hawker and Counselor Glenn. I know about Hawkerness, and I know that your father sent you there. He was trying to open communications with them to form a..."

"That's a lie!" Avalon yelled as she stood. Her chair scraped the floor behind her hasty legs and it crashed to the floor. The door opened quickly and two of the King's Guard stepped in, their swords already halfway out of the sheaths. "I am fine. You can leave us," Avalon commanded.

"I told you," Counselor Creighton said to Nelson. One of the guard approached the desk and righted Avalon's chair before leaving.

"You speak lies," Avalon said.

They sat in silence for a full minute before anyone spoke. Finally Counselor Nelson said, "I am glad to hear that."

Avalon didn't understand. Her face was red with impatience and her heart was racing, but she took a page from Creighton's book and waited.

"Your uncle had Counselor Glenn all worked up and so he shared their discussions with me. I did my own research in the library and recall some of the stories that my grandparents told me as a child. There aren't a lot of books available on the topic, but what I have found, it disturbs me."

"Counselor Nelson, I assure you that my father had no interest in contacting anyone in Hawkerness. That door closed over two hundred years ago when the Runners murdered our ancestors and ran us out of the castle."

He nodded. "So you are aware of the place?" he said with eyebrows raised.

Avalon stood slowly this time. She leaned over and placed her fists on the desktop, staring straight into Counselor Nelson's eyes and squinting hers to look more intimidating. "Of course I know. I am the King of Fontanasia. It is my job to know both our history and our future." Nelson squirmed under her stare. She had never seen the congenial man so uneasy. She was wondering who else had been discussing this topic.

"I should close the library if lies like this will come out of old books," Avalon said. She could see Creighton's half-smile.

"You should, Your Highness," Counselor Nelson agreed easily, too easily.

Avalon heard her father's words in her head. "No concessions, my son. You cannot trust those who would let you win. They are playing a different game altogether." Avalon thought of Taggerty. He never let her win anything, and she trusted him implicitly. She had known Counselor

Nelson her whole life, and she had trusted Creighton more than she trusted her father's old friend. Creighton challenged her, but Nelson seemed to give in too easily. Perhaps he wanted the library closed for his own purposes.

"You trust me, don't you?" Nelson asked, offended by her silence. Avalon looked at Counselor Nelson suspiciously, and he did not force her to answer. "I am one of the few people who know that your father did not die of an illness. I have kept your secret." Avalon was startled for a moment, and she couldn't help but straighten her jacket to make sure she was fully covered.

"Who else did Counselor Glenn talk to about this?" she asked as she sat down in her chair again.

"I don't know. Would you like me to question the other counselors?" Nelson asked innocently.

Avalon had made up her mind before she even noticed the discreet shake of Counselor Creighton's head. "No, not right now. This is a fabrication made up by either my Uncle Hawker or by Counselor Glenn, neither of which is here to defend himself. We should leave this between the three of us."

"Of course, Your Highness," Nelson said.

"You may take your leave," Avalon said. Both men rose and bowed their heads. Counselor Nelson retreated quickly to the door and was out before Creighton was half way around the large map table. Creighton turned back to Avalon, his eyebrows raised and his lips pursed. Avalon thought that his eyes were saying, I told you so, but she didn't know why.

Zaria found Avalon in the Council chamber sitting at a table and reading a book. It was dusk and torchlight flickered on the walls. Avalon was reading the journal that Creighton had given her. Her great grandfather seven times removed had been a scientist, and his journal was a mixture of notations and paragraphs on what he saw and what he felt. It was difficult reading, but Avalon had studied it for weeks. She wanted to know everything that he saw two hundred years earlier.

"I don't have time, Zaria. I have work to do."

"Just a moment, Avalon. I really need to talk to you."

"It can wait."

"But Avalon, it is important. I would go to father if I could." Her words stung, and Avalon was forced to have the conversation she had been dreading.

"I have met someone, Avalon. I think you know that. I will need the king's permission to marry."

"Fine, you have my permission," Avalon said on the verge of tears. She was leaning over the book trying not to meet Zaria's eyes. Thoughts of Taggerty had drained Avalon for months, and she wished her sister would leave before the tears came.

"He is not of noble birth, Avalon. So this is different." Zaria was right up in front of the table trying to get Avalon's nose out of the book. Avalon had stopped reading, but she could not look up at her sister. She glanced in Zaria's direction and then down at the table. Zaria was nervous but still graceful in her dress. Avalon could not compare to her sister's beauty, and it made her jealous. She was losing him for good.

"It's fine," Avalon said dismissively, and Zaria tensed. She was angry now too, and Avalon knew that they were about to have their first argument since their father's death.

"Avalon! This is a big moment for me. Don't just dismiss it." Zaria reached out for the book, but Avalon pulled it back and slammed it closed. She wanted to rip it into tiny pieces and throw it in her sister's face, but she placed it on the table and ground her teeth instead.

"Fine! We will talk about it. You couldn't have gone after anyone else? You had to go after the one person that you saw me noticing. You had to go after the one person that I liked!"

"What?" Zaria laughed but then caught herself. "You could never be that way with him. You are the king! This is your life." Zaria held her arms out to the Council room and looked around at the benches and tables.

"I understand that! Don't you think that after all of these years, I understand that more than anyone? But you don't have to throw it in my face. He could go off and have whatever life he is going to have in this city, but I don't have to be made to watch. I don't want to have to watch his happiness."

Zaria's mouth dropped open and her defensive anger subsided. Her look of understanding perched into a devilish smile. "You are talking about Taggerty," she said incredulously. "You have feelings for Taggerty?"

"Yes!" Avalon yelled, and her voice echoed around the room.

"He will be glad to hear that you don't actually hate him," Zaria said sarcastically.

"Of course I don't hate him."

"But I mean, you like him. You just admitted it to me. I knew there was a connection. I could tell the way he would look at you sometimes. And once he referred to your eyes as 'smoky' and I thought that was a strange complement for a man to his king."

"I don't get to like him, Zaria. I see what has been going on between you two."

"You don't see anything," Zaria suddenly snapped with uncharacteristic spite. "You never have your eyes open long enough to see anything in your paranoid little brain."

Avalon slumped back on the bench. She felt as though she was being slapped over and over, and her heart ached. "I'm not paranoid, Zaria," Avalon whispered and found herself again on the verge of tears.

Zaria sighed and the tension seeped from the room. "You think I'm in love with Taggerty?" Zaria asked with a gentle laugh. She walked around the table and put her hand on her sister's back. "I'm with Kensington," she said softly. "I want to marry Kensington, but he cannot ask for my hand. He is a commoner, although there is nothing common about him. He is smart and funny, and gentle. Avalon, You have to welcome him into the family if I am to have any happiness." Zaria's tone was humble and she was worried that Avalon would turn down her request.

Avalon's jaw dropped and she was unable to form words. She was completely shocked. She had lost Taggerty, and he had been found again. "What?" She fumbled for words. "I don't understand." But it all made sense to Avalon now. Kensington was always around the corner covering for Taggerty, but it had been Taggerty covering for Kensington. She relived so many moments in her mind, back to the night of the ball, back to the late dinners where Zaria and Taggerty just happened to have Kensington with them, back to the time Zaria had turned back to Kensington in the suite before she knew Avalon was there. All of these moments came together now and swept away her despair and anger. "What?"

Zaria put her hands on her younger sister's shoulders and they both had tears in their eyes. "I want to marry Kensington. He is wonderful. He makes me laugh all of the time, and he doesn't expect me to act with him. I can just be myself. I don't know when or how it happened, but there it is. Please, Avalon, say something. Say that you will give us your blessing."

"I don't know," was all Avalon could force out. She was both stunned and offended. "Why didn't you tell me before?"

"I didn't mean to hurt you, Avalon. I didn't even know you could have feelings like that." Zaria didn't want to upset Avalon further, so she clarified, "I just didn't realize how much you have truly grown up, Avalon."

"You're with Kensington?" Avalon asked. "How did I completely miss it?" Avalon's smile turned into a laugh and Zaria took a deep breath. They sat on a bench together, the setting sun pushing through the glass onto their faces. The warmth felt wonderful, and it reminded Avalon how she used to have time to explore the countryside, to relax, and to play. She would often rest in the grass or on a rock, allowing the sun to warm her body. She had forgotten the simple pleasures but remembered them now as her heart soaked in the good news. In the glory of the moment, she allowed herself to think of Taggerty and his curly black hair, and the way he walked a step back although with a forward lean like he wanted to walk next to her.

"Sister, you have my blessing. So, what can I do to uncommon a commoner?"

"You can make him head of your King's Guard," Zaria said eagerly. She was not expecting Avalon to object.

"I can't do that."

"You can do what you want. You are the king. Kensington has been serving alongside Taggerty all of this time. He loves Fontanasia, and he is a good man."

"But what of Taggerty?" Avalon asked rhetorically. She knew Gamon would not serve much longer, and Avalon had planned to give the position to Taggerty.

"Taggerty is willing to step aside to make the position available," Zaria offered.

Avalon rose from the bench and moved toward her own seat up above the benches. "Taggerty would do this for you?"

"Well, yes." Zaria approached her sister. "He would do this for me and Kensington. We love each other, and he agrees that a person's place of birth should not stop him from love. It was Taggerty's idea actually. Then it would be natural for Kensington to be seen with me and we would be able to get married."

"And Taggerty is willing to step aside, just like that?"

"Avalon, you were so happy a moment ago. Be happy for me. Do this for me." Avalon had never heard Zaria ask for anything. She was dutiful and played the part of princess like no other. It was ironic to Avalon that after all of her years of behaving the part, and after all of her suitors, Princess Zaria did not want to marry someone of a higher pedigree.

"Oh, Avalon, I know you are too young to understand love, but do this for me and I won't ask for anything else for as long as I live." Zaria was kneeling in front of Avalon, holding her sister's hands, and she was truly begging. Avalon wondered for a moment what her father would do, but her father was not here.

"Ok. Zaria. I will do it." Zaria jumped up and squeezed Avalon with a squeal of delight.

"Thank you, Avalon! Thank you." She was sincere, and Avalon was glad to make her sister happy. One of them should be able to truly enjoy life.

Avalon had remained in the Council room alone for over an hour. She didn't spend a lot of time here, but it was her place now. Zaria would be married soon, and she would start her family, and Avalon would need to do the same. It was impossible, but she was the king and she would need an heir to the throne. Avalon laughed at the thought that had brought her father to lie about her gender, but she understood now why he had done it. As long as there was a King Hall, Fontanasia was safe from rulers like Hawker who would exploit the people for his own gains. Hawker was part of the Hall family too, though, but he was one bad apple in generations, and she had stopped him. It was actually Taggerty who had stopped Hawker, driving him through with a sword. Avalon didn't know how her uncle could have survived, but he had. And he was alive still, out among nature, working for his food and his shelter, or maybe he had perished, killed by an accident or from starvation. She could not dwell on that now.

As though he could sense her mood darken, Jackie scampered from her pocket and up to her shoulder, tickling her ear with his tiny licks. "Get away, Jackie!" Avalon laughed. She pulled him from her shoulder and set him on the table, digging into a fresh orange and feeding him the orange peel. She placed a slice of fresh orange half his size on the table and laughed when he bit into it, orange juice squirting into his mouth and on his face. He jumped away from the orange and ran into Avalon's sleeve where he rubbed his eyes until he could see again. Avalon chuckled remembering how he had grown larger than a horse when they had crossed over to Cormicks. "Some beast you are," she told him as he scampered back into her pocket.

The door to the Council chamber opened and Taggerty entered followed by Kensington. Zaria must have gone straight to Kensington with the news. Both men approached and bowed, and Avalon looked closely at Kensington for the first time. He was short but sturdy and nothing like any of Zaria's typical tall and handsome suitors. His muscles pushed at his clothing. His blond hair and beard were full of red highlights. He was serious, staring straight ahead and not looking directly at the king. He was a trained soldier and proud.

"Yes?" Avalon asked Taggerty.

"Your Highness, I have some discomforting news." Avalon was surprised at the serious tone he was taking. She had expected to hear from Kensington. Her heart fell as she thought Hawker must have found his way back.

"Is it Hawker?" Avalon asked.

"No," Taggerty answered flatly with a question on his face. "Hawker is no longer a threat. I am here because

Counselor Nelson is having his hunters gather a noticeably large quantity of meat for drying. He has sent hunters out for six weeks and the people in his district have taken notice. The gossip is starting to spread through the Fingers."

Avalon had no idea why Counselor Nelson would be doing this, but she didn't want to appear weak. "And why do you bring this news to me?"

She could see Taggerty's jaw tighten as he kept control of his temper. "King Avalon, Fontanasia is a peaceful place, and people have been leading the same lives here for generations. We hunt to feed our people, but we do not stockpile except during the fall harvest when preparing for winter."

"True," Avalon said without committing. She didn't know what Counselor Nelson was up to, but she didn't like that Taggerty assumed Nelson was acting on his own. Her eyebrows rose as if challenging him to ask the question.

"It is summer," he said.

"So it is," she replied.

"Did you order Counselor Nelson to do this? Are you planning to move the army to Cormicks?" Taggerty asked directly, finally meeting her eye. He was dead serious, but all Avalon could think was that he was free. He was not with Zaria.

She told Taggerty the truth. "Don't get your hopes up. I am not planning an offensive, Taggerty."

"You must make Counselor Nelson stop, this instant. People are talking and this is no time to have them questioning their counselors or their king."

"Are you giving me an order?" she asked defensively.

"No, Your Highness." He tipped his head forward and set his eyes on the ground, which helped Avalon break free of their hypnotic spell. She pulled her hand to her eyes and rubbed them, taking a moment to think. She didn't know what Counselor Nelson was doing, and she didn't like that he had seemed so friendly and open her whole life but had of late been taking his own steps. Steps toward what, she did not know.

"There is dissension in the Council, Your Grace. You are blind to it just as your father was. You need to disband the Council and prepare for Cormicks."

"That is what Hawker wanted! He wanted to remove the Council and have my father rule outright," Avalon yelled, her words echoing around the chamber as Taggerty and Kensington both flinched.

"Your Highness, I am just trying to help," Taggerty said just above a whisper.

"You're trying to help?" Avalon responded coolly, and then she bit the inside of her mouth to stop from speaking because she knew deep down inside that Taggerty was trying to help.

Taggerty waited a breath and then pressed on. "You need to let me go to Cormicks to see what we are up against. We need to see what they are planning."

"No." Avalon thought of the small band of Guides who were out in the woods, waiting by the elbagrass for any sign of the enemy.

"You told me that you don't want to send anyone to their death, but by waiting, you are condemning us all to our death by giving them the time they need to launch an assault and to come here, straight into the heart of Fontanasia."

This view was nothing new to Avalon. She had the same argument with herself daily. On one hand it was wrong to rush in, and on the other it was also wrong to wait.

"Kensington, you spend a lot of time with Taggerty, and you have carried out a specific... task for me," Avalon stumbled on her words as she looked at Zaria's husband-to-be. He would be family soon, and no matter his upbringing, Avalon would have to bring him into the fold. "What do you think is the best course of action?"

Kensington's eyes came alive and Avalon thought she saw a slight smile under his thick beard. She had ignored him since they had met at her birthday party, so she could understand his reaction.

"King Avalon, I could not presume to know all that you do, but I do have an opinion on the matter." He looked up at Avalon who waited with her eyebrows lifted. "I understand Taggerty's willingness to move forward, because that is what we do. We are soldiers, and we don't wait for an enemy's attack easily. That said, it has been almost a year since the incident, and there has been no sign of the enemy. I don't believe that they were able to find their way here. I think waiting is a wise decision." He looked at Taggerty who had glanced back with a shake of his head, but Avalon could tell that Taggerty wasn't surprised by Kensington's answer.

Avalon nodded slowly. She hadn't intended to give Zaria her wish so quickly, but she had her excuse and was already forming a new task for Taggerty in her mind. "I agree with you both. We should not wait to be slaughtered by our enemy, but it has been months and our enemy is not here. Maybe we should go to Cormicks in time, but for now we will wait." She looked directly into Taggerty's eyes. "That is why Walthan had to kill Brick before we returned to Fontanasia. He had to make sure that no one knew how to get here, and I believe his sacrifice has kept us safe."

Taggerty swallowed hard. They both shared Walthan's loss. Avalon wondered why they had never taken time to talk about that night. Maybe that was just how battle was, a living beast inside a memory, biting raw chunks from heart and soul if left too close to the surface.

"Walthan killed Brick?" Kensington asked slowly, glancing between Taggerty and Avalon. He was truly shocked. "He was buried in honor near Walthan, I just assumed..." Kensington trailed off and tried to regain his composure, but this knowledge was a blow. Like the rest of the Guard, he had looked up to Brick all of his life.

"Another time," Taggerty said, moving his eyes to Avalon. Kensington pulled back his shoulders and stood at attention reminded that he was in the presence of the king.

Avalon and Taggerty looked at each other, and Avalon's eyebrows folded down in question. She had not told anyone what had happened in Cormicks, and only she, Taggerty and his Uncle Chylyn knew that Brick had betrayed Fontanasia. Avalon assumed that Taggerty had told Kensington. The two had been gone for months disposing of Hawker in the wilderness, and yet Taggerty had not shared that information with his closest friend. Avalon knew the King's Guard as a band of brothers, and she was shocked to find they could keep secrets from each other.

Taggerty answered Avalon's stare with a shrug and a slight smile. He assumed that Avalon had told Zaria about Brick, but she could not. They had lost their father too soon, and Zaria was shaken. Avalon could not pull the safety of a life in Fontanasia out from under the citizens, much less Zaria.

Avalon broke the moment with a command. "Taggerty, we have discussed your being the future head of the King's Guard, but I remove you from that commitment. I think what the King's Guard needs is Kensington's thoughtful presence." Taggerty's forehead twisted up and he smiled in understanding.

"Yes, Your Highness," Taggerty said with an uncharacteristically deep bow to his king.

"You will tell Gamon that he is relieved of his duty. I will give him my thanks later. You will both work with Kensington until he is up to the task," Taggerty nodded and took a step back. "Kensington," Avalon said as she looked at the dismayed soldier. "My life and the life of all of Fontanasia is in your hands. Prove that you are worthy of the task."

Kensington knelt and bowed low trying to compose himself, but when he stood, Avalon could see the stream of tears that had escaped his eyes, and then she realized that with her words, she had changed the course of his life forever. He had not asked for Zaria's hand in marriage, but Avalon had just raised his position in society enough to make it plausible.

Kensington cleared his throat. "My life is yours, Your Highness. I will do everything within my power to secure Fontanasia."

"You are dismissed," she told them both. She needed to figure out what Counselor Nelson was up to, and she would need some time before she let Taggerty in on his new errand. The men bowed, and Taggerty glanced up at her with a wink. Avalon tried not to smile, but Taggerty waited until he could see the slight upturn of her lips before turning to leave.

Myra found Avalon in the king's suite staring out the window. Avalon was wishing that she could grip the Fingers and close that mountainous hand to scoop up all of Fontanasia and move her people to safety. That thought made her remember the Anthracites peeling up from the earth and trying to trample her, and she shuddered.

"Are you cold, Your Grace?" Myra asked sensing Avalon's mood. Avalon missed Myra using her name, but she had gotten used to the formal titles. And in those tender moments when Avalon could not find her way out of her thoughts or her despair, Myra would still call her Avalon.

"No, I'm fine, Myra. Just thinking."

"Do you care to share?" Myra asked. Just a year ago, when Avalon was Prince Avalon and still under Myra's tutelage, Myra would have pried more than asked.

"Sometimes I wish I was never born. My mother would not have died, and my father would still be here."

"Oh, pish posh," Myra said, but her mood was quickly dampened by Avalon's statement. "You cannot control everything. You are the king and your parents would be proud of you."

"Zaria could have learned to lead Fontanasia."

"You know that is not true, Avalon. Zaria might have the capacity to run the day to day, but she is not the leader that you are. Besides, that would never come to pass because she was born a girl. There has always been a king in Fontanasia, just as there was for all time, and that's just how it is. Don't say that you wish you were never born. You were meant to be a king."

"But why can't I just declare Zaria as the queen?"

Myra raised her eyebrow and smiled at Avalon. "Anything else on your mind?" she asked softly.

Avalon sighed. "How do you know which men are good and which ones are not? How can you see it on them?" Avalon had been thinking about Zaria and Kensington, but now she was talking about Hawker again.

Myra smiled tightly and stood next to Avalon taking in the scenery. Her tall, bulky frame somehow carried a lightness of being within it, and when Myra drew in a long breath, it was Avalon who let out another sigh. Myra chuckled. "Women have been trying to figure out that very question for centuries." The joke was lost on Avalon, so Myra set in for a serious conversation. Her voice softened, "I know that you are good to the core, Avalon."

"But I am not a..."

Myra cut her off, "You are the king, and you are good. That is all we need to know about that." She looked down at Avalon who waited patiently, and Myra took the hint. "You can't see it on a man, and you don't know by looking at him. A high-born man who is dressed well can be a traitor, and a man who is smeared in the dirt of his labor can be a prince at heart. Their mannerisms won't give it away either, although that is a good starting point. Study their outward demeanor for long enough and you will see their true nature."

"But I missed it with Hawker, and I knew him all of my life."

Myra nodded. "You were a child who was loved well by his uncle. You weren't studying Hawker, you accepted him for the man that he showed to you. If you had studied him though, you might have seen it earlier."

"Like you?" Avalon asked. "You never liked Hawker. You saw it in him."

"I grew up with Hawker, and I saw his nature early in life, before he hid it from the world. But he hadn't changed, he had only learned to tuck it away behind closed doors."

Avalon's brow furrowed, and she bit the inside of her lip to keep her tongue. She could talk about her Uncle Hawker for the next thirty years and still not understand.

"Do you know Kensington of the King's Guard?" Avalon asked, looking Myra full in the face for a clue as to whether she was in on the secret, but Myra simply answered with a straight face.

"Yes, I have met Kensington. A very fine sort, thank you for asking." It was a neutral response, but Avalon assumed that there was only one person Zaria would confide in about something so serious as marriage, and that was Myra.

"So you think that my father would have approved of him to marry Zaria?"

Myra's face turned red and her eyes opened wide, a response that made Avalon chuckle. "So I'm not the last one to know?" Avalon asked her.

"Zaria is marrying Kensington?" Myra asked still stunned.

"Do you approve of him?" Avalon pressed.

"Me?" Myra asked as she turned from the window and moved to lean on a chair.

"Please," Avalon said as she motioned to the chair.

Myra begrudgingly sat down. She had been the only mother that Avalon had known, and yet she remained the ever-faithful servant and would not presume to sit before her king. This news was too much though. Myra sat her bulk in the chair and placed a hand over her heart. Avalon could see Myra's eyes watering, her typical stoic demeanor shaken by the news. "Yes, of course, I do approve of him," Myra told Avalon. "When you were away, and King Birch was," Myra paused to look for the word but there was still no easy way to say it. "When your father was found dead, Zaria and I were locked in the suite for over ten days. We were unharmed, but it was Kensington who made sure we were safe and fed. He remained on duty for over fourteen hours each day, only leaving early afternoon to get some rest and return before night fall. I had no idea that he and Zaria had formed a bond of any sort."

"Well he hasn't formally asked me for her hand in marriage yet, but Zaria made it perfectly clear that he will, and soon."

Myra's head was bowed forward, and she pulled her smock up to wipe her eyes. "I only wish your parents were here to see it." Avalon returned to the window and gulped hard. She wished her parents were here too.

Chapter 8
New Prince

Avalon waited two days before sending for Counselor Nelson. Although she believed Taggerty, she had sent Gamon yesterday to see for himself as to whether his borough was stockpiling food. He had reported back that it was true. District West was cleaning and preparing a hundred pounds of meat almost each day. The skins were being dried along the walls and the meat trimmed and salted for storage. Avalon had trusted Counselor Nelson as her father had, and he had always been kind and honest. She couldn't begin to guess what he was up to. Avalon was learning to trust no one. She had never liked Counselor Glenn, so his betrayal was easier to accept, but she could hardly believe it of Counselor Nelson.

She heard two loud knocks on the door to the throne room, and Avalon stopped pacing and watched the door swing open. She quickly sat upon the throne without another thought as two of the King's Guard flanked Counselor Nelson. He approached Avalon with his typical disarming smile and she reflexively smiled back. Counselor Nelson stopped at the edge of the small step and bowed graciously. "King Avalon," he said as he bowed.

"Counselor Nelson," she said as she nodded to the guard who returned to the door but remained inside the room. "You have been very busy in your borough," Avalon said directly. She watched his face for a flicker of anger, but none was there. Counselor Nelson smiled graciously.

"We have. I hope you are pleased. We are making wonderful progress. I told the men to try to hunt a bit further out so there are still animals closer to the city for when it gets cold."

Avalon was taken aback at his eager honesty. He was not even trying to hide what he was doing. She wondered if he would share why he was stockpiling food. "Why so much?" she asked neutrally. At that Counselor Nelson's eyebrows lowered in question.

"Well, I hoped you would be pleased. Of course, we will need more space and we will bring the meat to the castle storehouses. It's just that Counselor Creighton said that you wished a six month supply, and at two pounds of meat per person each week, it is a tremendous undertaking." Counselor Nelson looked worried, but he tried to smile. "I'm not complaining though, Your Highness. I am proud that you have come to us to complete this task. District West holds the best hunters in Fontanasia."

Avalon was confused. She hadn't ordered anyone to stockpile food. Counselor Creighton was making up orders on her behalf, and it took a moment of realizing that before Avalon became furious. She held her breath though, because she didn't want to admit that she had been fooled. She nodded her head and tried to smile, but she could feel her pasty lips sticking to her teeth and it came out like a grimace.

"Did Counselor Creighton happen to mention any of the other food stores that I requested?" Avalon asked as confidently as she could.

Counselor Nelson looked surprised. "No, Your Highness, but with the help of the other boroughs, we will prepare whatever is needed."

"That won't be necessary," Avalon cut in. "I asked him to distribute the work evenly. You are dismissed." Avalon couldn't wait to be alone. She was shocked at the news, and she was angry. She needed to fire Counselor Creighton right away.

Counselor Nelson bowed, but he did not turn to leave. Avalon nodded at him, and he cleared his throat and smiled politely. "King Avalon, Counselor Creighton said that you would be convening the Council to discuss this matter of filling the stores so early, and in such a large quantity. Can you tell me when that meeting will be?"

"No," Avalon said flatly. She was the king, and she didn't have to explain her actions to anyone.

"Very good. It's just, the people are curious as to what is happening, and any news I can share with them might help dispel any rumors. You know how the gossips can be."

But Avalon didn't know about the gossip. She thought that moving along the streets in the morning kept her in touch, but she had been the prince, and now she was the king. She knew them as little as they knew her, but they were her people, and she had to protect them.

"I understand, Counselor Nelson," she agreed, but she offered him nothing further. He watched her for another moment and then bowed and turned to leave. The guards followed Counselor Nelson out of the room and closed the heavy doors behind them. Avalon sat on the throne. Her body felt heavy again as the weight of Fontanasia encompassed her. Her father had made ruling look so easy. He had his own opposition in Counselor Glenn, but no one had ever given commands in the name of the king before unless they were actual commands from the king. Avalon couldn't show weakness, and Counselor Creighton would have to be dealt with. He was an ally of her father's, and she had been so sure that he was going to be a supporter of hers.

Avalon's thought was disrupted by small footsteps approaching from behind the throne, and she heard the rustle of the heavy rug as it moved back against the wall. Chylyn appeared before her followed by another Guide, and Avalon was certain they had been there for a while, only purposefully making some noise now so that she would not be startled by their approach. Avalon stood and faced them. She knew about the secret passage through the walls of the castle up to the throne room, and had seen Guides approach her father on two occasions in the past.

"King Avalon," Chylyn said quietly. "We have come to ask you what your plans are for Cormicks." He was direct, and she appreciated the fact that they did not try to maneuver politically. They were concerned only with the safety of their people and of peace in Fontanasia, and there would never be a hidden agenda. "Have you seen something?" the second Guide asked. Avalon did not recognize him.

She realized then that they thought she had dreamt the future and that she must have been putting a last minute plan together, but she shook her head. She had not dreamt since the return of Taggerty and Kensington, and her dreams were few and far between.

"What are your plans, King Avalon? We have men in the wood and they have seen nothing since your return from Cormicks." They would not tell her what to do, but they were pressing her now because she was stockpiling food.

"I have no definite plans, but I feel that we must prepare none the less." She watched them for any reaction, but they remained stoic, their faces relaxed, not one move of the head.

"You should not move forward until you have looked back long enough to see the path that you are on," Chylyn said. Avalon was reminded of Myra's cryptic advice over the years, but she actually understood what he meant.

"All I do is look back, gentlemen. There is a path ahead, but it is not clear to me yet. I cannot sit still any longer though. I am worried for the future of the people." Avalon's statement surprised her. She was starting to see a way ahead, and she could not admit that her counselors were working on their own without a direct command from her.

"Then you are choosing a path without knowing if it is the right one."

"I must do something," she said louder than she had intended and they all reflexively looked toward the door. No one interrupted, so they continued.

Chylyn cleared his throat. "You can look back further, study all the roads, and the path will open up before you. If the window was to be opened, it would have happened by now. The Monarch, the Runners, they do not know patience. If they could get here, they would be here now." Avalon wanted to believe him. She wanted to tell Counselor Nelson to stand down, and for things to return to how they had always been. But she had seen the Runners and the Anthracites and the skin crawling everred spiders. Avalon had horrible daydreams about the evil that would befall Fontanasia if they were overrun and slaughtered. She did not have the patience to wait and see what would happen. Counselor Creighton had put some plan in motion, and she needed to find out what that plan was. And she needed to give Taggerty his wish.

"When I look back further, I see the slaughter of our people and our flight from Hawkerness. I don't intend to be the king who waited for that to happen again."

Chylyn nodded slowly as the other Guide spoke. "We will do our duty and watch the window, but we must do what is right for our people when the time comes."

"I understand," Avalon said curtly. Her trusted Guides would leave if the time came. She remembered on the hill overlooking Cormicks, how Taggerty's uncle had known before any of them that the Runners were surrounding them, and how he had been the only one to escape in time. She felt chills up her spine. She hoped that memory was not a sign of things to come.

"We will return if there is any news," he said, and then the two men turned and slipped silently behind the tapestry and out of sight.

"You know why I have summoned you?" Avalon asked before Julius Creighton had made his way to the dais. Avalon brushed the King's Guard off and they left Creighton to walk the rest of the short distance by himself. He had been summoned to the throne room by the king, and yet he walked with his typical slow, hunched gate. He didn't need to pretend with her, she knew that he was younger than he looked. And yet he stepped tentatively all the way to the bottom step and stopped, bowing slowly as though he had a stiff back.

"I have my suspicions, King Avalon."

"And I have my suspicions, Counselor Creighton," she snapped back. He just stood there without reacting, waiting for Avalon to respond. "Your services on the King's Council are no longer required," Avalon said calmly, all restraint in her voice.

Creighton barely reacted. He nodded his head slowly and rubbed his chin with his thumb and forefinger. "And yet if you dismiss me now, it will show as weakness to the Council. You have just recently appointed me. What will you tell them of my absence?" Creighton spoke softly and respectfully, and Avalon wondered if he had heard her correctly. Of course he had, she knew. He was clever, and his calm question made her curious.

"I am not playing games here."

"Nor am I, Your Highness." This time he gracefully knelt fully to the ground and bowed his head, a full sign of respect to his king. Avalon was finding it difficult to stay angry, and she was confused. "May I speak freely?" Creighton asked.

"Of course, but only if you say something direct and of value and without riddle," Avalon snapped back. Creighton smiled at that.

"Very good, King Avalon. I will be as direct as I can. If you remove me from the Council and tell Counselor Nelson to stop growing the food stores, he will know that the order originated from me and that I was working on my own. He also knows that it appears Counselor Glenn was working on his own, and even though he had suspicions about Hawker, he has kept that secret for you." Avalon remembered how well she had trusted Counselor Nelson all of these months, and she would not have been able to fake Hawker's death without his complicit silence on the matter. He had obeyed Avalon without question. "Will he keep this secret? Will he reconsider just how good a king you are if you can't keep rule in Fontanasia?" His voice didn't sound like he was threatening her, but the words were there and Avalon was taken aback.

"Are you threatening me?" she asked.

"I am counseling you, my king. It will look like weakness if you expose what I have started in motion."

"And what have you set in motion?" she asked.

"I have begun what you could not, or would not. It is best to be ready when the time comes. You will need enough food to defend the city, or you will need enough food to send the army out for war. In either case, it is best to prepare."

Avalon wanted to lash back, but she bit her tongue. Creighton was smart, calm, and he could see something she did not. Her father trusted him, but her father had died at the hand of someone he would not fathom could take his life, and yet his own brother was capable and willing. She did not fear Creighton, but she did not trust him either. She now understood Taggerty's plea for her to disband the Council, but she would let this pass with Creighton for now. She would reconsider keeping a Council in time though, because if she ruled alone, she could ensure all orders came straight from her. Avalon trusted Myra and Zaria, and Taggerty and now Kensington. The rest would remain at arms length.

After dinner with Zaria, Avalon sat alone in her room. She was glad that she and Zaria were getting along again. Avalon had pulled away in the past year and dining together was helping to bring them closer. Avalon turned the blade of her sword in her hand and studied the inscription again and again. This was her meditation, the new obsession that relaxed her. Avalon would turn the blade and think about her father and her uncle and her people. She would plan different solutions to the threat of Cormicks but take no real action. Maybe that was what Julius Creighton was doing by forcing her hand, she surmised. He was trying to break her of her inaction.

There was a knock and Avalon called, "Enter," without taking her eyes from the blade.

Thomas opened the door and took one step inside. "Your Highness, Kensington requests a meeting."

Avalon nodded slowly. She knew the time would come, but she hadn't expected it so soon. Zaria had been gushing about Kensington since Avalon had made him the head of her guard, but that had only taken place a week earlier. Surely they would wait for more than a week before announcing their engagement.

"Is he here, Thomas?"

"Yes, King Avalon. He is waiting in the suite."

"I think I am safe enough with the head of the King's Guard. You may leave us, Thomas."

"Yes, Your Highness," the guard responded. He closed the door behind him and Avalon heard his footsteps on the brick as he walked away. She returned the sword to her holster and dressed in her outer coat as Jackie raced toward her on the bed.

"Of course, Jackie," she said as she placed her hand on the bed. The red lizard raced up her sleeve and down into her waist pocket. "You will want to hear this. It will be a big day for the Hall family." Avalon patted her pocket and moved into the outer room of the suite.

She saw Kensington looking out the large window, surveying Fontanasia. He didn't notice her at first, and Avalon studied him from the hallway for a full minute in the waning light. He stood erect with his shoulders back. Where Taggerty was tall and lean, Kensington had a strong and stout frame. Avalon could not make out his chin as it was covered with a thick, red and blond beard. She noticed that he looked much older than Taggerty, but it might have been the faraway look in his eyes as he stared out the window.

His coat looked new, and it was buttoned up but tight over his bulging muscles. His pants in contrast were faded and his boots were polished but worn. She had not noticed his clothing or shoes before, or rather she had noticed their shoddiness, but she had dismissed Kensington. She was slightly ashamed for judging him so harshly on appearance. She did not know his full character yet, and they would have plenty of time to get to know each other, but Avalon needed to make sure he had some new clothes made. When the engagement was announced, Kensington would need to look the part.

Jackie crawled out of her pocket and made a move for Avalon's shoulder, but when Kensington turned from the window, the lizard raced back down to his hiding place.

"King Avalon," Kensington said as he dropped to one knee and bowed his head.

He remained still until she took three steps forward and said, "Rise."

He stood slowly and looked everywhere but directly at Avalon. She knew he was here to ask for Zaria's hand, and she would give her permission when he did, but she would make him say the words. She could hear him breathing, and he gulped loudly. She imagined his muscles that were already pushing at the outer coat's material bursting through. He was a warrior, and Avalon still didn't understand what Zaria saw in him. He was a brute compared to her other suitors and yet here he was in the king's suite, a few short steps from becoming a prince.

"Do you have something to report?" Avalon asked, realizing he would not speak until told to do so.

"Excuse me?" Kensington asked clumsily.

Avalon smiled. She felt nervous most of her life, nervous that someone would find out her truth. Kensington must have felt the same way right now, pressed into this coat that was obviously borrowed, trying to find the right thing to say. "The King's Guard, Kensington. Do you have something to report?"

"Uh, no, Your Highness." Kensington took a deep breath and remembered his position. He was the head of the King's Guard, and he had a right to be in the presence of his king now. He blew the breath out slowly and Avalon waited. She reached her thumb and forefinger into her waist pocket and pet Jackie as Kensington straightened up and collected himself.

"King Avalon, I thank you again for the position of leading your King's Guard. I have been in service for seven years, and I will use all of my knowledge to protect you and Fontanasia, and Princess Zaria."

So he was at least twenty-five, Avalon thought. That was a good age to start a family, but maybe young for the head of her guard. She smiled at that. She would have given Taggerty that position and he was but nineteen. Taggerty's cavalier exterior covering his constant worry made him seem much older though. Avalon cleared her throat to bring herself back from her thoughts, and Kensington took that as his cue. He squared his shoulders and spoke with complete self-assuredness.

"Your Highness, I will be frank with you." He did not wait for her to respond. "I love Princess Zaria with all of my heart, and I believe she loves me too. I know that I might not be what your family expected for her, but I am devoted and true. I will spend all of my days in service to Princess Zaria and to your kingdom."

Avalon was reminded of Walthan now, with his muscular bulk and resolute assuredness. She was certain that Kensington meant what he said, and although she had no real idea of who this man was, Zaria had made up her mind.

Kensington looked at the floor, his words coming softer now. "King Avalon, I ask you for your sister's hand in marriage." His voice had shaken at the end and made Avalon's heart flutter. She breathed in deeply and didn't answer until she was sure she had her emotions in check.

"This is fast. I just made you the head of my guard a week ago," she said not committing to an answer yet.

"Yes, Your Highness, I agree. But I do not dare make Princess Zaria wait one minute longer. I live to serve the princess."

Avalon's eyebrows rose at his answer. It was honest and didn't seem rehearsed.

"Does it serve the princess to rush into marriage?" Avalon asked, although she knew they weren't rushing. Zaria had met him a year ago, and all of the time she thought Zaria was spending with Taggerty, she had been spending with Kensington. Zaria and Kensington knew each other well, and Zaria had not lost interest. She was gushing over him.

"We will wait as long as you command, sire, but neither of us feel rushed. We are in love." It was a second open and honest answer, and Avalon could see that waiting would serve no one.

"What is your full name, Kensington?" Avalon did not know this question was coming until it was already out in the room.

"Your Highness?"

"Who is your family? What is your full name?"

Kensington looked up at her now, his face turning red. He was not sure where the king was going with this questioning, and he started to sweat. "I am Kensington of the Reaches. My mother was Teresa Brown and my father was Tom Kensington, a hunter. Some people call me Kensington Brown, but my mother called me Kensington." He had grit his teeth, the vetting process not going as smoothly as Zaria and Taggerty must have prepared him for.

"What did your father call you?" she asked.

"My father died before I was born," Kensington said curtly, and Avalon felt a pang of remorse for having asked. Still, she was the king and she needed to know who would be entering her family.

"I'm sorry," she said softly. He cleared his throat, looking at Avalon now. His face was serious and questioning, and he was doing all he could to not beg. "I give you permission to marry my sister, but I have one condition."

"Anything, King Avalon," Kensington said hopeful again.

"My sister will not become Zaria Kensington, or Zaria Brown or whatever you were thinking. I am not questioning your past, but I cannot have an uncertain past make for a shaky future. You do not have to take my family's name, but your children will be of the Hall bloodline, and they will take the surname Hall. This is not a request." Again, Avalon had said it before she knew what she was doing, but as soon as she had said it, she was certain it was the right thing to do. Zaria would continue the Hall family name as Avalon could not. Avalon would never have a son, but she could not allow hundreds of years of Hall rule to come to an end. It was her turn to sigh. Any of Zaria's previous suitors of Fontanasia society would have had a proud last name to carry on. Avalon couldn't believe her luck.

"Anything, Your Highness." Kensington gulped down hard, although she didn't think he was offended, but more that he realized his children would carry the name of royalty.

"Then I will allow it," Avalon said, sounding more and more like her father.

"Thank you, King Avalon." Kensington bowed his head and then stood straight, bouncing lightly on his toes. Avalon could see that he was bursting with happiness, and she needed to let him go tell Zaria.

"Send Taggerty here before you see Princess Zaria, and do not see her unescorted. She is not yours until you are wed."

Kensington bowed again. "As you command," he said, and then he turned to go. He opened the door to the suite and Avalon heard the guards outside snap to attention. Avalon could see Taggerty had been waiting just outside the door, no doubt trying to hear the conversation. Her heart warmed at the sight of him so she faced the window to hide her expression and to gather herself. Before she turned away, she saw Taggerty and Kensington smile and grab each other's arms at the elbow, a tight sign of embrace for soldiers. Avalon took Jackie out of her pocket to distract herself for the moment. She held him up to her chin and pet his head until she heard the door close behind her, and the jakkow started to squirm in her hand.

"King Avalon," Taggerty said. She did not turn toward him, and he moved to the far side of the window and looked out. Jackie squirmed in her hand again, and Avalon put the red lizard on the windowsill and watched him scramble down to Taggerty who opened his hands freely.

"Jackie," he said, "don't grow up on me now." Taggerty said that on the few occasions he saw the jakkow who had grown larger than a horse when they had crossed over into Cormicks. The lizard curled into a tight ball in his palm, and Taggerty walked the pet back to Avalon. She held out her hand, and Taggerty gently passed the lizard over. Their fingers touched for a moment and Avalon held her breath.

"You have made a wise decision," Taggerty told her.

"So you aren't jealous that Zaria is going to marry Kensington?" she asked as a joke, but she could see that Taggerty did not find it funny in the least.

"I am truly happy for my friend. He is a good match for Zaria, inwardly if not outwardly."

"Yes, how am I going to sell that to the people?"

Taggerty looked at her quizzically.

"I like him, he's just so different than what I expected of Zaria."

"I should have found him a larger waistcoat," Taggerty said, and they shared a laugh. From the corner of her eye, she could see Taggerty look down at her, but she could not turn to meet his gaze. "He will do anything for Zaria, just as I will do anything for you." His voice was serious, and for a moment Avalon forgot she was king. Her face reddened and she looked down, moving Jackie to her pocket. "What of my future, Avalon? What will you have me do?"

She willed herself not to look into his eyes. His question sounded so personal, and she felt foolish. What was he asking her? Avalon felt embarrassed at her own thoughts because she knew there was no way he meant to say what she was hearing. She bit her lip and changed the tone of conversation. "You gave up leading the King's Guard. That was your future."

"Stop trying to protect me!" Taggerty said with frustration, and Avalon stepped back. He was angry in that moment, and when she turned to face him, he looked out the window. She watched him compose himself as quickly as he had lost control.

Avalon's mouth hung open for a moment. He had startled her, and she didn't know what to say. Her mouth was still hanging open when Taggerty turned from the window and looked at her. The waning light of day left gold specs to dance in the green of his eyes. Avalon closed her mouth and held her breath. She wanted what Zaria and Kensington had, but there was no future for her and Taggerty. Still, she couldn't help but think he was not talking business at this moment.

Taggerty reached his hand out and then dropped it, looking quickly to the door. Avalon looked at the door reflexively, but it was still closed, and they were still alone. She felt a lump in her throat. "If I am the future of the king..." Taggerty raised his hands palm up, open for her to see. "If there is anything that you didn't tell me, that you need to tell me, you need to tell me right now." Taggerty took a half step forward and curled his hands into fists before dropping them to his side.

Avalon couldn't help but realize that they were now standing close enough to embrace. What was she supposed to say, "I like you?" It was the truth but also sounded ridiculous to her. She couldn't help but blush. She cleared her throat and took a step back, glancing again at the door. She was the king, and she would remain king no matter what. It wouldn't do for her to be seen standing so close to anyone. She turned her back on Taggerty and walked to the sitting area, offering him a chair with her hand. She could hear him sigh before he took a seat opposite her. Avalon let Jackie out of her pocket and he zipped around the furniture unaware of the heavy atmosphere in the room.

"I wasn't going to put this plan in motion yet, but there is no reason you can't start working on it. I need you to figure out how to get the soldiers to the window. We can't leave a permanent trail like a bridge, and they need to do it without bringing too many supplies." Taggerty smiled outwardly and Avalon put her hand up to stop his reverie. "We aren't going now, or soon. I just need to have a plan in place for when the time comes."

"Is that why you haven't stopped Counselor Nelson from building the food stores?" he asked.

"Maybe," Avalon answered.

Taggerty gave Avalon the look that Myra did when she didn't tell the full truth and Myra expected more. Avalon smiled at the thought, but didn't offer Taggerty any further explanation.

"Assume that we will be sending fifty soldiers at some time, and make plans for the entire trip to the window. Then make a list of supplies needed if they were to stay at the window for a full six months."

"As you command," Taggerty said.

"Then make a list of rotating supplies if the men were to do one month rotations at the window." Taggerty nodded but pursed his lips. "Yes?" she asked.

"The King's Guard and soldiers are loyal and will do your bidding, Your Highness, but you realize that you will run the risk of everyone in Fontanasia finding out about Cormicks. It's one thing for the men to go hunting for a week or ten days, but to be gone for a month, and to return tour after tour and not to say anything, that will be difficult."

"You are right, Taggerty, but I can't rely on the Guides," she stopped herself and chose her words more carefully. "I can rely on the Guides, of course, but I can't expect them to be away from their families for months at a time without extending any assistance."

"I agree, but please ask the Guides what they think before you send your men out."

Avalon was surprised at Taggerty. "I thought you wanted me to attack Cormicks. Why the change of heart?"

Taggerty smiled, a glint in his eyes. "I do want to attack, but if all you want to do is watch the window, the Guides will be glad to continue the duty as long as it will continue to keep the window secret." His smile faded and he leaned forward in his chair. "Don't send soldiers unless you are serious about moving forward."

A shiver of electricity ran up Avalon's spine, and she thought she could feel the hair rise on the back of her head. Taggerty's confidence was electricity to her and she fought back doe eyes and a half smile. "I will consider your advice," she said. She bit her lip and dismissed Taggerty. He rose, clapped his boot heels together and tipped his head in an informal bow. He was halfway to the door when he reached up to the back of his shoulder and scolded the tiny red lizard who had climbed on him some time during the conversation. "Jackie, stay!" Taggerty said as he placed the lizard on an end table and left the suite.

Avalon smiled and then placed her hand over her heart. She closed her eyes and remembered how he had stood so close to her. She played the conversation over in her head until she had locked every detail in her mind. She could live on that moment for the rest of her life.

Chapter 9
Secret Wall

Zaria had come directly to Avalon that very night and woke Avalon out of a sound sleep. She hugged her sister and started a tickle fight like they were little kids again. Zaria was engaged to be married, and she was ecstatic. She lay in bed next to her sister and they reminisced for the first time in years.

"So you weren't actually already engaged when Kensington approached me?" Avalon asked. She thought for sure that Zaria had gotten engaged before that, and Kensington's visit was a mere formality.

"No!" Zaria protested. "I hinted, but Kensington never acted. He wanted to do everything properly." Zaria rolled onto her elbow and looked at Avalon. "He is honorable, I hope you can see that."

"The man who broke Princess Zaria's spell?" Zaria tickled Avalon again, and Avalon's strong arms could have easily fended her off, but it was nice to share a moment together. Times like these were long past, and since their father had died the world had become a much more serious place.

Avalon finally protested when she could hardly breath, and Zaria sat back and they both let the laughter run its course. Then Zaria sighed, and Avalon could see tears running down her face. "I wish father could have met Kensington," Zaria said through salty lips.

Avalon nodded. "Kensington has been on the King's Guard for a while, perhaps they did."

"Kensington stood guard a few times, but he was never introduced. I wish they could have gotten to know each other."

"I know what you mean," Avalon said regretfully. "He does remind me a little of someone father knew quite well though."

"Who's that?"

"Walthan."

Zaria smiled wide. "He does have that 'all for the kingdom' soldier outlook. I think it's instilled from his training under Walthan."

"And he isn't so tall, but he has Walthan's muscular build," Avalon added, not knowing Kensington well enough to comment on his character.

"Does he really remind you of Walthan?" Zaria asked.

"Yes," Avalon said definitively.

Zaria laughed again, wiping the remaining tears from her cheek. "Never tell Kensington that. It will go straight to his head, and I will have to hear about it every day."

They shared a laugh and then stayed up half the night as Zaria talked about the wedding she wanted to have. Avalon said that she would throw an engagement party, but then regretted it when she realized she had no idea how to plan such an event. Still, they were family and Avalon would do her duty.

It took only three weeks for Myra to plan the engagement party. Of course the orders came from the king, but it was Myra who sat with Avalon and planned every detail, and Avalon who gave Myra the order to execute the plans as she saw fit.

Myra could have put the party together in only a couple of days, but Avalon needed extra time to make sure Kensington's wardrobe was new, and most of it was created from scratch. Avalon never used a tailor, having Myra do all of her measurements and the tailor making patterns from those. But for Kensington, Avalon had the tailor brought to her own suite, and she summoned Kensington to be fitted. Avalon ordered three full outfits with coat, one outer coat for winter, and three separate uniforms. He was the head of the King's Guard, and he should look the part. Avalon had also decided that giving him a new uniform might make him look the part as the man worthy of the Princess of Fontanasia.

Avalon was to escort her sister to the engagement party, and she found Myra getting Zaria ready in her room. Zaria was enjoying her reflection in the mirror and looking for something to fix in her already perfect hair.

"You look beautiful," Myra said, her words wavering with emotion.

"Yes, you do," Avalon said. They both turned to Avalon.

"You really think so?" Zaria asked, completely thrilled with her new evening gown. Avalon stepped in and closed the door behind her.

"Yes, absolutely. As long as you aren't going to make me try that dress on next year." She smiled and Myra and Zaria burst with laughter.

"You would look good in this dress," Zaria said.

"I admit, it's getting harder to hide," Avalon said. "My shape would fill out these dresses now much better than they did last year." Myra looked at Avalon and tipped her head sideways, and Avalon knew what was coming. "No! I'm done with those days, Myra." They shared another laugh and headed to the party. Myra had coordinated the event, and she would be there as a guest, but as a servant to the Hall family, she would not allow herself to walk down with the king. Avalon knew that Myra would spend her time prompting the staff instead of relaxing as a true party guest.

The party was small but elegant, decorated in late summer flowers. Most of the guests were extended aunts, uncles and cousins coming from their mother's side of the family. The counselors were also invited, and Avalon spent a moment with each of them to try to assess their involvement with Hawker, and whether they liked the addition of Julius Creighton to the Council. She had been distracted for weeks by Zaria's engagement, but she still needed to deal with the Council. Her conversation with Counselor Nelson about Hawkerness had scared Avalon. She felt that she had dealt with it in the right way, but she still had questions.

Counselors Igway and Dekarecol had a short conversation with Avalon, and they were more interested in talking about improvements in their own boroughs to be concerned with Counselor Nelson and any orders from the king that didn't affect their borough directly. They also didn't have teenage daughters to introduce to the king, so they allowed Avalon to excuse herself early in the conversation. It was Counselor Jennings who stopped her in her tracks.

"King Avalon," Counselor Jennings bowed gracefully. He was counselor of the Reaches, which was a small area below Seaside where a lot of the boating people lived. He had thick, shiny black hair and piercing blue eyes so vivid that they were mesmerizing.

"Counselor Jennings, I hope you are enjoying yourself," Avalon said cordially. The typically serious Jennings looked around for anyone within earshot before leaning in.

"I am, Your Highness, thank you. Kensington is from the Reaches, you know, and we are always happy when one of our own is chosen to lead. You know, King Avalon, I wish for you to meet my daughter this evening, but it seems she has gone off to gossip with some of the other girls here." Jennings' eyes moved around the room.

"Next time," Avalon said flippantly. She had no desire to spend the evening dodging advances.

"I certainly hope not!" Jennings shot back, gaining Avalon's full attention. "Well," he explained, "there is only one princess, and therefore only one engagement." Jennings was smiling and it took a moment for Avalon to realize he was making a joke. She tried to force a chuckle.

"Of course," she said, ready to extricate herself from conversation with him, but he pressed on, lowering his voice conspiratorially, and Avalon froze in place.

"You are making a move on Hawkerness?" he asked in a whisper. Avalon's breathing stopped at the mention of the city, and she looked at him, her mouth hanging open. She tried to recover, but she was shocked at his question.

"Excuse me?" Avalon finally asked.

"I see that you have ordered Counselor Nelson to begin stockpiling the rations, and I can only assume that it means one thing. Frankly, I have been waiting for you to call Council and give your commands to the rest of us, but since you have not, and you have been too busy to see me, I could only take this moment to ask." Jennings' explanation seemed genuine, but Avalon wondered if he was in some way trying to blackmail her.

"I have been busy with my sister's engagement party, counselor," Avalon mustered. She had received Jennings' notes but had ignored them, and she regretted that now.

"Of course, Your Highness. I didn't mean to disturb the evening. I just wanted you to know that it is important that we all work together on this matter."

Again, Avalon was stunned. She needed to know what he knew and who else was talking about Hawkerness. "Counselor, you are right, and I shouldn't put this off any longer. Will you meet me in the throne room after I toast my sister and her groom to be?"

Counselor Jennings' face lit up at the suggestion. "Of course, King Avalon."

"Then I shall make the toast sooner than later so we can get on with our business," Avalon said in haste.

"Shall I gather the Council?" Jennings asked.

"No," Avalon said. "I spoke to Counselor Nelson alone, and I would like to continue the discussion with you."

"As you wish," Jennings said with a bow as Avalon turned her back and looked through the crowd for Taggerty. She spotted Counselor Creighton talking to Counselor Nelson and almost made a beeline for them, but she changed her mind. This was no place for a scene, and she had deduced shortly after their meeting that Creighton was right, and she had to pretend the order to stockpile food came from the king.

Taggerty wasn't apparent in the crowd, but she knew that he would be present tonight. Avalon made her way toward Zaria who was entertaining their cousins from their mother's side. Avalon had spent some time with them when she was young, but when she had found out that she was a girl she had pulled away from them ending any further friendship. They were family to her, but distant family now. Yet Zaria had always kept in touch, having fun gatherings and throwing small parties throughout the year to stay close. Avalon had been invited to these gatherings, Zaria encouraging her to be social and get to know them, but Avalon was protecting her secret. It didn't help that seeing them reminded her of her mother. Zaria had told Avalon many times that she should speak with her aunts to get a better sense of who their mother was, but Avalon could only remember that she had killed her mother in child birth, and she preferred the stories that their father had told about Queen Samantha. Avalon looked at her polished boots and shook her thoughts away.

"Please, excuse us," Zaria said when she saw Avalon approach. Avalon tipped her head at her cousins who were bowing and curtsying to their king. When they were several steps away, Zaria took Avalon's arm. "They think you are pompous for the way you ignore them," she told Avalon.

"I am not a pompous king," Avalon retorted.

"You haven't interacted with them since you were a child. Sometimes I think you are still a child," Zaria quipped back with a smile. "You are only fifteen, you are practically a baby." A year ago, Avalon would have entered into an argument with her sister, but she had grown years since she had become king, and she remained calm, understanding that her sister was just toying with her.

"Well, this child intends to make a toast to her much older, practically ancient sister and her fiancé the Neanderthal." Avalon smiled as Zaria had, but she could see that Zaria was nervous with the remark about Kensington. "I am only joking. I like Kensington very much," Avalon reassured Zaria, but her sister didn't look confident in the words. "Hey," Avalon said, stopping their stroll and looking straight into Zaria's eyes. "He will be my brother soon. He will be family. You must let me have fun with him, that is how men bond."

Zaria looked at Avalon quizzically and then laughed, looking over Avalon's shoulder and spotting Kensington and Taggerty. "That could be true," she whispered, "but for someone who has spent a life studying the habits of men, you hardly know them at all." Zaria stepped away from Avalon and took Kensington's outstretched hand. Avalon could see her sister blush, and she could tell that they were absolutely in love. It was a sight Avalon had never truly seen before, and she held her breath to stop the tears. She cleared her throat and looked to the bandleader who had been playing a waltz, but always had his eye on the king to make sure he was ready for the cue. Avalon simply nodded, and the band stopped playing. The bandleader nodded to the headwaiter, and ten wait staff with trays full of champagne glasses poured into the room as the chatter of the party faded into silence.

Avalon moved to the step in front of the band and taking a glass of champagne, she held it up, keeping her eyes on Zaria. "Ladies and gentlemen, thank you for coming this evening. It is my great pleasure to announce the marriage of my sister, Princess Zaria, to Kensington of the Reaches." Avalon was grateful when all eyes turned from her to Zaria. Avalon let her eyes move to the wall at the back of the room so she could keep her composure. She was sure that if she kept watching Zaria's reaction to her speech, they would both begin to cry.

"For any of you who don't know Kensington, he has been in the King's Guard for over seven years, and he trained closely with Walthan." Avalon had exaggerated this point, but it had the reaction she knew it would as the crowd gave its muffled approval. "Kensington is the head of the King's Guard, and he has sworn his life to me, to Zaria, and to the people of Fontanasia. The only regret that Zaria and I have is that our father is not here to give this toast himself. I know that our father would have found in Kensington a great warrior, a true heart, and a second son. As for myself, I have found a brother." Avalon's voice remained strong. "Let us raise our glasses and toast Princess Zaria and Kensington. May they have a long and loving life together."

"Here, here!" the crowd boomed, and everyone drank their champagne. All eyes were on the engaged couple except Taggerty, who was looking directly at Avalon with a smile. She looked down, feeling the heat of a blush running through her face before she caught herself. She realized now that this was her subconscious reaction to Taggerty's attention, to look at the floor. Others might mistake that as a bow of her head though, and as king, she was not to lower her head to anyone. She needed to control herself, to not react. He was starting to make her feel a little crazy.

Avalon turned toward the bandleader. She smiled at the musicians and raised her eyebrows as they bowed their heads and then the bandleader called off the next song. Avalon took a step down, and the crowd parted the dance floor, allowing Kensington and Zaria to begin the dance.

Avalon didn't take her eyes off the couple as Taggerty approached and stood next to her, and they watched Kensington lead Zaria around the dance floor. They were the same height with Zaria in heels, and Avalon was very surprised to see how graceful Kensington was in the dance. He had the shape of a brute, and Avalon expected two left feet. Zaria beamed with pleasure, and Avalon could see the remnants of tears in Kensington's eyes.

"Now that Zaria is set, are you going to start thinking about your future?" Taggerty asked, not taking his eyes off of the couple.

"Excuse me?" Avalon asked. She looked away from Taggerty and her eyes fell upon a small gathering of young ladies who were intent on the king. She tapped Taggerty with her elbow and he looked away from Kensington and Zaria, noticing the same girls that Avalon had. "I'm surprised you're not over there looking for the next best thing, I mean, since Zaria dumped you."

"Dumped me?" Taggerty asked flabbergasted. Still watching the dance, they both smiled. "Actually, I'm trying to decide which would be worse torture."

Avalon's eyebrows pulled down in question.

"Those girls are dying for a dance with the king. Is it worse if you don't dance with any of them, or if you ask only one of them?"

"I don't approve of torture, Taggerty, and I don't have time to dance," Avalon said with all seriousness. "We must meet with Counselor Jennings right now. What he has to say is disturbing, and I need you with me. When this song ends, bring Jennings and Kensington to the throne room."

"As you command," Taggerty said, bowing to Avalon, one hand on the hilt of his sword, the other hand over his heart. He turned and moved away quickly. Avalon smiled and began moving to the door. Many of the guests raised their glass and bowed as she passed by, and Avalon tried to look relaxed, like she was enjoying the evening, but inside she was terrified. Counselor Jennings must tell her everything he knew.

Avalon didn't want to raise any eyebrows so she left the party discreetly. When she stepped from the room, four of the King's Guard escorted King Avalon around the main level to the throne room. She waved her hand to dismiss the two guards who had entered the room with her. They walked the perimeter of the brick room, and when they were satisfied that no one was there, they exited through the side door that led to the Hall of Kings. She knew they were posted outside the door still, keeping their king safe.

Avalon paced the floor for a moment, the large gray stones smooth under foot. The throne room was large enough to hold an audience, but not audacious in any way. There were several benches along the sides of the room, but most of the space was open allowing for the easy flow of business. Avalon looked up at the heavy tapestry that was hung behind the throne. It was the Hall coat of arms. She stared at it for several minutes, proud of the symbols but also weary of the lineage of kings that would die with her. Avalon was only fifteen though, and she hoped she had many years to consider a successor.

She moved up the steps to sit upon the throne but walked behind it instead. Avalon looked to the side door and the main door to make sure she was alone, and then she knelt, pulling back the corner of the tapestry to reveal the wall behind it. Avalon knew that the secret passage was here, although she had a hard time seeing it in the dimly lit room. She listened for a moment and then said, "hello," to no one. Satisfied that she was alone, Avalon sat the throne just as the guards opened the main doors. Taggerty and Kensington walked in behind Counselor Jennings and then the doors closed behind them. The three men walked to the bottom of the steps and bowed.

"Counselor Jennings, I am interested in your questions about Hawkerness," Avalon said. To his credit, Kensington remained silent, and Avalon wondered if Kensington knew the story of the old city that their people hailed from, either from old folk tales, or from Taggerty.

"Yes, King Avalon," Jennings responded. "The Reaches are small, but we can be put to any task you need. Where are you in your plans?"

"The plans," Avalon said slowly. "What do you know of my plans?"

"Nothing," Jennings answered openly. "I only know that Counselor Nelson has been put to task, and I would like to take up the cause if we are to invade Hawkerness."

Avalon swallowed hard and made a point of not clenching her jaw. She hadn't decided to invade, but she was terrified that the Council might be talking about Cormicks. Still, Jennings again referred to the city as Hawkerness which meant his information was not current. He was either fishing for information, or he was truly in the dark.

"Why do you think I should invade Hawkerness?" Avalon asked.

Jennings was surprised by the question, and he thought about it for a moment. "May I speak honestly, Your Highness?"

"Please, do!" Avalon was surprised at the question. If the counselors could not speak freely to the king, then what was their purpose?

Jennings took a deep breath and let it slip slowly through his teeth. "Counselor Glenn told Counselor Nelson and I about Hawkerness just a month before your father died. We didn't take him seriously at first. We thought he was trying to resurrect fairy tales, and we couldn't understand what he meant by it." Jennings looked at Avalon, but she waited for him to explain further, and her silence gave him the courage to continue. "He said that Hawkerness was a danger to Fontanasia, and that the Council needed to put together a plan and present it to King Birch, so that we might keep our city safe."

Avalon pondered the information. It was speculation at best, and all of the information could have been gleaned from the old stories. She looked at Kensington and he shrugged a little, his eyebrows moving up his forehead. She looked to Taggerty, and his slight nod told Avalon that it could be fairy tales. Still, she felt her heart beat in her neck and the blood pounded in her ears. It was anger or fear ramping up her heart, and she sensed true danger in these words.

Avalon tried to keep her tone level. "It has been almost a year since my father died. Why have you not come forward before now to speak of this?"

"I didn't believe Counselor Glenn in the first place," Jennings said plainly. "He had no proof. Our city has lived in peace for hundreds of years. Frankly, I couldn't see what he was getting at."

Avalon knew what Counselor Glenn was getting at though. It was Hawker. He was using Counselor Glenn as his puppet. Dead or alive, banished or buried, Hawker's poison was still spreading.

"But when I heard about Counselor Nelson and the entire District West being put to task, I reconsidered. Of course, Counselor Nelson would tell me nothing but that you tasked him with filling the stores with six months worth of meat." Jennings shifted his weight to one leg and

Avalon could see he was getting tired of standing. She would not move this to a table discussion though; she needed to be on the throne. She needed Counselor Jennings to respect her position.

Avalon could stop the stocking of the food stores and put the rumor to rest, or she could inform the Council of the true threat of Cormicks and move forward with a plan. She was watching the window, and she would keep her people safe from the Monarch, the Runners, and safe from fear. She looked at Taggerty and was certain in an instant that keeping the secret of Cormicks was the most important task. Taggerty watched her, waiting for her command, and Avalon caught his eye and tipped her head ever so slightly toward Jennings. Taggerty's response was just as slight of a nod forward, and Avalon's heart warmed in her chest. She was sure that without words and with the barest of motions, they completely understood each other.

"Counselor Jennings, I appreciate your candor. There is more that I would like to discuss with you. Can you wait for me in the Council room?"

"Yes," Jennings responded eagerly.

"Good," Avalon smiled coolly, but her mind was buzzing.

"Your Highness, it might be a long night. Perhaps Counselor Jennings family would like to be escorted home?" Taggerty added.

"Congratulations to you and Princess Zaria," Jennings said, turning graciously to Kensington. Jennings held the front of his vest with both hands and tipped his head forward with a smile. "My wife and daughter are both at the party," Jennings added.

"I know your daughter, Sarah," Taggerty volunteered. "I will let them know that you are in council and will make certain of their safe return home."

"I would appreciate that," Jennings said. Avalon caught herself rolling her eyes. Of course Taggerty knew Sarah Jennings. She pushed back a pang of jealousy.

Kensington looked at Avalon, and when the king did not speak, he did. "I will escort Counselor Jennings to the Council room, and then before I return to the party, I will make sure to send in some refreshments while he waits for you, sire."

Before Avalon could reply, there was a double knock upon the door and a guard stepped in, loudly announcing Counselor Julius Creighton to the three people in the room as though the room was full. Julius Creighton came forward, slowly moving toward the throne, a little hunched, each step prepared before taken. Avalon saw a young, clever man faking his status. She almost laughed out loud at that thought. Creighton was pretending to be old, Avalon was pretending to be a boy, Kensington was pretending to be royalty, and Taggerty had been born a Guide, yet Jennings in his true nature was under suspicion.

"Carry on," Avalon said, nodding at Kensington and Taggerty. The three men bowed to the king and turned to leave. They nodded to Creighton, only the two counselors speaking a short greeting as they passed. Avalon took a deep breath and tried to steel herself for her meeting with Creighton. He had been an ally to her father and something in her told her that he could be trusted, and yet he had given an order to Counselor Nelson that she did not give. He was making moves that she had not decided to make yet, and because of that she could not allow herself to give in to trusting him.

"Counselor Creighton," Avalon said as he stopped to bow. She noticed the slow way he half bent his knee as though it might give out underneath him. The patience he had was incredible, and Avalon marveled at it until she realized that it gave him time to take in every room, to look at every situation before it presented itself, and that moving slow might actually be an advantage.

"King Avalon, I expected to find you at the engagement party, and yet here you are having stolen the groom-to-be from his celebration and conducting business when you should be celebrating." He said in a jovial tone as though they were at the party now.

"I fault you for that," Avalon said directly.

Creighton's eyebrows rose. "Me?" he asked lightly, but Avalon could see that Creighton had tensed.

"If it wasn't for you telling Counselor Nelson to begin fortifying the food stores, then Counselor Jennings would have tucked the information he had into the past, and we all could go on as we were for hundreds of years more."

"What did he tell you?" Creighton asked directly, and Avalon wondered if he was worried that a secret they shared was coming to light. She decided to tell Creighton what she knew.

"He told me that he wants to help in preparing for the invasion into Hawkerness." She watched Creighton process the information.

"Hawkerness?" he asked. Then he nodded his head and let his eyes wander around the floor, putting his thoughts in order. He had been so prepared in their previous meetings, and Avalon realized that she had never seen him in deep thought before, working things out on the fly. He had always known each angle of the conversation and had waited for things to develop before him. Tonight, he was working things out in front of her.

"Then Counselor Jennings can be trusted. That is good news."

"May I ask how you have come to this conclusion?" Avalon asked.

"Your Highness, none of the counselors have referred to Cormicks by its name, they only know it as Hawkerness.

This means that they only know what Counselor Glenn told them, and that..."

"All of the counselors know?" Avalon was surprised. In the past year, none of them had approached her before Counselor Nelson a few weeks ago. "And how is that good?"

"It is good because it means that there are no traitors on your Council."

"No traitors?" Avalon asked. "How is it that Counselor Nelson would take it upon your word to start a process that would bring all eyes on him and his borough?" Avalon didn't truly suspect Nelson of treachery, but she was still wounded by the action.

"King Avalon, we are counselors. We all counsel our king as to what is happening in our boroughs so that Fontanasia is cared for as a whole. As leaders, we work together on issues to make sure that this city runs well. When the king is not meeting in Council with us, we still must meet to ensure everything is going along as it should. We trust each other at our word. It is not Counselor Nelson's fault that he is eager to please the king."

It was true, Avalon had not met with the Council for the first ten months she was king, and they had kept about the business of running Fontanasia. But she wasn't going to be scolded by a counselor, even if her father did trust him. "Why did you come here, Counselor Creighton? You too could be enjoying the engagement party. Or are you just spying on me and making sure that I am making the moves you want me to?"

Creighton smiled at Avalon's comment, but then his face turned apologetic. "I am not toying with you, my King." And although he sounded sincere, Avalon couldn't help but feel like a cat who was chasing a ball of string.

"I came to find you at the party because you need to see what I have found, and I don't think it can wait any longer. I have tried to get you to look before, but you have been preoccupied. It is time. I have a question first though. I need you to answer me truthfully."

She stared at the hunched over counselor and his long robes, her mouth agape.

"Can you, King Avalon, answer me in truth no matter what I ask?" he prodded.

"I will answer you," was all Avalon could muster.

"Is Hawker Hall truly dead?" he asked, his stare cutting into hers. Avalon tried not to react, but her eyebrows pulled in on themselves. She had said nothing, but Creighton shook his head slowly in disappointment. "So he is alive," he whispered. Creighton was looking at Avalon in all seriousness, and the hair stood up on the back of her neck. The constricting fear she had felt when trapped in the dungeon of Cormicks returned to her, and Avalon had to remind herself to take a breath.

Avalon had agreed to accompany Counselor Creighton to the archives. He would not hint as to what he had found, and Avalon didn't like following his summons again, but she went nonetheless. The three walked in silence, Avalon lost in her thoughts as to what Julius Creighton could be up to, Creighton slowing the party down with his fake old man walk, and her guard Thomas walking tall, moving his eyes everywhere as they shuffled down the dark steps, past the iron works, and to the archives. Avalon remembered that Thomas had been on duty the last time that Creighton had visited her at night, and felt a pang of panic wondering if the two were plotting something, but then Avalon realized that Thomas always stood watch at night, and it was just a coincidence. She hated that her thoughts always turned to paranoia.

"Wait here, Thomas," Avalon commanded at the door to the archives.

"I will lead you in, sire, and then I will stand the door." Avalon nodded at Thomas who pulled the huge wooden door open. Avalon expected a loud creek, but the door was well oiled and it swung open easily on its heavy hinges. Thomas lit three mounted torch stanchions and took a quick look around the space, not really expecting to find anyone in the archives in the dead of night. When he was sure the room was clear, he stepped outside and pushed the door almost fully closed. Avalon turned her attention to Creighton who smiled and gestured his arm toward the back wall. He pulled one of the lit torches and led the king to a long desk, using the torch to light several candles.

"Were you ever here with your Uncle Hawker?" Creighton asked.

"Yes."

"What did he show you?"

"I was around ten years old and I wanted to see where he spent his time."

"And where was that?" Creighton asked suspiciously, his eyebrows rising in question.

Avalon shrugged. "Here, in this room pouring over the books." Avalon walked Creighton over to Hawker's small study area on the side of the archives. It was the same desk Creighton had shown Avalon to the last time they had met here. There were many books stacked on the desk, some still open on the table as though Hawker might walk in behind them and pick up where he had left off.

Creighton nodded slowly. "I worked with Hawker here in the archives researching history together and learning about Cormicks together. Of course, in the old files our native city was called Hawkerness, as you know." Creighton walked along the table flipping the pages of some open books, but Avalon got the feeling he could recall every book in front of him if he needed to. He continued as though he had read her mind. "I've read most of the books in this room," he said, moving his arm around with a slow practiced movement. "I became a very good resource for Prince Hawker once he realized that. We spent hours together, studying, learning, and debating."

The hairs on Avalon's neck rose again and she fingered the knife in her pocket. She wanted to trust Julius Creighton but felt her traitor uncle in her presence at the mention of his name. Creighton was being honest with her, she thought that or she wouldn't have come with him to the archives, but Avalon still didn't truly know how to decipher who to trust and not to trust.

Creighton kept silent allowing Avalon a moment to look over the book titles that lay before her. Below a large metal arm with a glass affixed to the top, there were very old and faded journals. Avalon pointed at the arm and Creighton moved in quickly to slide the contraption over the book. His normal pace was slow, and his quick movement startled Avalon and she fingered the hilt of her knife again. The tomb-like library gave her the creeps, and the torches did little to light the space. She stepped away from Creighton who smiled and slid a candle closer to the page. Through the glass mechanism, Avalon saw the faded print jump to life under the flickering light. The glass made the tiny, faded prints legible, and her eyes opened wide.

"I had it made so Hawker and I could read every volume in here, even the oldest books. The beveled glass makes it possible." Avalon's jaw dropped open. She had never seen anything like it. "I am pleased to have pleased a king. I can have one made for you if you would like." Avalon nodded her head imagining her tiny, red jakkow lizard magnify in front of her face.

"I would like that." She looked at the open volumes, stopping at one that showed how to tie different knots. "I know this one," she said pointing at the book. "My father presented me with a copy when I turned seven."

Creighton nodded. "A fine gift for a young prince. This copy was given to Hawker by his father, your grandfather, just as your father received one."

"I'm surprised to see Hawker has the same book. He didn't seem to go for physical crafts." As she was speaking, the words were almost choked back in her throat as Avalon remembered how lithe her Uncle Hawker had been with a sword when he was trying to kill her.

"It was a misbelief that Hawker didn't like to study things like this. He was indoors all the time, that is true, but he was skilled. He could tie any knot he wished whether he practiced or not. And he didn't go hunting, but he did kill animals for sport. He was actually quite cruel. I have seen him hit a rat with a knife at thirty feet, right here in this library."

Avalon choked back the bile in her throat and she hoped that the dim torchlight did not reveal the disgust on her face. "It would take me a lifetime to read all of these books."

"Prince Hawker read most books in this space, many more than once. He is smart, cunning, and not to be trusted." Avalon looked at Creighton with a question but did not say anything. "Your Grace," Creighton said directly but with a reverence that Avalon had yet to hear from him, "I didn't realize Hawker was who he was, but if I had, your father might still be alive. The only thing that scares me is that I have met a man smarter than myself, a man who was able to outwit me." Creighton's tone wasn't arrogant. It was simply to the point. "I don't know what you have done with Prince Hawker, but wherever he is, he is still a threat."

Avalon pursed her lips together. She had learned early in life the value of keeping secrets. She wasn't ready to share with anyone that Taggerty had disposed of Hawker far away on horseback and left him at a point unknown somewhere in the woods. "You mentioned that there was something important that I needed to see," she deflected, looking down at the books on the table and trying to guess which one he had brought her here to see.

Avalon was secretly planning a reconnaissance mission and a full incursion into Cormicks if the time came, and if there was more to learn, she needed to know it. Kings before her had protected the secret window between Fontanasia and Cormicks. For generations the people of her city had lived peacefully, allowing the stories of their ancestors to fade into myth. Only Avalon and a few others knew the truth, and now the Monarch of Cormicks wanted blood. She had to move forward with her plans, and whatever Creighton had uncovered might be detrimental.

Creighton blew out the small candles he had lit on the worktable and took the torch from its holder. He nodded his head to the right and Avalon followed him into the shadows. "I was in here for about ten days during the lockdown, and I had a lot of time on my hands. I wouldn't normally invade a prince's private study, but it got pretty boring even with a mind like mine." He stopped at the end of two tall library stacks and faced a stone bust of an old forgotten librarian.

"It wasn't really trespassing."

Creighton gestured toward the statue and Avalon took a step toward it. The torchlight danced in the dark making the rock face move in the shadows. Avalon waited, impatient and frightened.

"Hawker's private study is in his chambers."

Creighton studied Avalon's face and then nodded to himself. "Yes, but Prince Hawker's secret study is in these archives." He quickly tossed the torch into his right hand and reached out with his left. Avalon jumped back against the wall, which was a fool of a defensive move, but Creighton didn't lay a hand on her. He slid his hand down the back of the pillar that held the stone bust, and Avalon heard a click. Then she felt a breeze on the back of her neck, and she jumped away from the wall and reached for her sword.

Avalon swept between Julius Creighton and the stacks of books, feeling a stab of pain as her ribs connected with the wood shelving. She wielded her sword up in front of her for protection and slowly backed out of the stack before Creighton could make a move for her. The rest of the library was pitch black except where Thomas had lit the torches by the door, and she turned her head in that direction to make her escape and then stopped abruptly. Julius Creighton wasn't moving toward her. He wasn't trying to stop her from leaving. He was standing with the torch in one hand and his other hand beckoning into the darkness that had opened up behind the statue.

"I researched history with Hawker, but I did not realize who he really was. None of us did. Not me, not you, nor your father." Creighton waited by the opening that was canvased in the dark, and Avalon was stunned by indecision. "Your Grace, I worked with Hawker, but I mean you no harm. You can call Thomas in if you wish, but you might not want him too close to the material inside."

Avalon lowered her sword but she didn't move back into the stacks. Creighton could somehow read her expression in the darkness and he smiled softly. "You have to trust someone at some point." But Avalon had no way of deciphering the difference between the people who were lying to her face and the people who were being honest with her. A tear crept to her eye as she felt the sting her Uncle Hawker's treachery had left on her heart, and then she sheathed her sword.

"My King," Thomas whispered next to her.

"Ahh!" Avalon yelled, jumping scared out of her wits into the far shelf. She spun, eyes wide at Thomas who looked terrified. His sword was drawn and pointed down the stack toward Julius Creighton.

"Thomas," Julius Creighton said easily in greeting.

"Counselor Creighton. I heard the sound of a sword being drawn and I had to check on King Avalon." Avalon didn't like that Thomas seemed to be apologizing to Creighton.

"Yes, of course," Creighton told Thomas. Then he looked at Avalon. "King Hall, will you be needing Thomas at this time?"

Avalon removed her hand from her chest and straightened her jacket feeling foolish that she had been so startled. Her hands were shaking and she wanted to go back to her chambers immediately, but she could not turn back now. Creighton was right. She needed to trust someone, and he seemed genuine. He must have known her father well for Thomas to see his king with sword drawn and not to have immediately reacted against Creighton.

"Return to your post outside, Thomas," she said to the soldier.

Thomas sheathed his sword, bowed, and sank back into the darkness. Avalon took a moment to steady her nerves. She was already on edge down here in the tomb-like archives late at night in the pitch black, but the quick movements of Julius Creighton and the wall opening was too much already, and she didn't need Thomas scaring the wits out of her.

Counselor Creighton waited patiently in the mouth of the opening, and Avalon thought she could see the faintest smirk on his face. Just when she had caught her breath, she saw a glint of steel in the dancing torchlight. Before she knew what was happening, Counselor Nelson pounced from the darkness and lunged toward her, a sword in his outstretched arm. Avalon and Creighton yelled at the same time, Counselor Nelson's sword moving toward Avalon's face. She was leaning back into the shelf and was caught off balance. She grabbed for her trusted knife as Counselor Nelson thrust forward. Avalon ducked under his blade and brought the knife up into his torso.

They had crashed together and Avalon heard a horrid guttural noise emanate from Nelson's throat as her knife thrust into his stomach. His outstretched arm was over her shoulder and he was leaning his weight on Avalon, his old muscles holding tight to her arm. Avalon was horrified.

"My King," Counselor Nelson grunted. "My King." Avalon pulled her knife back and he slid down, pulling his sword arm back in. When he did, Avalon heard a thump as the books behind her head crashed back to the ground in the next row. Avalon held her knife in her hand, the blood glinting black in the darkness as Counselor Creighton ran up the aisle with the torch.

"Are you okay?" he yelled at Avalon who was frozen in place.

"Yes," she whispered, looking down at Counselor Nelson as he clutched his stomach, his sword clanging to the ground beside him.

"King Avalon!" Thomas yelled as he made his way in the dark.

"Here!" Avalon called back, picking up the sword and standing guard over Counselor Nelson. "Counselor Nelson?" Avalon asked, still stunned that he would try to kill her.

The injured man looked up at her, his robes starting to soak up the blood, and he smiled. "My King," he said again. Counselor Creighton moved around the stack of books to the one behind Avalon.

"Who sent you?" Creighton said sternly, waking Avalon from her frozen position. Thomas held his sword at Counselor Nelson's neck as Avalon walked backward around the shelf. Julius Creighton knelt over the figure of a man, but Avalon could not see his face. He held a long knife in his hand, and books covered his legs and half buried his torso. Avalon moved to see the face, and she was shocked to see that it was a very old man. He had been hiding in the books behind her.

"Who sent you?" Creighton repeated loudly, but when Avalon moved to the side she could see a pool of blood seeping onto the floor. Counselor Nelson's sword had penetrated the back of the man's head and he was bleeding profusely.

"Prince Hawker is the rightful heir to the throne. He will protect us from the Runners." The old man coughed, and Avalon recognized the old librarian who had greeted her on her last visit to the archives. "The old stories are true, how we came to be in Fontanasia," he whispered. "King Avalon will not protect us." A trickle of blood oozed from the side of his mouth and his eyes looked at Avalon, but they did not see her anymore.

"He's dead," Creighton said, prying the long knife from his fingers and sliding it away into the darkness. He stood swiftly and walked around Avalon. She followed him so not to be left in the dark next to the dead librarian.

"Counselor Nelson, can you hear me?" Creighton asked as he handed Thomas the torch and knelt down. He pushed Thomas' sword away from Nelson's throat with his fingers. "He saved the king's life," Creighton said without looking up. He opened Counselor Nelson's robe and saw where the blood was the worst. Avalon watched as he tore some cloth from the robe and bunched it up over the wound.

"I saw him waiting down the hall from the archive with a knife in his hand, and I found an old sword near the armory. When he followed Thomas in," Nelson stopped talking and tried to smile at Creighton. "I'm not used to this sort of thing you know."

"You did well. You saved King Avalon's life."

Counselor Nelson cringed with pain as Creighton applied pressure to the wound, and Avalon finally came to her senses. "Thomas, go get three men and a stretcher.

Have someone alert the doctor that you will be bringing Counselor Nelson to him."

"Sire, I cannot leave you unprotected," Thomas said. He looked at Counselor Nelson for a moment and then nodded. "Can you bolt the door when I leave, Your Highness?" he asked as he turned to leave.

"Yes," Avalon replied. "Don't alert anyone else as to what has happened. I don't want to ruin my sister's engagement party."

"Yes, King Avalon," Thomas said, pulling the door closed behind him, Avalon throwing the bolt in the same instant. She returned with a second torch and wished she hadn't brought more light. She could see a lot of blood pooling purple in the glimmering torchlight. It oozed over Creighton's hands as he applied pressure to the wound.

"I'm sorry," Avalon said.

"It is my honor to serve the king," Counselor Nelson said dazedly.

"The doctor will be here soon," Creighton said. "Save your strength." Avalon watched as he tore strips of cloth from the bottom of his robe and packed it on top of Counselor Nelson's wound. He looked at Avalon and jerked his head toward the opened passage. "You need to see what I have found, King Avalon." Creighton stared at Avalon with such intense sincerity, that she did not wait a moment longer.

Avalon placed one of the two torches in the wall mount. She turned to the opening in the brick wall with her torch, nothing but darkness before her. She moved slowly down the stack of books and beyond the statue, holding the torch in front of her to reveal a small hallway.

The short passage opened up to a small room where Avalon could make out tall tables along the gray, stone walls. She walked slowly around the room noticing books about poisons, archery, and combat. She found a book about first aid and thought of Counselor Nelson bleeding out in the next room. She flipped through it quickly, looking at the pictures and trying to gain some knowledge on how to stop Nelson from dying. Avalon felt hopeless and terrified. She sensed someone behind her and turned to see Julius Creighton in the doorway, streaks of blood covering his robe where he had wiped his hands clean.

"You let Hawker live. Have you dreamed of him?" His tone was passive, but Avalon felt accused and stunned.

"My uncle is dead," she told him. Did Creighton know of her dreams? Impossible, she thought, ignoring that part of his question.

"Then this won't bother you." He moved to a table and pointed to a large volume. "Hawker taught himself to navigate by the stars." This puzzled Avalon, so he continued. "Hawker learned where the stars are in the sky at certain times of the year. The Guides have practiced this, but no one else in Fontanasia has taken the time, except your Uncle Hawker. He can recognize the sky from wherever he might find himself, and use the stars to navigate a path."

Avalon felt stupid. She had looked at the stars all her life, but had never taken the time to find a pattern in them. As she stood dumbfounded, Creighton walked to her and took the torch from her hand. He lit a second torch on the wall and placed the one he was holding in a holder on the opposite wall, lighting up more of the books, revealing something that stunned Avalon. It was the large map that her father had shown her before her trip to Cormicks. It had the same writing and was lined with the same gold braid. She hadn't removed it from the wall or even looked at it since her father showed it to her. This should not be down here, and Avalon was worried. Was this a duplicate or had Hawker stolen her father's map from it's hiding place?

Creighton pointed to the map, his face betraying its usual control and contorting into anger. "What did you do with Hawker? He is not locked away, I have checked the cells," Creighton pressed, raising his voice and startling Avalon. He took a step toward her and repeated his question even louder. "What did you do with Hawker?"

Avalon's hand moved to the knife hilt in her pocket. "What do you want?" was all she could think to say.

"I want what you want, King Avalon. I want Fontanasia to remain as it has for generations to come. But Hawker has other plans." She regretted not killing Hawker when she had the chance, and then immediately regretted the thought of killing anyone.

Avalon gripped the knife tighter and stepped back, her eyes squinting in suspicion. "Hawker is no longer a threat. You were working with him. Why have you brought me here?" It got darker as she backed into the passageway.

"I stayed close to Hawker because someone had to see what he was up to. He has always had an eye for the throne, and I told that to your father." He moved to the wall and pulled a torch from its holder and held it out toward Avalon. She panicked, stumbling backwards and falling to the floor, her knife flying loose as she tried to catch herself. Creighton took two quick steps forward and all Avalon could see was the torch coming for her. She screamed as her arms rose to cover her head, but the torch moved back quickly.

"King Avalon, I did not mean to startle you," Creighton said in an even tone.

"Stay away from me!" Avalon yelled. Julius Creighton took slow steps back and put the torch back in the wall holder. He seemed to make an effortless change back to his slow-moving self, and Avalon was even more suspicious. It was the same way her Uncle Hawker had pretended to be a studious klutz only to swiftly wield his sword in her face. She should not have come down here.

"King Avalon, you need to see everything that Prince Hawker was studying." Creighton sounded disappointed, and Avalon wondered why this bothered her. He lowered his slouched frame into a chair and waited for Avalon to stand up. She did, walking back to the table like a cat, each step quiet and purposeful, her eyes stuck on Creighton. She stopped where the map lay, the gold braid around the edge held flat with grotesque metal statues of figures that Avalon had never seen before. They were animal, not human, but reminded her of the barbarian-like soldiers used by the Monarch in Cormicks.

She rotated sideways to the table and glanced at Creighton who was content to wait in the chair. Avalon studied the map for the second time in her life. This map was identical to the one that her father had shown her. Seeing Cormicks so close to Fontanasia turned her stomach. There was real danger in the world, danger that could wipe out the population of her land. She held her stomach tight and swallowed down the thought as she allowed her eyes to move over books that Hawker had laid out on the long, high table.

She turned the pages of a book about the practices of the Guides. She realized that Hawker was studying how the Guides track, and how they use landmarks. She saw several more books about survival, food that grew in the woods, and poisonous leaves. Avalon shook her head involuntarily. Hawker hated the outdoors, and he never went camping or hunting. He preferred life in the castle and was known to leave only to watch the Festival of Fontanasia. His skin was white as milk, and Avalon could remember begging him to go practice the bow and swords, and Hawker saying he abhorred the outdoors. Avalon's brow furrowed as her thoughts churned, and she tried to focus.

"What do you see?" Julius Creighton asked from his seat.

Avalon didn't answer, sifting through more of the volumes on the table. Then she saw the drawing of the jet-black Anthracites and her heart stopped. The picture before her would not seem menacing to the onlooker, but the

Anthracites had attacked Avalon. She had felt the ground shake as the huge rock forms ripped from the ground and their mountainous feet crushed everything before them.

Julius Creighton spoke in a faraway voice. "Imagine someone goes off on an adventure and awakens a sleeping beast, and then they capture the beast, torture it, and kill it. Is it the beast's fault for being a beast? Are they justified in killing that beast, or should they not have wandered into the beast's territory in the first place?"

Avalon could tell that he was speaking hypothetically, but he didn't know how right he was. He didn't know that Avalon had awoken the Anthracites. He didn't know that for the first time in hundreds of years, the Monarch of Cormicks was aware of Fontanasia's existence. All he knew is that he found a book about Anthracites and a map to Cormicks, and he seemed to be certain that Hawker was still alive, despite the elaborate funeral.

Every thought rushed into Avalon's mind at once. She needed to send a recon team of Guides to Cormicks to make sure Fontanasia was safe, but if Hawker knew about the elbagrass and the window to Cormicks, and if he studied the power of the Anthracites, he could still be a threat. He had the great warrior Brick side with him and turn traitor on the other side of the window. Brick who had tried to kill his own king's son on Hawker's behalf. She worried that if she sent soldiers into the forest to protect the window to Cormicks, she was really leading Hawker's followers to their end game. Avalon's dry throat gulped at the thought.

"What is it, King Avalon?" Creighton asked again.

"I don't know," Avalon answered, but as soon as the words left her mouth, she knew the question her mind had been forming, and she needed to see Taggerty immediately.

"I will look at the rest when I am ready. But right now, we leave." Avalon needed to get out of this stone tomb. She had to talk to Taggerty to find out where he had left

Hawker. If Hawker could read the stars, he could find the window.

"We must discuss what has become of Hawker," Creighton pressed, but his face showed concern, and he seemed to know what Avalon was thinking. Avalon moved around him and took both torches from the walls. "There is much you don't know," he told her as she handed him a torch.

Avalon wanted to tell him that he had no idea, but she held her tongue. She moved in front of him through the short passageway and back into the library. Counselor Nelson lay on the ground, still awake. The pile of bandages made from Creighton's robe was still clean on top, and Avalon was glad that the bleeding had slowed. Creighton flicked the switch behind the statue, and Avalon heard the wall close, the torchlight dancing for a moment with the rush of the air.

"What will you do?" Creighton demanded. "I know you barely trust me, but you will trust my counsel just as your father did. I don't know who else was with Hawker, and if you change anything right now, if you take action, anyone who has been waiting, they will notice, and you will lose the hunt before it has begun."

"Lose the hunt," Avalon said to no one, her voice trailing off into her thoughts.

"King Avalon," Creighton pressed, but Avalon wasn't listening.

She looked at Counselor Nelson, who had been watching her in silence, and then she turned to Julius Creighton, a terrifying thought manifesting in her mind. "It is our end, unless I can stop him. When is the next full moon?" But she already knew the answer to that. She had tracked the cycle of the moon since she had returned from Cormicks. Avalon ran through the stacks to the outer door.

"Stop who?" Creighton echoed after her.

"Hawker!" she yelled back as she threw the bolt and sprinted to the stairs, leaving both counselors in the dark.

Chapter 10
Final Words

Hawker had been wandering for months, looking at the sky each night trying to find a constellation that he recognized. He killed animals and ate berries for food, and he found streams or collected rain for water. He cursed Birch and Avalon. One night during a thunderstorm while he was nestled under a pine tree, shivering and scared for the first time in his life, he had even cursed his own mother. She had told him that he was the son of a king, and he was entitled to rule Fontanasia. She had cursed when Avalon was born, and she had died soon after, but not before she had made Hawker promise to take the throne for himself.

Hawker waited out the storm, angrier than he had ever been. He hated the situation he was in, but he hated Avalon more for making him doubt his mother. He hated Avalon for making him doubt his own desires. He thought he might die this night, among the flashes of lightning and the flood of water that seemed to come down the hill from nowhere and try to wash him away. For the first time in his life, Hawker felt a moment of despair. And then he had a dream.

Hawker dreamt that he was walking east, and he came upon a field of tall grass. He had almost stepped into the folds of grass to make his way across before he noticed the small dead animals on the edge of the field. He knew then that he had found the field of elbagrass, and he needed but to wait for the full moon to make his way across. His dream was a revelation, and Hawker woke with tears in his eyes. For the first time he could remember, he cried tears of joy.

He broke camp at first light and headed east, his eyes expectant hour after hour. He came to a thicket of trees and had to try to keep going in the same direction. He refused to take a break, knowing that his dream would come true this day. When Hawker Hall dreamed, his dreams always came true.

Avalon ran from the archives up the three flights to her study. She had to see if the map her father had shown her was still in its hiding place, but she already knew the answer.

Avalon removed the painting of the small pond in the tall grass just as her father had, and reached her arm into the hole behind, but the space was empty. The map in Hawker's secret study was the original that her father had shown her. Avalon grit her teeth as she lit a torch, and pushed the flames closer to the small opening just to make sure the space was empty, but the torch just got in the way, so she pulled it back and shoved her arm into the hole up to her shoulder. She reached around slowly, but there was nothing. She heard a crinkle when her wrist hit the back wall, and she turned her palm over, her fingers feeling a small piece of parchment. Avalon pulled it out slowly and went to the large table. Her father's purple seal was on the folded paper, and Avalon assumed Hawker had read the letter when he stole the map because the dried wax had been snapped open already. As she unfolded the letter, she almost dropped the torch on it when she recognized her father's writing. Avalon took a moment to steel back her tears so she could read the words.

Dearest Avalon,

If you have found this letter, then I have not had the chance to throw it away upon your return from Cormicks. I dreamt last night that the castle was locked down and there was no way in or out. Upon waking this morning, I can find no changes to the day, and I am baffled by the dream. You know as well as I that a dream brings the truth in its own way, but this was the first dream I have had in my life that I wasn't in, Avalon, and it scares me.

I love you, and I am so proud of you. I know you will always do the right thing for the people, and I hope that someday you will be able to do the right thing for yourself no matter what lies I have told. I am here always, Avalon. If you need me, look inside yourself. The best of your mother and myself will live within you always.

Love,
Your father, King Birch.

Avalon stepped back from the table and dropped the torch as she crumpled to her knees. Tears streamed in rivers down her face. She remained on all fours for a long time, letting the hurt try to purge itself from her body until she could cry no more. When she thought that the ache might stop her heart and she might never be able to stand up and live again, she thought of the people of Fontanasia. If she didn't protect them, Hawker would most certainly return and make the city his own. Avalon knew she had made a mistake in allowing him to live. She needed to prepare for the worst.

The light from the torch had smothered out and Avalon didn't know how long she lay on the floor of the study. She'd heard running footsteps outside the door several times, and she knew that the guards would be looking for their king. At one point the door slammed open and she heard steps approaching her. It was Kensington. She had waved him off and he had left, but not before posting guards outside the door.

She wanted to know if Counselor Nelson had lived, and the thought brought her back to Hawker's secret room and to the phase of the moon. Avalon had waited too long, and the mistake might cost her all of Fontanasia. Hawker had studied botany, hunting, water collection, the stars, and Cormicks, and she had let him go. Her only hope was that he was so far away and lost that he would never make it back to Fontanasia nor find his way to Cormicks. But he had studied the route, stealing her father's map, her map, and making it his own. Avalon didn't think she could find her way to the window without the Guides and she had been there once before. She hoped that even though Hawker was one of the smartest people she knew, that he would not be able to find his way.

Avalon stood and took a deep breath, walking outside of the study. Two guards followed her down the hall to the parapet that overlooked the city. She didn't know what time it was, and she looked down at the Fingers, dark but for the fires that lit some of the streets. Then she moved her eyes to the sky and looked at the moon. It would be full tonight, just a small sliver in darkness. The bright spots glittered brightly and Avalon appreciated the beauty of her moon. She could imagine the elbagrass burning brightly tonight, the alleya leaf ripe for the picking. She hoped upon hope that Hawker was far from that place, but her heart felt heavy knowing he was out there, still plotting, making his way back home.

Avalon walked purposefully down the stairs and through the main hall near the castle entrance. The guard on watch saw her and snapped to attention, and she walked by him without a word. She was going to the barracks where the King's Guard trained and lived. Another guard snapped to attention upon seeing the king, and when he saw that Avalon was headed to the training area, he stepped in behind her intending to open the door for the king. When they got to the entrance to the courtyard, Avalon stopped and allowed the guard to pull the heavy door open further so she would not need to squeeze through.

"That will be all," she told the four guards who melted away and let the king pass through alone. They would have orders to follow her, but she was headed toward their barracks where there was only the King's Guard, so they knew she was safe. Avalon moved through the doorway and walked down the long, stone hallway. No fires were lit when she got to the courtyard, but the moon was all she needed to see the different buildings.

Avalon went to the only two-story house. She had been there before, when she was a child, before she knew that she was a girl. She had snuck down with Connor to see where the great soldier, Walthan, lived. There had been many men working drills in the yard, but they all stopped when they saw the small prince walking among them. Avalon remembered how strong she felt at that moment, the future king and ruler of these men. She vowed as their righteous leader that she would always stay competent with weapons for the rest of her life. She had kept that promise so far, but she hadn't returned to this place after that day. She found out that she was a girl months later, and in her insecurity she had not wanted any close eyes scrutinizing her.

Avalon looked around the courtyard, but it was deserted. She stepped up to the heavy wood door and knocked. The head of the King's Guard occupied this house, but Avalon knew Taggerty had been living here because this was Kensington's house now, and Avalon knew that the two were thick as thieves.

The door opened at once, and Avalon's mouth hung open when she saw Taggerty standing in front of her with his shirt wide open, his bare chest and stomach visible under the full moon. Avalon looked away instinctively, and then forced herself to look back at Taggerty. She was a man, he was a man, and there was nothing to be embarrassed about.

"Your Highness, I'm so glad you are unharmed," Taggerty said, stepping aside to allow her to enter the house. Avalon looked in and saw that the furnishings hadn't changed at all in the seven years since she had last looked inside.

"I thought that Kensington would have taken this space by now," Avalon said, taking one step inside to allow Taggerty to close the door. He didn't close it right away though, and she turned to see him nod his head out the door into the darkness of the night. Avalon was confused when he made a low hand gesture, and then she understood when she saw a guard materialize from behind a shrub, bow, and walk back toward the castle. Avalon let out a loud breath. "He didn't think I was safe enough in the domicile of my own guard?" She was flippant for a moment, and then her words came back to her. They had both watched her own uncle try to kill her. She was never safe.

Taggerty ignored the question and closed the door. "Please, excuse me, King Avalon. I only just returned to change out of my party clothes. Kensington is still with Princess Zaria." Avalon slowly looked around the room. She didn't know what she was looking for at first, but the tight feeling in her chest told her that she was jealous. Although she knew it was impossible, she was looking for any sign that Jennings' daughter might have been here.

"The party?" Avalon asked. She didn't know how long she had been lying on the floor of her father's study.

"Yes. Well, most of the guests have retired, but they do have a small party continuing in one of the smaller rooms. You know how Zaria likes a gathering," he said as Avalon watched him button up his shirt. She smiled because she knew a comment like that a month ago would have filled her with jealousy. Taggerty pulled on his sword belt and then his coat. "I will take you to Kensington," he said dutifully.

"We can talk first," Avalon said, not wanting to tell Taggerty that she came here looking for him. She walked over to an old wood chair with a worn blanket thrown over the back.

"We should keep this place up," Taggerty said, embarrassed. Avalon took a seat and Taggerty remained standing.

"Please," she said, offering him the couch opposite her chair. Taggerty sat down but did not relax. He stared at Avalon and she looked back unconsciously biting her lip. She didn't have time to decide how she felt about him right now. She needed to act before Hawker did any more damage.

"I have been thinking about Counselor Glenn's death," she said, surprising Taggerty. This was not the direction that he'd expected the conversation to go. He nodded though, and Avalon continued. "I acted in haste and out of anger that day, and in the end I was on the floor, and I couldn't defend myself."

"You were wounded," Taggerty said.

"I should have stood up. If I could have taken control of the situation..." Avalon shook her head. "I can't help but think that fear and indecision kept me on that floor."

"You were not afraid," Taggerty said gently. "You did what you had to. You stormed into that room and you defended your father. Don't second guess that."

"Maybe," she said. Taggerty was still sitting forward on the couch and Avalon couldn't remember ever seeing that expression on his face before. He was looking at her as though she was a child, none of his usual cavalier importance showing. She felt self-conscious but comfortable in the moment. "I will never let fear or uncertainty slow me ever again." Her eyes met his, and he was smiling. She planned to ask Taggerty to leave, and she swallowed hard.

"I am at your command," Taggerty said eagerly, somehow reading her mind.

Avalon hated what she was going to ask Taggerty to do, but she had to move forward and she could not be scared into inaction. She could not wait for Cormicks to attack.

"Avalon," he said softly. He had spoken her name without the pomp reserved for a king, and she liked it. "I am at your command. If there is anything you need to tell me, anything at all, I am your man."

Avalon's heart leapt into her throat and she froze. She was confused now as to what he was talking about because she could sense something deeper in Taggerty's meaning.

"You still think that I should disband the Council?" she asked.

Taggerty nodded and sighed, and Avalon saw regret in his eyes and opened her mouth to speak, but then closed it just as quickly. Taggerty was behaving oddly. His tone was soft and gentle. He rubbed his eyes and then moved his hand down his cheeks to his chin. "Ok," he said loudly. He slapped his hands on his thighs. "Yes, I still think you should disband the Council."

"I'm not going to," Avalon told him.

"Then why did you ask me?" Taggerty threw back in frustration. Avalon watched his growing uneasiness. "I'm sorry, Your Highness. Please, continue." Taggerty sat back into the couch and crossed his legs, and Avalon leaned forward in her chair.

"The power is in the perception," Avalon said. She didn't know she was going to say this, but when she did, Avalon realized that she had been forming a plan for months, a plan that she had been afraid to implement, and this night she would execute that plan.

"Hawker had a plan, and he made Counselor Glenn his pawn. He used Counselor Glenn to further his agenda by spreading the right amount of lies with the right amount of truth. Counselor Jennings knows about Hawkerness, because that is the lie that Hawker spread based on old information. He tried to make the Council fear Hawkerness and the Runners, so that they would take some action. Hawker needed the Council to do his bidding. He knew that my father would never have moved against Cormicks because my father knew that no one in Cormicks knew about Fontanasia."

"Did you talk to Jennings?"

"No, not yet. But I have been thinking about this for months, the things Hawker would say to my father at dinner, and some things I overheard. It's ironic. It was my father who gave Hawker a greater voice within the Council..." Avalon trailed off. How could her father have known that to trust his own brother would be foolish? It was like allowing your new puppy to nibble on you only to realize too late that he had grown into a large animal with a big appetite. She shook her head. "I think I am going to interview all of the counselors."

Taggerty stood, ready to leave, and Avalon was sorry that the moment had come to an end. She was talking business, but she still relished being alone with Taggerty. "I will help you," Taggerty said as Avalon followed him to the door. "The quicker you interview the counselors, the quicker you will decide to disband the Council."

"I'm not going to do that," Avalon said in defense.

"You have to," Taggerty told her. Avalon was taken aback by how easily Taggerty talked to her. No one else would address the king in this manner, and she relished his candor. Still, she was the king, so she needed to protest.

"I have to?" she asked him.

They were both standing near the door ready to leave, and Avalon saw Taggerty's smile in the darkness. It should have bothered her, but it excited her instead. Taggerty took a step closer and Avalon almost took a step back, but she held her place and was within arms reach of Taggerty.

"You don't have to, King Avalon, but you should. Hawker had the power of perception. He was King Birch's brother, and he said he was talking for the king when he talked to the counselors, and they took him at his word."

"I do not have a brother, and Zaria would never betray me," Avalon backtracked the conversation. "Besides, Zaria has no political aspirations. She is going to get married and start a family."

"Yes," Taggerty agreed, his voice getting softer in the dark. "That is exactly what your father thought of his brother."

"Are you saying that Zaria will betray me?" Avalon asked with a laugh in her throat.

"No, of course she won't, and neither will Kensington. He is your brother now. But Counselor Creighton spoke for you when he had Counselor Nelson increase the food stores, and you had no recourse. The truth and the perception of the truth are two very different things. You just said as much." Shivers ran up Avalon's spine, and she wondered if Taggerty was still talking about the Council.

Taggerty stepped closer. "And that old librarian, who knows what Hawker told him? That old man has never seen Cormicks. It was only the lost and forgotten legends and stories that Hawker had resurrected. It was perception. How could he believe it was real just from words? How could he believe it without seeing it?"

"Most people believe what they hear and ignore what they see with their own eyes," Avalon said softly. She was a girl, and she was the king. She knew this to be true. Taggerty stared at Avalon as though he was waiting for her to continue. She blushed in the gray light and cleared her throat.

"Well, you are right about perception, but not about the Council. I can't bring the people together and fight a war if we are not united, and I need the counselors to carry my orders to the people if the time comes." Avalon had changed her mind several times in as many days. "I have gone back and forth on this, but I'm just not ready."

Taggerty's voice rose and he seemed anxious. "You don't need the counselors. The Council does not represent the heart of the people." Avalon could see the passion dancing on his face in the dim firelight. Suddenly he took a step forward and grabbed Avalon's hand. She was startled and frozen in shock. Taggerty pulled her hand up in front of her and barely touching her fingers, he squeezed the king's ring. It had been passed down for generations and it was Avalon's now. He ran his thumb over the engraving. "If you will tell the truth," he said looking at the ring. His eyes moved up to meet hers and Avalon steadied her nerves.

Do you know my secret? Avalon almost said aloud.

Taggerty repeated his words softer now, staring directly into her eyes. "If you tell the truth, your people will follow you. They love you. They are faithful to their king," he said and he showed her the ring that held the seal of the King of Fontanasia.

"They love me?" Avalon croaked. She looked up and made out the green of his eyes in the dim light, and she waited.

"They do," Taggerty said sincerely. Avalon blinked. She could imagine Taggerty leaning down and kissing her lips as Kensington had kissed her sister, but that would never happen. Taggerty was always decisive, and he had paused, watching her. Surely if there was anything else he wanted to do, he would have. Avalon felt hope, and then hope turned to despair as he let go of her hand.

"You have to leave," Avalon said suddenly. Taggerty was startled and looked hurt, and Avalon realized she had said that harshly. She took the final step to the door and explained. "I need you to go to the window and prepare the way for the troops. We must enforce our defenses."

"I will," Taggerty said, shaking his head. Avalon thought she saw a flicker of remorse on his face but then it was gone.

"You need to go as soon as you can. It's Hawker, he is why I came here. He knows everything, and I think he is going to try to find Cormicks."

"Hawker?" Taggerty asked. "That's not possible. I was with him for months, and he's useless out in the wilderness."

"That is what we both thought, but I found his hidden study in the archives, and he knows how to hunt and forage, he knows how to find water and make fire, and he knows how to guide himself using the stars."

Avalon saw a flash of concern on Taggerty's face. "That's not possible," he said.

Avalon didn't know what Taggerty knew about the stars in the sky, but she knew that she had to beat Hawker to the elbagrass.

"I'm sure that where you left him was far enough away, Taggerty, but Hawker was even more cunning than we knew. He will try to cross over to Cormicks and finish what he started with Brick. We have to stop him." Taggerty watched Avalon for his instruction, and she mulled her plan over before giving him the command. "Go to the elbagrass with a few men. Take food and supplies and ready the way."

Taggerty nodded and then opened the door and they both stepped out into the darkness. It was a bright full moon tonight, and Avalon would typically have felt better knowing that the elbagrass was shining blue on her side of the window and that the Monarch of Cormicks could not attack right now, but she couldn't feel safe knowing that Hawker had the wit and the skills to find his way to the window.

They walked in silence, and Avalon remembered the day she had first met Taggerty. He had kept up with her quick self-righteous pace and walked a few steps behind her the entire way up through the Fingers and back to the castle. She hated him then, his pompous air and the way he had ignored her at the Festival of Fontanasia so he could flirt with Princess Zaria. Avalon knew now that her hate had been jealousy, and she smiled in the darkness enjoying Taggerty's company on their silent walk to the castle. Avalon didn't have time to play games that could lead nowhere, and she would put her jealousy behind her forever. She was a boy to Fontanasia, a king, and she needed to make decisions for the future of her people.

Taggerty stepped in front of Avalon to open the large wooden doors. The same guard who had followed Avalon out was still waiting, and he snapped to attention when he saw the king. Avalon swept past, and Taggerty followed her up to the door of the king's suite. She stepped inside but he did not follow, and she turned to face him. Avalon was resigned to her fate, yet it it was still difficult to say goodbye.

"I will leave at first light in three days. I have already worked through most of my plans for trekking the ravine," Taggerty said.

"Good. Leave the ropes in place. I will follow with fifty men in two weeks. Leave one man to guard the ravine in case Hawker tries to cross in that same spot."

"You cannot come to the elbagrass. You are safe here. Do not expose yourself to Hawker, my King." Taggerty was sincere.

"Did you hear the part when I said I would be traveling with fifty men?" Avalon asked and smiled. She had the same worries as Taggerty, but she could not be stunted by fear. She had done that long enough.

"I will see you in three weeks then," Taggerty said. He looked at Avalon for a long moment, and then he spun on his heels and disappeared into the darkness of the castle.

Avalon awoke to Myra sitting at the foot of her bed. The room was dark, the heavy curtains fighting the bright sun. It was already mid morning, and Avalon couldn't believe that she had slept so long.

"Myra, you should have woken me," Avalon said. When she was younger, Myra would have pulled the curtains aside at dawn to wake Avalon, but now that she was king, Myra had backed off, waking her only when she thought Avalon was sleeping too often.

"Pish posh," Myra said, disregarding what Avalon wanted. "A king needs sleep too." She moved to the window and moved the curtain aside slowly, letting Avalon's eyes have time to adjust. She returned to the foot of the bed and sat, looking at Avalon expectantly.

"What is it?" Avalon asked slowly.

"Nothing," Myra said, but there was obviously something on her mind, so Avalon waited. Myra smiled. "So, you are traveling?" she asked.

Avalon thought about lying, but she hung her head. Myra must have been waiting in the suite when Avalon had returned, and overheard her talking to Taggerty.

"I might be," Avalon said with a smile.

"And you won't listen to Taggerty, that it is too dangerous?"

"You know, Myra, I hardly listen to anyone anymore. Now that I am king, I just make up my mind about it and there is nothing else to be said." Avalon smiled. She had quoted Myra's words and was having fun with the only mother she had ever known.

"And how will you know that you can trust these fifty men?" Myra asked.

Avalon shrugged. "They are of the King's Guard, and they would not harm the king." Avalon knew different, but Myra did not know about Brick, and Avalon wasn't about to tell her.

"That isn't all together true." Myra stood and moved to sit on the bed at Avalon's side. Avalon kept her face neutral, but she was worried that Myra had found out that Hawker had help, and she wasn't ready to admit to Myra how paranoid she felt.

"What do you mean?" Avalon asked.

"Well, there was a hunting accident shortly before you were born. It was a mishap where your father killed one of the King's Guard who were hunting with him."

Avalon was shocked to hear this. "What happened?"

Your father said that the man had tripped and fell on his blade, but we all know that isn't the truth. King Birch never admitted what really happened.

"And why are you bringing this up to me?"

"I can see that you will do what you will," Myra said as she stood and headed to the door. "You will take Kensington with you. You can trust him and he is family now." Avalon raised her eyebrows in protest, but she did not argue. She had already decided to bring Kensington. He needed to see the elbagrass and know the full threat. Myra reached the door and turned to watch Avalon.

"Okay, I will take Kensington," she said in mock disagreement. "But Zaria is not going to be pleased."

"Good," Myra smiled and opened the door to leave before turning back to Avalon. "And you will take my nephews, Jakon, and Davev who are in the King's Guard. Then I will be able to sleep at night."

"Oh, I will? Is there anything else?" Avalon asked in good humor although she knew this was a serious moment for Myra who would never tell a king what to do.

"Well, you could take Connor too, but he isn't old enough for the guard yet. Jakon and Davev are his older brothers. They will protect you." Myra left before Avalon could disagree, but she was thankful for Myra's advice. The George family had been protectors and servants of the Hall kings for generations, and Avalon knew they would be true to their family name. She had known Connor since they were babies. He didn't sign up for swords in the Festival of Fontanasia last year because he refused to fight the prince out of deference. If his older brothers were anything like that, she knew they were equal to the task.

Taggerty would leave in three days, and Avalon in two weeks. She needed to get her Council in line to make sure that the kingdom ran smoothly. She wanted the people to go on with their peaceful lives, to protect them from the thought of danger as her father and the kings before him had. She thought about her father's Council, the one she had inherited. Aside from appointing Julius Creighton in Counselor Glenn's place, the rest of the leaders were seasoned. It was Avalon's turn to trust now. Just as Myra trusted her nephews, Avalon needed to trust the counselors until they gave her a reason not to.

Avalon padded to the door and opened it, surprised to find Thomas at his post in the hallway. "How is Counselor Nelson?" she asked.

"Your Highness, Counselor Nelson has lived, but he is not in a fair condition yet. The doctor says that he will recover, in time." Avalon was relieved. She had an image of Counselor Nelson jumping out of the darkness, his sword coming toward her face and then the thrust of her knife into his stomach. She shuddered.

"I'm glad to hear it," she said abruptly and then stood up straight. "I want Kensington and Gamon in the Council chambers in thirty minutes, and the rest of the Council in one hour, save Counselor Nelson. Where is he now? I will go to him."

"He is on the first level, sire. The doctor didn't want to move him. And Kensington has been waiting for you. I am to send someone for him when you awake."

"He can see me in thirty minutes." Avalon didn't say anything else, so Thomas tipped his head and swept from the suite. She would show her cards to the Council and test their merit.

Chapter 11
Tall Tales

Kensington was waiting for her when she arrived in the Council chamber twenty minutes later. He bowed when she walked in, but he didn't say anything. Avalon crossed and moved up the step to be seated. She rubbed her thumb in the wood on the arm of the chair and tried to draw on the spirit of kings before her. Jackie crawled to the edge of her waist pocket and Avalon clicked her tongue causing him to run up her chest and onto her shoulder. She didn't typically let Jackie scamper around in public places, but when she had first introduced Kensington to the lizard, he had been shocked into silence for the rest of dinner, and Zaria had laughed profusely at his demeanor.

"How was the rest of the party?" Avalon asked.

Kensington's mouth hung open for a moment as he watched Jackie perched on her shoulder, and then Avalon patted her pocket and the tiny, red figure ran back down her torso and into her pocket. Kensington took a deep breath.

"It was a wonderful party, Your Highness. Princess Zaria is very pleased."

"Are you not pleased?" Avalon asked.

"No, King Avalon! I am very happy. Thank you for the party. Thank you for everything." Kensington's solid frame seemed to shrink as he looked at the floor. "It's just, Princess Zaria was so delighted that you took the time. She was especially moved." Avalon could see that Kensington's happiness really did hang on Zaria's, and this pleased her.

"Well, I'm glad," Avalon said.

Kensington cleared his throat. "I have taken the liberty to speak with Counselor Jennings," Kensington said, still looking at the floor.

Avalon bristled, but then she realized that she had to trust Kensington. Taggerty trusted him, and Kensington was family now. He had worked with Taggerty for months in taking a Prince of Fontanasia out into the wilderness, and leaving him there without a real explanation. He had not asked why Hawker had been buried in a funeral procession for all the people to see when truthfully he had been banished from the land. Kensington was loyal to a fault, and Avalon felt grateful that she was inheriting him as a brother.

Besides, Avalon had forgotten to talk to Jennings last night when she returned to the castle, so he'd done her a favor.

"What did Counselor Jennings have to say?" Avalon asked.

"I will try to convey his sentiment, King Avalon, but I must admit, it is Council business, and I don't know what he was talking about." Avalon nodded, and Kensington cleared is throat. "He said that after King Birch died, Counselor Glenn told him about the enemy at Hawkerness and that we must prepare for war. Then Counselor Glenn died and nothing became of it. When he saw you adding to the food stores, he assumed there was truth to what

Counselor Glenn had told him, and he came to you to offer his assistance."

She could see the confusion on his face, and Avalon nodded. "Thank you, Kensington." She swallowed back fear mixed with relief. There had been no war because Brick had been stopped in Cormicks.

"I am going to tell you a story now, before the Council arrives. I need you to keep an open mind, and I need you to swear that you will tell no one of this." Kensington nodded gravely, but Avalon needed to make it perfectly clear what she was asking. She looked at the solid warrior who was to marry her sister. "You must not tell Princess Zaria. I have not told her, and you must not either." Avalon didn't want her sister to have to start her marriage out on a lie, but there was nothing else to be done.

"I understand, King Avalon," Kensington said.

Avalon pointed to the benches behind him. "Please, sit down," Avalon said. Kensington looked at her ominously as he took his seat.

After months of second-guessing herself and remaining stagnant with inaction, Avalon was certain that she knew what to do. She could see the next steps of her reign more clearly than if she had dreamt the moment.

Avalon had decided that she wouldn't disband the Council at this time. Each counselor was a leader in his respective borough.

Avalon knew about Cormicks, and some or all of the counselors might have known about Hawkerness, but none of them knew of the current state of the old city and what the Runners were up to now. She needed to come clean with Kensington so that he could understand the weight of the situation and help her with her plan.

"You may have heard the old stories of Hawkerness, the city that our people hailed from. These stories have been passed down for generations, and now are mostly tall tales told to children." Kensington was frowning as he nodded affirmation. Avalon took a deep breath and tried to think clearly.

"These stories are real. There is an enemy that means to crush us, and we must keep Fontanasia safe from the Runners who still live in our old city of origin." Avalon watched for a reaction, and it only took a moment for Kensington's eyes to open wide.

"My Uncle Hawker was trying to open up the passageway and bring war to Fontanasia."

Kensington's face flushed red. "Taggerty and I took him to a place where he could never find his way back. He is useless in the wilderness. Honestly, he is most likely dead by now."

Avalon shook her head and Kensington took a deep breath as the color slowly drained from his face.

"We must assume that Hawker is alive," Avalon said with certainty. "I have found his secret study, and he has been learning about hunting, botany, and he has learned to read the stars to guide his way."

"Read the stars?"

"It's an ancient art," Avalon affirmed, "and I'm certain that no matter where you left him, Hawker will find his way."

"We should put men on the outer wall and send out some scouts," Kensington said. "He will not get the chance to kill you, King Avalon."

She nodded, but the weight of her situation didn't give her a moment's relief. "Thank you, but I don't think Hawker is coming back here." Kensington was cunning and quickly understood the situation.

"We must send men to block the passage to Hawkerness."

"We are," Avalon said. "Taggerty leaves in two days to ready the way, and I intend to go in two weeks with fifty men to ensure that my Uncle Hawker never gets close to his goal. Kensington, you will come with me, but first instruct Gamon to fortify our defenses."

"You must not go," Kensington told Avalon. "I'm sorry, my King. Fontanasia needs you, and Hawker will not hesitate to try to kill you if he sees you again."

"I'm not worried about my own mortality." The statement sounded strange, like something Myra George would say, and Avalon regrouped her thoughts.

"There is a bright blue sea of tall grass under the full moon waiting for anyone who dares approach it. If you can wade to the center of this field in the light of the full moon, you can pass into Cormicks. That is what Hawkerness is called now, and that is where the Runners are. It is the door to destruction, and I will do everything I can to keep it closed." Kensington was saddened and horrified, and yet he was resigned to his fate.

"This blue grass," he said, "my grandmother spoke of it when I was very young, but I have not heard the story since she died. It is fiction." Kensington was willing to help his king, but he seemed to be battling the reality of all of his years with an enemy he had never heard of nor seen.

"It is no fairy tale," Avalon said.

"How is it possible?" Kensington whispered.

Avalon clucked her tongue and Jackie scampered from her pocket onto her outstretched hand. He took a moment to look at Kensington before he scurried around to explore the design on the wood chair.

"It is as real as this red jakkow lizard, Kensington." He was taking it all in and Avalon read the concern on his face.

"We have five Guides watching the field, and they will not allow Hawker to pass," Avalon said confidently, although the thought made her stomach turn. The Guides were watching the elbagrass for the enemy, not the woods for anyone approaching from the rear.

"So the Fingers that Walthan was so passionate about building all those years ago, this was the reason, and he kept it from all of us." Kensington spoke reverently. Walthan had done his duty to the fullest extent that he could without letting even the soldiers know that there was a real enemy.

"Yes, that was why Walthan created the Fingers. I have taken the passage to Cormicks, and I have seen our enemy. Walthan died protecting me on that trip." Avalon's voice cracked. She thought after all these months that she could have her emotions in check about Walthan's death, but she could not put it behind her.

Avalon cleared her throat. "We will leave in two weeks. Assemble forty-eight men and as much food as we can carry on our backs. Bring rope, swords, and knives. We will build the rest of our defenses when we arrive at the field of elbagrass." Avalon had described the bright blue elbagrass, but she wondered how Kensington would react when he actually saw the field. It was a stunning sight, and a lot to take in.

"You can tell the men that we are going hunting so they won't have time to spread rumors. Have Gamon assemble any townsmen who look like they could fight. Train them, run drills, and ready the walls. I leave him in charge of carrying out Walthan's plan of defense for this city. Tell him whatever you need to, Kensington. I need him to protect Zaria."

Kensington met Avalon's eyes. He knew what was at stake. There was a loud double knock on the door, and then a guard took one step in and announced the counselors. Avalon clucked her tongue and when Jackie was tucked safely in her pocket, she waved them in. "Stay here for the Council meeting, then you can go start your work."

Kensington nodded and moved to the side but stayed within steps of the king, and Avalon did not correct his position. He was the head of the King's Guard, and he was about to be family. It would do the Council good to see Kensington take a more central position.

Avalon had apologized to Counselor Jennings for not returning to speak with him the night before. He was gracious, and she felt that he genuinely wanted to help. It was good that Kensington had spoken to Jennings though. Avalon needed to be a strong king who asked for advice but knew when to stop asking and start leading. She didn't want to appear weak to anyone, and she needed to make sure to impart that here in Council today.

All of the counselors were present except for Counselor Nelson who was resting and recovering from his wound. Counselor Creighton had been the last counselor to appear. He walked as slow as ever and bowed to Avalon with the typical easy grin on his lips, but Avalon saw that his eyes were tired and cloudy with a look of worry.

"Thank you all for coming today," Avalon said graciously. "I believe that the Council is necessary for the health and well being of the people of Fontanasia, who we have all sworn to protect." Avalon took a moment to meet each of the counselor's eyes so that they knew that she was talking to them. "I need you all. I need you to lead the dealings in your boroughs and to work together so that Fontanasia can run smoothly. And I need you to take my direction and make my decisions your priority."

"Of course, Your Highness," Counselor Jennings said. The rest of the counselors were nodding.

"We are preparing for an excursion. I have asked Counselor Nelson to add food stores because I will be taking my men on a trek of the surrounding lands." Avalon watched their faces.

"In my absence, you may entertain Princess Zaria's instruction. She is my sister, and I trust her implicitly."

Avalon looked at the counselors and her eyes stopped on Counselor Creighton. He now had a gleam in his eye. He was entertained, Avalon knew. Perhaps she was taking a course he had not predicted leaving him pleasantly surprised.

After a moment of silence as the counselors looked at each other, Counselor Creighton said, "King Avalon, is that wise? The outing, I mean."

Avalon stiffened at Creighton's challenge, and she almost snapped at him. She tried to control her breathing because she did not want her face to turn red.

"What issue do you have with my excursion?" she asked haughtily. She was the king, and she wanted the counselors to be almost afraid to find reason, or at least afraid to speak up.

No one said anything, so Counselor Robert cleared his throat. "You are the King, and you may do as you wish. It's just that in the past year we have not had much time to talk about Fontanasia and further improvements or changes we could be making. This is but your second Council meeting, Your Highness. We are counselors, and we want to be of use to our King, but if you leave now, we will have to wait for you to return." Robert was smiling, and as always, he conveyed his point graciously and without inciting any tempers.

Avalon looked at Creighton who was pinching his lips together in a smile. He was enjoying this.

"I don't expect to be gone for more than one month," Avalon said. She knew that if the Monarch got the Runners across the window, no improvements to Fontanasia could save any of them, and she was losing patience.

"Counselor Jennings," Avalon said, looking directly at him. She paused a moment and let him watch her face, trying to silently gain his confidence. "We have had some discussions of late. It has been over a hundred years since a king trekked the land. Do you not think it wise, for the safety of Fontanasia and her people such as your daughter, that we make sure we know what is beyond our own records?"

Avalon was giving Jennings reason to believe that the king was concerned for his daughter, and that piqued his interest. His eyebrows raised and Avalon could see him immediately sit up taller in his seat. It did not take long for him to take the hint.

"King Avalon, I would be remiss if I didn't tell you that we as a Council need our king present to lead us. But if your concern for people such as my daughter keep you from ruling with a clean conscience, then I must agree that this expedition should be taken immediately, so that you may return to us as soon as possible."

Avalon smiled knowing Jennings had taken the bait.

"Then it is settled, and we cannot change your mind," Counselor Creighton added. "We will continue to make sure everything in Fontanasia is handled to the best of our ability until your return."

"Thank you," Avalon said. She could see that Creighton was moving the meeting along and wrapping things up for her, and she appreciated it, although she didn't like that he was always a step ahead of her. "Do not speak of this trek to anyone. We are planning to surprise the men, as a sort of drill."

The counselors agreed and filed out one by one, each of them wishing Avalon a safe and speedy trip. Counselor Creighton moved slowly and made sure that he was the last one in the room, and Avalon could tell that he wanted a moment. She dismissed Kensington, and the two were left alone in the chamber.

"So you think I should or should not take this trip?" Avalon asked.

"You are still a boy, King Avalon. A man would not explain himself; he would just do what he wants. And a king would not beckon the advice of his counselors."

But Avalon didn't have time to pose. "There is too much at stake right now to worry about compromising my authority. These counselors might feel that I owe them an explanation, but I don't have time to play politics right now. My men will follow me when the time comes." Avalon was certain of that.

Creighton nodded and then chuckled. "You told the counselors to approach Princess Zaria if they needed something while you were gone. Do you expect them to actually do that, or do you imagine that they will do what they like?"

"They can do what they like!" Avalon yelled. He was laughing at a woman being in charge and Avalon was furious. The joke was on him though. A girl stood in front of him, ruler of Fontanasia.

She wanted to slap his face. She wanted to make him kneel before her to show him that he was the one who was laughable. Avalon was surprised at this thought because it did not embarrass her like it should. She was angry, and she didn't care.

"And now you will leave and give the Council rule over Fontanasia because you can't see that they will never approach Princess Zaria."

"We both know that I did next to nothing for months after my father died, and the counselors moved on with their lives and kept the daily business in the Fingers. They have each been part of the Council for years," Avalon spat. Avalon stopped her rant. She noticed that Creighton was not so much arguing with her as studying her reactions. She felt uneasy in his presence again. "Are you protesting because you need help in your borough?" she asked.

Creighton casually rolled his eyes and smiled, and Avalon realized he had been drawing her out, and she had fallen for his ruse. She sighed and shook her head.

"What do you gain by insulting my sister?" Avalon wondered aloud.

Julius Creighton sat on the stone table in the front row. "I am not trying to insult the princess, but this would be a good time to let Kensington earn the respect of the counselors."

"Leave Kensington in charge before they are married? They will trust me even less."

"Leave Princess Zaria in charge, but leave Kensington with her. The counselors will see that as an indirect order they cannot circumvent. They can go to Princess Zaria, which they will not, or they can go to their future prince."

Avalon laughed at the thought. In all this time, she had not placed the title 'prince' with Kensington. He was a soldier, and he needed a few years of refinement to earn that title. "I need Kensington with me. He has to know." Avalon's words were grave, and there was a long pause as they both considered options.

"Then leave someone else in charge, one of your cousins perhaps," Creighton said neutrally.

"My cousins?" Avalon repeated. She had never considered it. Avalon had spent little time with her extended family since half a life ago she had found out that she was truly a girl. She didn't know any of them very well. Her choice was her trustworthy sister, Zaria.

"Certainly," Creighton said. "You are not a direct descendant to the kings of Hawkerness." Avalon knew that when the Runners had stormed Hawkerness, the king and his immediate family had all been killed. It was a distant cousin to the king who had escaped and led the survivors to the safety of Fontanasia. Avalon's lineage hailed from that cousin.

"I will consider it," Avalon said half-heartedly.

"You are upset because you believe in your sister. Have you read the book about the Anthracites yet?" Creighton asked.

"Yes," Avalon said, taken aback. She didn't know what he was getting at.

"Men rule Fontanasia for a reason, King Avalon. If you had really understood that book, you would know why."

Chapter 12
Truth

$\mathcal{A}$t first light on the third day, Avalon made her way down to the castle's main entrance hall. She milled about in the torchlight for a few minutes. There was no guard on the door to the hall that led to the barracks for the King's Guard, and Avalon took a deep breath and squeezed through the opening. The torches were still lit through the brick hallway, and she walked silently but purposefully on. When she reached the edge of the courtyard in the first gray light of dawn, she paused and scanned the opening. Avalon hadn't talked to Taggerty in two days, since they had confirmed their plans in Kensington's house. She could have approached him at any time since then, but she had not wanted to seem too eager, so she had waited. She had not slept well last night, and now she was here, trying to get a glance of his small party leaving for the window. Avalon walked the block to the stables and listened, but there were no sounds of men or horses rustling about, and her heart sank. She had missed him. Avalon felt Jackie squirm in her pocket as she spun to make her way back to the castle. Her heart almost stopped when Kensington surprised her.

"Your Highness," Kensington said in a gruff whisper. "I did not expect to see you here."

Avalon swallowed back a scream and her hand leapt to her heart. "Kensington, you scared the wits out of me," she admitted.

He smiled. "If you are here to check on the preparations, I would be glad to show you."

"Yes," she managed as she straightened up. He turned and held his hand out, showing Avalon what direction to step. Once she started walking, Kensington stepped in next to and just behind her. She swiveled her head around slowly, still hoping to catch a glimpse of Taggerty, but the courtyard was empty.

Kensington led her into a large, brick building that was a meeting hall and indoor training space. Torches were lit in their sconces, and Avalon could see rows of packs lined up along the wall with supplies neatly arranged on the floor and ready to put in each pack. Avalon was surprised that so much had been done in so little time.

"Taggerty left two hours ago. We have had a small team working on the packs for the last two days. Taggerty wanted to make sure that we traveled as light but as fortified as possible." Avalon walked around the room and inspected the contents. Kensington picked up a cloth sack and handed it to Avalon. It seemed to be loaded with rocks. "These packages simulate the food that will be carried." Avalon moved her arm up and down as though she was weighing the cloth against something.

"Very clever," Avalon said.

"Thank you," Kensington said with relish, and she knew that he had come up with that idea. "Weapons will be carried on the belt," he told Avalon as she crouched and inspected the packs more closely. Jackie raced from her pocket to the ground, running in and out of the items, and getting lost in the multitude of packs.

"Don't forget to put a few nuts in your pocket for my jakkow. He might want to make some of the trip with you," Avalon teased Kensington as he watched the tiny, red lizard with the same expression of concern that a woman might make at the presence of a mouse. Avalon chuckled as she inspected more of the contents. There was flint to make fire, small knives, axes and saws, and dried lamb skin sheets. "Those can be used in case of rain, and it can double as a blanket or small tent," Kensington said confidently.

"You have made great progress in a short amount of time."

Kensington nodded and looked around the room, his expression of pride changing to serious understanding for the weight of the trip they would be making. "Taggerty and I took our experience from our latest long excursion and applied it to this. We had to make some of these items on our last journey, so it was just natural to incorporate them."

Avalon nodded slowly. They had been gone months with Hawker, and she didn't realize on the outset that there was no way that they could have brought enough supplies for the entire trip without a convoy of horses to carry their packs. They had to live off the land as her small army would in some way with fifty men on a one month trip. She felt even greater appreciation for Taggerty and Kensington. She had been so naive when she had sent them out into the wilderness to banish Hawker, and yet Taggerty had never complained. He had never come to her with the problem of food or supplies on such a long trek. He had taken charge of the orders and solved the problem without burdening her.

"I don't see rope," Avalon said.

"Yes," Kensington responded. "Taggerty and his men carry very little food and other supplies. They took with them all the rope that they could carry. We will only bring a small amount."

"Why did he take so much rope?" Avalon asked.

"It is difficult to explain, Your Highness. And if you will allow Taggerty his druthers, he does not want you to be burdened with the small details. He wishes for you to see his plan with your own eyes." Still kneeling over the items, Avalon smiled to herself. Taggerty was thinking of her. Then she let the moment pass, and she sighed. He'd thought of preparations for his king, not of Avalon the girl.

Avalon tapped her ring on the hilt of a knife, and the clicking sound caused Jackie to scurry from the pack and up her arm. "Will we be able to leave sooner?" Avalon asked as she stood.

"We will do as you command, sire, but if you can wait the full two weeks as planned, it will give Taggerty the time that he needs to prepare for the large amount of men," Kensington said apologetically. "It's the ravine. He said you would understand."

Avalon's curiosity piqued, and she was impatient, but Kensington needed time to prepare the packs and choose the men who would accompany them.

"You have much work ahead of you, Kensington. I can wait."

Avalon sat in the king's suite and cradled Jackie in her hand slowly stroking his head and back. It had been ten days since Taggerty had gone, and the upcoming journey filled her with both impatience and trepidation. She was still frightened that the Monarch would find his way across, and now she was also worried that Hawker might find his way to the window. In the back of her mind, she was also concerned that the counselors would band together to move against her when she was gone. She had admitted to herself that Creighton was right and they would not approach Zaria for business. Avalon had asked Zaria about their cousins and what their character was, but the conversation proved fruitless. Avalon could not trust a stranger to rule, and she knew the counselors would be offended.

Avalon hadn't told Zaria that she would be leaving in four days either, but it was time. She would lie to Zaria that she was simply going on a trek of the countryside, and she hoped that Kensington could keep the secret. Avalon wanted to tell Zaria the truth, but she couldn't bear to frighten her sister. Zaria would be worried enough with Avalon away because the last time she had left, their father had been poisoned. And now Kensington would be leaving as well.

Avalon was thinking of the dream she had the night before Taggerty's return from banishing Hawker. It had been a true vision of the future. She was supposed to see Kensington with Zaria in the dream, but she had missed that. She remembered how angry she had been at Zaria because she was jealous about Taggerty, but she could see now that her dream was telling her the truth. The dream was showing Zaria looking toward Kensington, and Taggerty trying to introduce Kensington. Zaria swept into the suite just then, as though she knew Avalon had been thinking of her.

"Zaria," Avalon said.

"Avalon!" Zaria said with a start. Avalon had not been hiding, but Zaria hadn't noticed her.

"Come and sit with me."

Zaria rolled her eyes but smiled at the same time. She crossed the room and sat on the other side of the low table, opposite Avalon. "Sitting alone? You are turning into father."

It was Avalon's turn to roll her eyes, but she could see the similarity. Avalon had often found her father sitting alone in this chair. "I wanted to talk to you."

Sensing Avalon's seriousness, Zaria lost her smile. "What's wrong?" she asked.

"Nothing is wrong," Avalon said cryptically. "You are going to be married to Kensington soon enough, and then you will be moving into your own suite and I will be left here alone."

"Yes, but you will still have Myra," Zaria said with a smile.

"Until you have babies, and then I will lose her to you," Avalon jibed back.

"Babies!" Zaria said with a blush.

Avalon laughed and allowed herself to enjoy the moment. "Zaria, I will be going on a trip, a hike if you will. I leave in four days."

"Do you have to go?" Zaria asked. She rose from her chair and moved next to Avalon, sitting on the arm of Avalon's chair. Avalon had seen her sit here for years, listening to their father talk, watching him look at Zaria in a way he had never looked at Avalon, with the soft twinkle of a father watching his beautiful daughter grow into a woman.

"Yes," Avalon said. "And Kensington must come with me."

"No," Zaria said and then stopped herself. "Why does he have to leave again?"

Avalon had spent days trying to figure out what she would tell Zaria, and she still didn't want to share her true plan with her sister. She trusted Zaria implicitly, but Avalon wanted Zaria to live without worry. It gave Avalon a small amount of joy in a world that hinged on the brightness of the moon. If Avalon could keep her enemy at bay, then there was no reason for Zaria to change her pure outlook on the world. There was no reason to spoil the dream with a nightmare.

"Don't you want me and Kensington to get closer?" Avalon asked.

"Of course I do. He is the head of the King's Guard, and I know you trust him. You have even shown him Jackie."

The tiny lizard heard his name and jumped from Avalon's hand and scrambled to the edge of Avalon's knee. Zaria saw the lizard and waited a moment before touching her dress at the thigh, allowing Jackie to climb onto the yellow fabric of her dress. The lizard walked carefully up to Zaria's belt and curled up into a ball.

"But why do you both have to leave me?"

Avalon could see that Zaria's worry stemmed from the last time she was away. "I need to trust Kensington and to accept him as my brother. I want him to take this trek with me so that we can bond." Zaria didn't say anything, so Avalon continued. "It's a man thing. You wouldn't understand."

Zaria smiled politely, but she didn't laugh. "It's a man thing?"

"Yes, it is," Avalon said, knowing that she would get a ribbing from her sister. "I have been studying their behavior for over seven years, and I know what a man thing is, and this is it. Don't you want Kensington to feel that he has my utmost confidence?" Avalon deflected with another question.

"Yes, of course."

"Then this is what it takes. How will he feel if I go on a trek with fifty men, and he is not one of them?"

"That is more than father ever took hunting," Zaria noted aloud.

"I'm not hunting. I am trekking the land, marking the terrain. It's a small expedition. We will be back in less than a full cycle of the moon," Avalon reassured, but she knew this short timetable might be a lie.

Zaria pursed her lips, but Avalon knew that she would not argue. "I guess it is important for him to be there," she acquiesced. "And you will need someone to look out for you."

"I am the king, all of my men will be looking out for me," Avalon said as she stood confidently.

"You know what I mean," Zaria said, looking up at Avalon. Avalon pulled her shoulders back and did not answer. She knew that Zaria meant she would need someone she could trust to help keep her secret, but Avalon had not planned to tell Kensington or anyone that she was a girl. Her father had instructed Walthan that she deserved her privacy as a Prince of Fontanasia, but he didn't tell Walthan the truth. Avalon was the king now, and she could command as she liked.

"I will find my own way. I am the king, have a little faith in me," Avalon said.

"You know that I have faith in you, Avalon," Zaria said aloud, but her face showed concern and she wasn't saying what was really on her mind.

"Do you know that I had a dream about you and Kensington?" Avalon asked and Zaria brightened instantly.

"You did! What happened?" Avalon could tell that Zaria thought this dream was to take place this week, and she snickered at her older sister.

"I had a dream back when you hosted my birthday celebration. I saw that Kensington and Taggerty would return that night."

"That sounds like a dream about Taggerty and Kensington," Zaria said. "Or maybe a dream about Taggerty?" she asked mischievously.

Avalon grit her teeth but did not take the bait. "In the dream, Taggerty and Kensington came to the ball and at the time, all I could see was Taggerty looking for you. I know now that I was supposed to see my introduction to Kensington that night. That was what was momentous in the dream. My dream was trying to show me your fate and fortune, and I should have seen it, but I didn't."

Zaria smiled. "Thank you, Avalon." She leaned over and took Avalon's hand in hers. Avalon's hands were dry and calloused, and Zaria's were silky smooth.

"You're welcome," Avalon said. They sat and smiled for a minute, Jackie scampering from Zaria's lap to her arm and across to Avalon's jacket. Zaria shivered at the tiny feet across her bare skin. They giggled at the lizard, enjoying the moment for what it was, trying to forget about the long separation that was to come.

"Speaking of fate and fortune, don't the Guides believe that Taggerty is the future of the king or something like that?"

"Well, he did save my life," Avalon replied quickly.

"I'm serious," Zaria pushed. "I know that you like him. You have since the day you first saw him at the Festival of Fontanasia last year."

"I have not!" Avalon defended weakly, knowing it was true. She pinched her lips together to keep herself from sounding defensive, but Zaria pressed on.

"You should talk to Taggerty, Avalon. He can be trusted."

"I know he can be trusted, Zaria," Avalon said with regret. "Imagine it, finding out your king is a girl." Avalon looked at Zaria who was smiling. "You can't imagine it because you have always known. Imagine if you found out dad was a girl," Avalon said weakly.

"That's ridiculous, Avalon."

"And that's what he would say! It's too much to even comprehend. I am the king. I cannot ask Taggerty to accept a lie. He deserves much more than that."

"Like what?" Zaria challenged.

"I don't know," Avalon said, but she was thinking of Taggerty having his own family.

"What if he wants to be with you?" Zaria asked.

Avalon pushed a laugh out of her lungs although the prospect made her want to cry. She had been through this in her mind a thousand times, and there was just no way to make it work. She gulped back her sentiment and stood, straightening her jacket as Jackie scampered into her pocket. In this moment, Avalon actually found herself wishing that Zaria and Taggerty were together because then Taggerty would be spoken for. That might be the only way for her to put this behind and move on with her destiny. She was the King of Fontanasia, and there was nothing else.

"Avalon, there is something I need to tell you, and I need you to not be angry," Zaria said quietly. She stood and followed Avalon to the window. "Promise," Zaria said.

"How can someone promise not to get angry?" Avalon challenged. "It's not possible to know your reaction."

Zaria smiled at her thoughtful sister. "Yes, but it is possible to be angry and not fly off the handle, if you promise."

"Fine," Avalon said. "I promise not to be angry."

Zaria turned to face Avalon and took her hands, forcing her to turn away from the view outside and to look up at her older sister. "Avalon, Taggerty knows that you are a girl."

Zaria's soft words were like an explosion in Avalon's head, and she stumbled two steps backwards, Zaria's grip keeping her upright. Avalon couldn't speak. She stood staring at her sister with her mouth hanging open as every emotion she'd ever felt swirled through her chest. Her mouth opened and closed three more times, her words blocked by the lump in her throat. Avalon didn't feel angry, she felt embarrassed.

"I don't understand," Avalon finally said, and Zaria smiled.

"He knows, Avalon, and I told you that he can be trusted. He has known for a year."

Avalon was shocked, and then she remembered that Taggerty had been raised to protect the king from the moment that the Guides had pronounced him the future of the king. Taggerty would protect Avalon no matter what. "He knows that I'm a girl," Avalon said.

"Yes. We slipped after all of these years. It was the night you and Taggerty found me and Myra sequestered in the suite, after father died."

"That's not possible." Avalon was terrified. Taggerty had known she was a girl for almost a full year, and he had not even hinted to her.

"He likes you. I know he does. He has a crush on you." Zaria was smiling and trying to calm Avalon who was visibly upset.

"He has spent most of the year with you, not me," Avalon told her.

"He has spent most of his time chaperoning me so that Kensington and I could be together. And you haven't helped Taggerty get close, have you? You don't let anyone get near you."

"That's not fair. You know what's at stake," Avalon said. Zaria nodded and said nothing further.

Avalon remembered two weeks ago when she stood alone with Taggerty in Kensington's house. "If you tell the truth," he had said to her. He'd moved in so close that Avalon had hoped he would lean down and kiss her lips. "If you tell the truth..." she heard. He was asking her to trust him with her secret, and she hadn't.

Chapter 13
Blood Moon

They left in late morning on horses followed by four wagons. Counselor Creighton wheeled Counselor Nelson to the front of the castle so they could bid goodbye to their king. Avalon said nothing as she mounted her horse and sat tall in the saddle. Zaria stood with the counselors, but she did not say anything to Avalon or Kensington. She had cried the night before and had asked both Avalon and Kensington not to go, and both had comforted her. In the end, they would leave her. She held her head high, watching in the rising heat of the sun as the men moved out.

They did not leave in secret like Avalon had last time she went to Cormicks, via the locked gate and through the Guide's camp. They left through the Fingers for all to see. Many citizens of Fontanasia had turned out on the path that led through the center of the city and down to the plains. They cheered for the men and for their king. Avalon nodded and tried to make eye contact with as many people as she could. She wanted the best for them, and she wanted them to know that she saw them.

Kensington and Gamon rode with Avalon, and his young sons chased Gamon along the path. He was not going on the trip with Avalon, but he would see the king and the rest of the men to the outer wall. Before long they were out of the Downs and looking over the plains to the outer wall. Avalon felt her tense shoulders relax a little when they got beyond the citizens of the city.

They didn't ride away from Fontanasia fast, but they weren't going in secret this time. They came over the low rise and Avalon saw the outer wall. She felt a pang of regret as she thought of Walthan who had the wall erected before Avalon was born. It was the perfect place for an outer defense, running from the Helon Sea and across the open plain, doubling back around to the base of the mountain that Fontanasia had been built into. From this position, her army could attack with bow and arrow at any aggressors as they approached on the other side of the wall. The low plains gave no cover, and an army could be severely decreased in size before even reaching this outer barrier.

She led her men down to the wall, her eyes scanning for the crease in the brick that would give away the opening. To her great frustration, she could not find it. The wall had been built so that anyone not walking along the edge would not be able to find the opening. As they trotted their horses closer and closer, Avalon felt a panic, and Kensington, understanding without a word, led her to the opening.

"Your Highness, I'm practically riding on top of you. I apologize," he said, guiding his horse to the right and flashing a smile at Avalon. She looked back at him and his eyes moved to the right and he squinted, telling Avalon that he saw the opening and that she should turn the convoy slightly. She gladly took the hint and made a note to revisit this area alone with Kensington so that she no longer needed help getting in or out of her city.

Gamon pulled next to Avalon, his hand resting over his heart. "I leave you here, King Avalon. I will do my duty." Avalon nodded and Gamon turned away. They moved down the ridge, and with a little more guidance from Kensington she was upon the opening where the left side of the wall overlapped the right, and a ten foot wide corridor appeared. Avalon led the men through, and then they were out on the plains, moving slowly so the wagons could keep up.

It took several hours to get to the edge of the woods where they would camp. As they approached their stopping point for the day, Avalon could see three horses in the grass.

"Perfect," Kensington said and he spurred his horse ahead. Three figures that had been lying in the grass stood up. They were Guides waiting for the party of soldiers to arrive. As she approached, Avalon could see that they had set up a long rope to tie off the horses, and the soldiers followed Kensington's lead. There were already full pails of water with ladles on the ground for the soldiers who were grateful to the Guides for the refreshment. Avalon was surprised to see them here, and she realized that Taggerty and Kensington had done a lot of preparing in the short time, leaving no detail to chance.

Everyone had dismounted and the wagons were unloaded, the men having some time in the late afternoon to relax. The sky was still clear at dusk and the air warm, and the men did not need to set up the small sheep skin tent coverings. Avalon walked along the line of horses, not knowing how or when to break away from the men for some privacy.

"Rest here, Your Highness. The men have already started setting up your tent," Kensington said. He left Avalon seated on a makeshift chair next to the woods.

Avalon would have been glad to take a small tent, but Kensington had erected a tent that was fifteen feet square and looked spacious compared to the small sacks that the men would crowd into. When Avalon saw the men putting the sleeping bags on the ground, she felt bad but she did not show it, and she did not turn down the tent that Kensington had built for her. He had planned for everything. She was the king and Kensington would make sure that everyone remembered.

"King Avalon," Kensington called when the tent was erected. Avalon stood and walked by the men who had come on this journey with her. They were hearty men, strong soldiers, and none of them complained for the work. She noticed some of the men looking tentatively into the woods. When she got to the tent opening, Kensington turned to follow Avalon's gaze back at the men.

"Some of the men don't look like they've been camping before," Avalon said.

"You noticed that?" Kensington asked. "We always lead the hunting parties away from these woods because they believe that these woods are haunted."

"I have heard of that," she said.

"It's an old wives tale that I can laugh at now, only because I know where we are going. If I didn't know the truth, I would be just as anxious as those men."

"The founders of Fontanasia wanted to protect the passage to Hawkerness so they started that rumor to keep people from trekking these woods," Avalon admitted. Her father had divulged that the night he had told her about Cormicks. She had played that conversation out in her head hundreds of times, trying to remember all of the wisdom he had imparted to her just days before his murder.

Kensington pulled the tent flap back and followed Avalon in. "You didn't have to make such a nice tent for me, Kensington, but I do appreciate it." There was a small table with some tea, fruit, and bread for supper and Avalon was grateful. She held her hand out to the chair opposite her at the small table and Kensington sat and watched her eat the bread and tea for dinner.

"Won't you eat?" Avalon asked.

"I will when my men have eaten," he said proudly, and Avalon was reminded of the honor Walthan felt in leading his men.

"You have thought of everything, haven't you?" she said to Kensington with a smile, and he smiled back.

"I thought of some things, Your Highness, but it was Taggerty who thought of everything." Kensington rose from his chair and bowed. "Please, excuse me for leaving you alone, but I have several duties waiting. There is a pan of water on the table for your use, and there is another pan on the floor that you can fill when you need the bathroom. We did not bring a steward on this mission because we needed the soldiers, but we can manage assisting you for a month." Kensington smiled and headed for the flap that served as the door.

"Thank you, Kensington," Avalon said, truly grateful.

"Your Highness," he said as he bowed and turned, leaving Avalon alone.

So, it was Taggerty, knowing that she was a girl, who had planned for everything. Taggerty, who had been on the previous mission to Cormicks with her and most likely had remembered that she needed to go into the woods alone to use the bathroom. He knew that she was a girl and so he knew why she required privacy. And here she was with fifty men outside the tent and she did not have to worry or want for anything, except for another moment alone with Taggerty so she could explain herself.

Hawker had taken no pleasure in killing the Guide, but he had to get to Cormicks, and he knew that the Guide was there to stop him from entering the elbagrass. He had respected the Guides as a whole, and many of the books he had studied were created from interviews with the Guides. He had learned how to read the stars, how to stay warm in any weather, and how to find the window to Cormicks. It was all there to be discovered by anyone willing to read and study for years to decode the puzzle. And here Hawker was, across the window, and on the verge of being a king in his own right.

He'd been worried about the timing of the plan he had been forming. Once out of the elbagrass and through the thicket of trees, he needed to find the castle and convince the Runners to attack Fontanasia right away. It was two weeks until the elbagrass would not be poisonous, and Hawker needed the Monarch to see the urgency of his plan. The fact that there were Guides at the elbagrass told Hawker that Avalon was not all trusting, but since there was not an army waiting there, Hawker knew that Avalon was failing as a king. Hawker needed to get an army of Runners across the window right now, before the Guides could warn Fontanasia and build up defenses.

Hawker found a rock outcropping the first night and slept there, hunched down and shivering against the wind in his meager robes. On the second day he woke to the frantic movements of little white birds with red freckles. They swarmed over a bush that held berries and Hawker greedily swatted the tiny birds away to keep the berries for himself. He found tracks in the dirt that were easy to follow, and he walked swiftly and out in the open. He had only the concealed knife and two sharp rocks and his wits to defend himself, but he was certain that he would be taken alive. These people would be curious as to where he had come from, and if Brick had done his job, then they might even be waiting for him. Hawker imagined the Runners bowing at his feet as he walked into Cormicks, and he allowed the fantasy, although he knew it would not be quite that easy.

He came around the side of a small mountain that looked like the side had caved in. There was a pile of boulders and rocks at the bottom and huge tracks of black dirt in the ground. It wasn't until Hawker climbed half way up that he realized those were the remnants of Anthracite tracks. His cold heart stirred, and he knew that he was close. He continued his climb and stood erect at the top of the mountain and saw a castle off in the distance. When he looked down upon it, he imagined sitting on top of an Anthracite and walking into Fontanasia. He would crush the Fingers, take the castle, and stand on the parapet to look down at the people in the boroughs as they came to beg him for mercy. They would be his people soon enough.

Hawker slept at the bottom of the mountain in a blanket he had found mixed in with the rocks. He climbed back up the next day to watch the castle. He saw a weak lot of scavengers living inside the walls, but the soldiers that patrolled the walls were serious brutes. After two days of watching, Hawker knew he had to make his move. He walked over the mountaintop and down the other side, strolling right up to the gates of Cormicks. The guards at the gate had knocked him down, but he did not fight back. He knew that they would take him to their master, and Hawker's heart rate increased with excitement as they dragged him inside. He was marched into the center of a large hall and paraded in front of white robed counselors who had beast-like men flanking them. Hawker had noticed that the farther he made it into the castle, the more the faces of the guards were tattooed. He concluded that they wore their rank on their flesh for all to see, which made sense to him knowing this was a society of killers and brutes. He also noticed that the white robed men were shaven bald, each forehead bearing a small yet different mark than the next.

Hawker was thrown down on the floor in front of the Monarch of Cormicks who laughed at him and taunted him, but Hawker kept his head and stuck to his plan. He had been barely listening to the Monarch as he watched the white-robed men. He could see that they were in factions, leaders of their boroughs or whatever they might call the different sections of Cormicks, and Hawker knew that these were the men who mattered.

The Monarch was a large figure, muscular and tattooed, more like the Runners who Hawker had read about. Hawker waited for his opening, and then he stood up tall, his height equaling the Monarch's, both taller than the dog like men who stood guard around the throne.

"I am Prince Hawker of Fontanasia, and I am the one who sent you the warrior Brick. He was to tell you of my plans to open up the window between our great cities. Where is Brick, by the way?" This short speech earned him a blow to the stomach. The Monarch abhorred being spoken to out of turn, and Hawker couldn't blame him for that. He was the ruler of a pack of wolves that would turn on him at the first sign of weakness.

As Hawker crouched on the floor and sucked in air, coughing and pretending the blow hurt him more than it had, he watched the faces of the white robes, and he knew that he had their attention. They knew who Brick was, and they were interested.

"Brick's inability as a warrior cost him his life," the Monarch bellowed and received grunts of pleasure from his guards.

Hawker picked his moment and stood up again, standing tall. Although he'd been expecting it, he was furious at the treatment and he was revising his plan as he interrupted the Monarch. "Well, that is a shame," Hawker said quickly with the careless wave of his hand. "You have little time to mount an army and cross over into Fontanasia. Their guard is down right now, but at the next full moon it will be too late. They will have soldiers standing by at that time, and it will be harder to..." He was cut off as one soldier belted him in the stomach and another cut him down at the knees causing him to fall to the floor in real pain this time. While he grunted and assessed his injuries, Hawker watched the faces of all in the hall very closely. There was a rustling of whispers among the white robed men, which caused a moment of panic to cross the Monarch's face.

Hawker recognized the hierarchy here immediately. The Monarch was in control, but the small men in white robes held power too. They all had their own large guards, like dogs protecting their masters. The white robes looked feeble next to their dogs, but then Hawker had always looked feeble next to his brother, King Birch. Yet Birch was dead, not Hawker. He liked these white robes, and he could tell by their covered interest that they were listening, but they would not let their Monarch know that. Hawker could read any situation, and he read this one. They were cautious, but they would be his.

Before he could say anything more, he was unceremoniously dragged away to a cell and tossed in, but Hawker didn't feel despair, and he laughed aloud for a long time. He ate the gruel that they brought him, and it took less than three days to be summoned back up to the Monarch. They were alone in a dining room this time without the White Robes, and Hawker knew that his short speech had caused a stir. The Monarch watched him for a few minutes and then he sat at the table to dine, allowing Hawker to stand and watch. At that moment, Hawker knew that he would get every wish he had.

"You sent us the warrior Brick," the Monarch said evenly. "Why?"

Hawker lowered his head to enhance the deceit that he was subservient and would be helping the Monarch. "He was to give you the signal and let you capture the party he was with. I wanted Prince Avalon dead so that I could take his place as King in Fontanasia. I was then going to come here and offer you my partnership."

"I don't have partners," the Monarch yelled as he slammed his fist into the table. Hawker folded his shoulders lower and pretended to be scared.

"That was the wrong word. I am sorry." Hawker looked around the ancient brick hall and admired how run down it was. "I only wanted your glory to be brought to Fontanasia. You know how to treat people. You understand that they are to be ruled with fear. We need you to open their eyes to the real world." Hawker was sincere, speaking from the depths of his blackened heart, and the Monarch nodded.

It took less than thirty minutes for Hawker to deceive the Monarch into believing that he was sincere in handing over Fontanasia. The Monarch was easily persuaded since he still felt the sting of losing some of his men to the prisoners who had broken out of the dungeon and escaped. He had tried to find them for months, but time had made him give up the fool's errand. Now he felt the sting again and his fury returned. He was ready to mount the army and take them where Hawker led, and to rule the rest of the world.

The Monarch told Hawker to sit with him, and Hawker sat folded low in his chair. The Monarch planted his large fist on the table in front of Hawker. "If I decide to do this, you will lead us to this city."

"As you command," Hawker offered, keeping his smile until he was safely tucked back in his dungeon cell. Hawker sat alone in the dark of the dungeon eating the disgusting stew day after day, but he didn't give up hope. He counted the days and noted the full moon pass on this side of the window, and he knew they would come for him.

The Monarch had Hawker escorted up several times to discuss the layout of Fontanasia, the defenses, and a plan of attack. Two weeks later, they put his hands in shackles and planted him on a horse that was led by one of the goliath soldiers. Hawker abhorred being on horseback. He preferred walking because he didn't trust animals. They were vile.

The Monarch took the lead with Hawker quietly giving direction as they went. They were setting out three days in advance of when they needed to, and Hawker soon saw the line of horse drawn carts surrounded by soldiers walking in regiments between. It was the convoy of the men he called White Robes, and Hawker knew they were coming to see the battle. This was the most important thing to have happened here in over two hundred years, and no one was going to miss the action. This made Hawker ecstatic, although he rode low on his horse and tried to look defeated. He would no longer try to gain the Monarch's trust. If he worked it out, Hawker could usurp the Monarch on this very trip.

It took the entire day to make it to the edge of the wood because they walked at a snails pace. Hawker saw patches of scorched ground along the way and wondered if the Anthracites had caused that, but he wouldn't make the mistake of asking any questions.

"This is the place," Hawker said. The Monarch barked a command and the soldier who had been leading Hawker's horse grabbed Hawker's arms in a vice grip and pulled him down in one move. Hawker's arms stung and he let out a grunt. He watched as the parade of wagons pulled up to the trees.

"This is not the place!" the Monarch yelled. "We were through this area a hundred times, and there is nothing but trees packed so tight we can't get through."

The soldier threw Hawker at the feet of the Monarch's horse and it whinnied and pushed up onto its back legs, terrifying Hawker that it would come down and crush him. He looked up to see a smile on the Monarch's lips and Hawker felt angry enough to stand up and end the Monarch right then, but he needed to wait until the time was right. He knew that as long as he had the blessing of the White Robes, they would let him take control of Cormicks with no recourse. They were counselors, and in this cutthroat place, none of them wanted to be in charge.

"I will take you through the trees tomorrow," Hawker told him, still on his knees.

The Monarch pulled back on the reigns and his horse backed up two steps before dropping to all fours again. Hawker looked at the ground and waited for the Monarch to dismount. "I have lost men in these woods," he said to Hawker in a low voice. "They go in and they never return."

Hawker knew that they were poisoned by the elbagrass, but he did not volunteer that information. "This is where I came from," he said quietly and was relieved when the Monarch turned away and began barking orders.

Avalon was exhausted. She hadn't done anything physically demanding aside from sitting astride her horse, but she found that being king drew all eyes to her, and she had to pretend to be a boy even harder. She was trying to pretend to be a man really, to fill her father's shoes, and she second-guessed each move she made and each word she spoke before taking action. It was exhausting.

Sleep had come easy that night. Avalon could hear the muffled voices of the men outside her tent until after the sun went down. She could see the orange light of the fires dancing on the white cloth of her tent. She had brought Jackie on this trip, and she put him down in the grass and watched him investigate the ground. He found a couple of leaves to eat and returned to Avalon. She scooped him up and placed him on her cot, and then she sat alone in the candlelight listening for a long time. She wanted to see Kensington so she could help him make his arrangements, but she felt safe with her secret inside the tent, and she knew that Kensington was strengthening his position as leader of the King's Guard with each command.

Avalon dozed off, and when she awoke, she sat straight up on her cot. She could hear muffled voices outside her tent, and she strained to hear what they were saying. It was dark, but she noticed a shallow glow forming, and she knew that it was dawn. She had slept soundly and was surprised to find that her muscles didn't ache when she stood up. She crept over to the pan on the floor to relieve herself hoping that no one outside could hear that she was awake. Avalon felt a little stupid sneaking around her own tent, but she needed time to dress herself properly, making certain that her clothes were fastened the right way and that she looked like a king. It would have been easier with a mirror, but that would have been too much to bring on this trip.

Jackie had been moving silently around in the grass, and he jumped to Avalon's arm when she knelt down to retrieve him. She tucked him safely in her pocket and then strode from her tent, expecting most of the men to be sleeping. Avalon was shocked to see that both wagons were empty, the packs lined up neatly in two rows. All of the men were awake and had rolled up their blankets, and they were seated in small circles eating bread and fruit for breakfast. Kensington was standing just outside the tent waiting for Avalon when she stepped through the flap.

"King Avalon," Kensington said loud enough for the men to hear him. They all began rising from the ground.

"As you were," Avalon commanded, and the men froze in place. Their eyes moved between Avalon and Kensington. "Finish your breakfast, men. We have a lot of ground to cover today." Kensington nodded and the men melted back into their small circles.

"Breakfast?" Kensington asked.

"Yes," Avalon said sternly, feeling foolish. She needed to command the men, to show them that she was in control. They were taking a journey with her and they would not believe what was at the journey's end. She needed to earn their trust.

Kensington produced a small bowl with fruit and a hot cup of tea. "This is a luxury, Your Highness. We will have some days of travel where there won't be much to eat but jerky, but Taggerty will have some proper meals ready when we arrive." Avalon ate the apple quickly and gulped down the tea. When she was sure none of the men were watching, she pulled a grape into two halves and dropped them into her pocket for Jackie. She felt his tiny body squirm and she knew that he was tearing into the fruit.

"We are ready to go," Kensington said as four men approached and disassembled Avalon's tent.

"Wait, I should say something to the men," Avalon said, acting calm while her heart pounded in her chest.

"The men would like that," Kensington replied genuinely.

Avalon stepped onto the back of the empty wagon so that all of the men could see her. She looked at their serious faces, some young and some older but all of them soldiers, her soldiers. "Warriors and most loyal soldiers," she began, "you might be wondering what the Guides are doing here. They are not usually present at hunting trips, but this is not a hunting trip and we are not trekking the land aimlessly. We have a path to follow. Many of you have heard that these woods are haunted," she said, immediately regretting it because some of the soldiers who had not been thinking that yet were thinking it now. "These woods are not haunted. These trees are just like any other trees, standing tall out of the ground. There is nothing sinister about them. The haunted woods, that is the story that our forefathers told to keep people out of this area of the forest." Avalon paused a moment and noticed the large smiles of two of the men who stood nearest her, and she knew in an instant that these were Myra's nephews. They had some of her smile on their faces, and one was large and sturdy like Myra. The other one stared at Avalon with Myra's eyes and intense brow.

"We are together, going down the path of our own history. I am taking you to the passageway to Hawkerness." Some of the men looked around, and Avalon didn't know if their confused faces reflected knowledge of Hawkerness or that they had no idea what this meant, but she continued. "Over two hundred years ago our families came out of these woods and built Fontanasia, but there is an old enemy still down that passageway. If we are lucky, they will never find Fontanasia, and if we are not lucky, we will be defending this passageway with our lives to make sure that our families, our friends, and our city survives."

Avalon looked at Kensington for assurance, and he was standing proud, his men following suit. This was the first time they would be tested as true soldiers, and they were ready.

"You will see things on this trip that your eyes will not want to believe, but on the memory of my father, what you see is real. Our enemies are beyond the sight of our eyes, and although we have not seen them in over two hundred years, they are as real as the ground that you are standing on. You are about to go down the forgotten path that has been traveled by few people in the past two hundred years. You've passed into that trusted group now, a group that includes kings before me, and soldiers like Walthan who died keeping us all safe. You are the men that I trust the most, and I am sure you will keep everything that you see a secret. That is a lot to ask of you, because you have family and friends that you will want to tell. You will want to warn them of the danger, but there is another way to live. You can live like Walthan. You can keep this secret and keep your families safe and happy in their lives. You can use this trip as a device, to think of better ways to protect your city."

Avalon looked at Kensington and her forehead crinkled with worry, but she stayed the course. "I have not told Princess Zaria, my sister of this secret. Kensington, my trusted advisor, has not told his bride-to-be of this secret. We do not wish to bring panic and worry to the one we love the most."

Avalon wanted to tell the men how Walthan had died keeping the secret, but she bit her lip and stepped down from the wagon, and that was the only signal that Kensington needed to round the men up. There was a stony faced Guide who stood alone at the edge of the forest who squinted at Avalon, and when she noticed him, he took the first few steps and disappeared into the trees. Kensington loaded a pack onto his back and followed Avalon into the trees. Like on her recon mission to Cormicks, there was nothing for her to carry on this trip either, but she did not argue. Many of the men picked up smaller packs and a few of the very large men pulled on huge packs, but no one complained as they followed King Avalon into the woods.

It was easy going the first day as they moved under the canopy of trees. The growth lessened with the shadowed sunlight, and all Avalon heard behind her was the crunching of footsteps on the dead leaves. Her nerves subsided, and she watched the Guide as he stopped next to a leafy boulder that was shaped like a thumb. Avalon was surprised how quietly the men traveled until she realized that if she moved in silence, they would follow her lead. She decided that small conversation might make the time pass quicker. Avalon looked around and noticed Kensington and Myra's nephews closest to her. She decided to get to know Myra's family.

"You are a George, are you not?" she asked the shorter of the two men.

He smiled widely. "Davev is my name, Your Highness. I'm not surprised that you know of me though. I am a great warrior."

"You are a great exaggerator is what you are," the taller one took up as he tightened the straps of his pack. His pack was larger than Avalon's body, yet he was not even breathing hard. "The king knows who you are because you look just like Aunt Myra."

Avalon smiled to herself, feeling at home with the men she had just met.

"I'm Jakon George, Your Highness. Don't mind my brother Davev. I'm the tall one, but he tells tales taller than these trees."

Avalon smiled at the rivalry. "You are brothers?" she asked.

"We are cousins," the tall Jakon replied.

"You are lucky to have such a close family," she told them, but she had nothing else to say. Avalon was not good at small talk. She had been listening and learning her whole life, but she did not know how to relate to anyone outside of her inner circle, and those around her did not know how to relate to a king. They walked on in silence again.

She remembered this part of the forest from the last time that she had been through here with Brick and Walthan, both seeming to keep an eye on the unknown Taggerty. On this trip she wasn't worried about the men's feet snapping twigs or leaving a path in the underbrush. They would worry about that on the other side of the ravine. For now, she wanted to make time to the window. She walked ten paces behind the Guide, and her men walked a few paces behind her, spread out through the thicket ten across. The Guide would slow sometimes, his head moving side to side, and Avalon had no idea what he could be using as signals telling him that he was on the right path. Then she noticed a brown rock overhang that she remembered from her first journey.

They walked for hours without a word, but when they came to the area of the woods where the shrubs disappeared and the dirt turned red, Avalon could hear the muffled whispers of some of the men commenting on the change. Avalon's calves ached and she knew that they would be stopping soon. A thousand steps later, the Guide turned to Avalon and nodded. She recognized the huge rock from her first trip, and Avalon simply stopped walking and sat down on a fallen tree. Jakon and Davev stopped near Avalon and Kensington ordered the other men to make camp and set up the king's tent. While Avalon waited, she saw the Guide climb to the top of the boulder and look around the woods. She remembered Chylyn seemed to be perched in the same position, and she wondered if this Guide would sleep tonight.

The red dirt had smeared the white fabric as the men set her tent up, and she dusted off her pants before moving inside. Avalon was grateful for the privacy of her tent. There was no grass for Jackie to stretch his legs on, and Avalon watched him scamper around in the dirt, the tiny, red lizard camouflaged on the red ground. When he realized he would find no food here, she picked him up and placed him on the small table, his tiny red footprints quickly covering the surface. Avalon again shared her fruit with her companion before blowing out her candle and lying on her cot. She listened as the tall trees swayed in the wind, the ripple of their leaves soothing her mind and helping her drift off to sleep.

The next day, Avalon and the fifty soldiers walked under the tree canopy for hours on end, the shrubs returning and wiping the red dirt from their boots and pants. They made the edge of a small valley mid day and rested in the dry heat of the sun before crossing the valley and taking to the woods again. Avalon walked on, her mind mixing this day with the memories of her previous trip. She felt that she had been a child a year ago and was now an adult. The entire world had changed for her on her last trip, and although she had no intention of crossing the field of elbagrass for revenge, her heart wept for Walthan as she followed the Guide through the woods.

They stepped from the edge of the trees just before sundown, the ravine stretching out in front of them. She could hear the quiet gasps of some of the soldiers as they saw the deep fissure. Avalon shuddered when she remembered the sand eels and how they had slithered up her legs and paralyzed her before she even knew what was happening. She subconsciously felt for the bag of keeley dust on her belt and was relieved to find it there. She would cross the ravine this time with her hand in the pouch, ready to spread the dust and kill the sand eels if the time came.

The Guide stepped up to the edge of the ravine and took his bearings. He looked back at Avalon and she thought that he was pointing to the setting sun. She nodded, but the lost look on her face made the Guide move his hand and point again. Avalon stepped to the edge of the ravine and squinted into the waning sun. A hundred paces up the ravine, she saw a rope net tied to the tops of the trees. It fell like a giant web down into the bottom of the ravine. Taggerty had been here, and he had made a way across the ravine. Avalon wanted to move up the edge to take a closer look, but night was upon them and there were preparations to be made.

"We will take a look in the morning," the Guide whispered, and Avalon nodded.

"We camp here tonight under the stars," she told Kensington.

"We stop here, men," was all that Kensington had to say, and men dropped packs all around the clearing. Avalon's tent was erected in ten minutes, and she was utterly grateful for the privacy that it afforded her. Her muscles were aching from the long walk, and she was sure the men were hurting after carrying the packs so far, yet not one had complained.

Avalon sat at the small table in front of the candle and drank three cups of water poured from a large canteen. This was the first time she found herself wondering if they had brought enough food and water for everyone. She ate a handful of grapes and gave two to Jackie who waited patiently on the table. Then Avalon sank her teeth into the tough jerky and ripped a piece off, smiling at the memory of her first taste of the rough food. Her cheeks even felt too tired to chew after the day's travel and she ate the rest slowly.

"King Avalon," she heard outside the tent flap.

"Enter," she said knowing that it would be Kensington.

Avalon held her hand out and Kensington took the small chair opposite her. "Help yourself," Avalon said, glad for the company.

"Thank you," Kensington said as he started in with the grapes. Jackie saw Kensington quickly gobbling up the rest of the grapes, and he scrambled to the edge of the table. Kensington stopped eating and watched the tiny, red jakkow lizard with both fascination and repulsion. It was an anomaly, something that Kensington was having a hard time grasping. He had lived enough of life to know the world, and to see this new creature had thrown everything he knew off balance.

"Perhaps I should show him to the rest of the men so that they too can prepare their minds for what they are about to see," Avalon said with a smile.

Kensington shook his head slowly but said, "Perhaps."

"Jackie is the least of it," Avalon told him. "You know where you are going in name, but you have no idea, Kensington."

They ate the jerky and drank water in silence, both too tired for small talk. Then the stout soldier tore two grapes in half and reached his hand out, allowing Jackie for the first time to scramble into his hand and eat. "You are right, of course," he acquiesced. Then he sighed heavily, and when Jackie was done eating and had returned to the table, Kensington stood and bowed to excuse himself.

Avalon lay down on the cot. She was exhausted but her mind would not allow sleep to come. She had seen only a portion of the rope net that Taggerty had erected, and she willed the sun to rise so that she could take it all in.

She was greatly impressed by all the preparations Taggerty had made in such a short time. He had helped Kensington ready the packs for the men. He had packed his own materials for his small party of men, and he had put together a private yet practical tent for her own use. Avalon would have typically brushed off any excitement she might have felt knowing that Taggerty was thinking of her as more than just the king. But she allowed herself to soak in the knowledge that Taggerty had known for a long time that she was a girl, and that he had built this tent for her privacy and comfort. He had not exposed her, but instead he had protected her.

The more she thought about it, Avalon realized that Taggerty could not have accomplished all of these things in the three days before he left. He had been preparing for many men to cross the ravine. He had been devising plans, making lists, making her tent, and working out the details for the moment that Avalon changed her mind about moving men to Cormicks. Avalon's heart stirred, and she realized that if Taggerty was with her right now, she might be angry with him. She had been making decisions to stand down, but he had been going ahead on his own with what he thought would be best. It should have angered her, but she giggled to herself, and then she blushed and clamped her hand over her mouth. After months of trying to ignore all emotion, she was surprised to admit to herself that she was in love with Taggerty.

Avalon hoped that no one outside the tent had heard her laugh, and she listened intently in the dark. When there was only silence, she rolled from her cot and pulled on her outer clothes and wrapped a blanket over her shoulders. She pushed the tent flap open slowly and noticed the gray lumps of men sleeping on the ground in the dark. She moved to the edge of the ravine where the Guide camped alone, and she was surprised to find him awake. It was early still, but they all needed their rest. He seemed to read her mind.

"King Avalon, you should be sleeping. We still have a lot of work ahead of us."

"My body is tired but my mind is restless."

"Can I help?" the Guide asked. Avalon had no intention of discussing Taggerty.

"Yes, you can. I am concerned that with this many men, we won't have enough water."

The Guide smiled with approval at the question. He pointed over Avalon's shoulder. "There is a rock outcropping ten minutes away. The hard stone is carved out to form large basins, and it stores water for us when it rains. We will not go thirsty."

Avalon could tell by the Guide's satisfied tone that at some time in the past, the Guides had carved the stone basins themselves. "Very good," she said. Avalon looked up at the curtain of stars, and for the first time she noticed the moon. She was shocked to see a vivid red ball in the sky tonight. The Guide followed her eyes toward the heavens. "What is it?" Avalon asked.

"That is the blood moon," the Guide answered matter of fact.

"I feel like it's an omen," Avalon whispered.

"It is not." He sounded certain of that, but Avalon felt heavy in her chest. She wondered if Taggerty could see the moon tonight.

"What does it mean?" Avalon asked.

"It is what it is," the Guide replied.

"Well, what is it?" she asked again.

"It is the blood moon," he repeated without changing the level tone in his voice. The Guide turned back to stoke his small fire, but Avalon couldn't take her eyes off of the red ball in the sky.

Chapter 14
Keeley Dust

She lit the candle and quietly packed her bag. It was close to dawn Avalon knew, and she wanted to walk down to the rope structures to see exactly what Taggerty had devised to get this many men across the ravine both quickly and without leaving a trail. She tucked Jackie in her pocket and when she stepped through the tent flap, she almost screamed at the black figure standing just outside. She clamped her hand over her mouth and realized that it was Kensington.

"I want to see it too," was all he said before stepping away from the camp. Avalon moved in step next to Kensington. The blood moon was gone, and they used the gray light to make their way up the ravine. Avalon liked Kensington more and more as time went by. He didn't have a suitable family background, but he was diligent, he was loyal, and he was intelligent. Avalon knew of no young men from any of the prominent families who could have handled this trip so heartily, and she was grateful that Zaria had found him.

They came upon the rope structures and stood silently, allowing ten minutes to pass until the sky allowed them enough light to get a good view of the ropes. Taggerty's design was simple, yet the large scale he had been able to implement was amazing. Avalon saw what looked like a wide rope net that was tied off near the tops of two trees so that the net extended down into the ravine without actually touching the side wall. The bottoms of the net were tied off to what looked like the trunks of large trees that were rotting at the bottom of the ravine. Avalon wanted a closer look, but she would have to wait until they climbed down.

"It's amazing," she told Kensington.

"It is," he agreed with a wide smile, and Avalon knew that they were both feeling proud of Taggerty at this moment. The design was perfect. The men could get in and out of the ravine without leaving any marks on the ravine walls and limit the tracking of their path if their enemy came across the window.

"How did he do this?" Avalon asked.

"It looks much like the small nets that the children in the Fingers play on, but on a greater scale," Kensington answered. Avalon nodded, remembering that she had seen something like it at the Festival of Fontanasia when she was young. The children's legs would get tangled in the rope, which was amusing, but for the strong soldiers, it should not be much of an issue.

"Will they climb down with their packs on?" Avalon asked. "It seems like that might be a bit much, even for the heartiest of men."

Kensington walked to the side of the netting and showed Avalon a rope that was tied off. "We can slide the packs down on this and pull them up on the other side," he told her. Avalon nodded. She looked up to where the ropes were tied off on the trees above and let her eyes follow slowly down the ravine.

"You first?" she asked with a smile, and Kensington laughed.

"I will wake the men," he told her. "Will you be needing your tent?"

"No, I'm done." She patted her pocket. "Jackie and I will be here when you are ready," she told him. Kensington handed Avalon a small cloth and a canteen.

"Eat, King Avalon. It's going to be a fun morning," he said as he walked back along the edge of the ravine to where the soldiers camped. Avalon looked at the rope netting from every angle that she could. She chewed on the dry bread and jerky that Kensington had left with her and sipped from the canteen while she leaned on one of the trees that had the rope tied off to it. It was a tall tree with very few branches near the bottom, and she wondered how he had gotten up the tree to tie the ropes off.

"Your Highness," a voice thundered, and Avalon looked along the ravine to see the smaller Davev outrunning Jakon to the netting. They were running all out, both with full packs on their backs, but neither looked exerted in the least. Jakon punched Davev on the shoulder when he finally caught up.

Avalon waited for Jackie to climb from the tree trunk down into her pocket before calling, "Here I am!" The men bowed in unison, already tying their packs to the mule rope.

"King Avalon, may we go down into the ravine ahead of you to make sure that the rope is safe?" Jakon asked. Avalon knew that these men were adventurers and they wanted to go before the other men, so she didn't argue their point.

"As you wish," Avalon said, "but did Kensington tell you of the dangers?"

The men looked at each other with smiles that said they could defeat anything, but they waited for Avalon's instruction.

"There are sand eels at the bottom in the dirt." She drew questioning looks, but again they silently waited for Avalon to explain. "They are large flat snake creatures that you can't see until it's too late. They will paralyze your legs and slowly devour you whole." Avalon paused to make sure the men had heard. "Stay on the rocks the entire way across the bottom of the ravine. Don't rest until you have crossed all the way. There is a rock shelf on the other side where you will be safe."

"We are not afraid of snakes, Your Highness," Jakon offered respectfully.

"You are not afraid of anything, I gather, but do not take my words lightly. The sand eels are both invisible and deadly."

"Yes, King Avalon," they said in unison with a bow.

"Go," Avalon said, and the men lifted their heads and darted to the webbing. They lifted the side rope and both packs started their slow slide to the bottom of the ravine. She thought they would slingshot down at that angle, but the men had to bounce the rope up and down to take away enough friction to make the packs move.

Once the packs were at the bottom, both men reached up and heaved themselves over the side and onto the rope net. The net sagged a little but did not touch the edge of the ravine. Jakon was much taller and he had hoisted his weight up first, but the small and stout Davev was right behind him, and with his tight frame, he was quicker on the descent. They shot verbal jabs at each other the whole way down, and Avalon stood at the top of the ravine leaning over to watch. They were both quick and made it look easy. As Davev reached the bottom first, he hopped off onto the black rock. Jakon jumped off the other side and landed on the same rock, and Avalon cringed when she thought both men would be splayed out into the dust as prey for the sand eels. They were nimble though, and they clasped wrists and wobbled a second before throwing up hearty laughs. When they looked up and saw that Avalon was watching, both men turned and started hopping across the stones to the far side of the ravine.

Avalon sighed heavily, and when she turned away from the ravine she saw that the soldiers were coming up to the obstacle with their packs. They approached as a group and Avalon waited until the last had come up from the back. The Guide smiled at Avalon as he swung his body onto the net and started to descend, his small pack still on his back. Avalon waited until he was halfway down the net and then she addressed Kensington.

"Did Taggerty tell you anything about the ravine?"

"He said that you would address the men," he told her as he put his two packs at the edge of the ravine.

"Men," Avalon called, and they all turned their attention to her. "Once you are at the bottom of the ravine, you will stay on the rocks as you cross the bottom. Do not step on the dirt, it is loose, and there are creatures in it that can harm you." She repeated the description that she had given Jakon and Davev to make sure the men understood.

The men nodded and Kensington pointed to the closest of the men who picked up their packs and put them where Kensington had put his. "Ten at a time, men," Kensington yelled. The rope next to him bounced a little and Avalon realized that Jakon and Davev were half way across the bottom already retrieving their packs.

"Would you like to go now, King Avalon?" Kensington asked.

"I will go last," she told him and he nodded, expecting this answer. She stood next to the rope where the men hooked their packs, and as they worked their bags down by bouncing the rope up and down, Avalon made sure they each heard her warning about staying on the rocks.

Kensington stood closer to the net where he spread the men out into pairs so that there weren't too many in one place at any time. The soldiers swung up onto the net and climbed down more deliberately than Jakon and Davev had. They worked without talking as everyone focused on the task at hand, and soon it was Avalon's turn.

"Your Highness," Kensington said when there were two men left. "These men will stay on this side of the ravine. It is only you and I now." Kensington clasped wrists with the remaining soldiers before they bowed to Avalon. They stood off to the side to let Avalon and Kensington mount the net.

Kensington reached over his head and grabbed the side of the net with his large hands, pulling it down with his weight. Avalon grabbed the rope on her side. It was rough, but her hands were well calloused from sword practice and the rope didn't hurt. She kicked her legs over her head to somersault onto the net and heard a small squeal, realizing that she had forgotten to secure the pocket where Jackie was hiding. As she landed upright, her boots pressed into the rope, and she looked down and clutched a hand over her pocket. She was relieved to feel Jackie inside, and his tiny talons had kept him clung to the fabric.

"Sorry," Avalon whispered. She moved her eyes over her shirt making sure all of the buttons had stayed in place and that the bottom was still tight under her belt. She started to climb down as though she was backing down a ladder. The net didn't rock much, but it took all the arm strength she had to hold her weight upright on the rope. Climbing down was harder than the soldiers had made it look. She was facing down at an angle, with her weight on all four limbs as she went which tasked muscles she didn't have to use very often. She was sweating before she made the bottom. Kensington climbed slowly and Avalon was able to dismount the net safely and move to the next rock before he reached the bottom. Kensington let his weight drop from six feet and landed nimbly on the rock, again surprising Avalon with his agility. He was a sturdy man, but he was spry.

"Do you need to take a moment?" Avalon asked, her limbs already tired but her mind anxious to get to the other side quickly. She felt exposed, and she had her hand in her pocket loosening the strap on the pouch of keeley dust. She remembered the last time she was here and the soft feeling of paralysis as she lost the use of her legs and fell over in the dirt. Avalon was sweating now because of her two layers of pants on the bottom and three layers of shirts on the top, but that extra layer had kept her secret a year ago so she would have to sweat it out today and be grateful instead of annoyed.

"I'm ready," Kensington told her. He looked forward to the edge of the ravine and saw two heads peering over the edge, and then he set his gaze on Avalon. "We will go straight across, and if there are any men still at the bottom, you are to go around them to the net and go up the other side." He put his finger up before she could speak. "Please don't argue with me, King Avalon. I know you want to be strong for the men, but you are their leader and their king, and they will want you safe as much as I do. It's easier on us all if we know you are out of danger. We train for this..." Kensington looked around the bottom of the ravine and chuckled. "Well, not this, but we train to protect our king." Avalon felt a surge of pride and nodded in agreement. She wondered if Kensington had come up with that speech on his own or if it was rehearsed.

Avalon turned and looked across to the far wall before letting her eyes settle on the ground in front of her. She could see the ropes tied off to the bottom of the ravine on tree trunks and marveled that the old wood had held the weight of fifty men rocking the ropes. She set off, finding as many rocks as she could in the loose, crunchy dirt that made up the ground. The boots of the men who had gone in front of her had dusted off the rocks, and the path was easy to make out. Avalon hopped from stone to stone, going faster than she had last time. Brick had been slowing her down then, on purpose she now knew, and she shook off the deceit and set her mind to the task. Avalon tried to keep her eyes out ahead of her, but she felt scared and had to look down every few minutes to make sure there were no sand eels attaching themselves to her legs.

She passed branches and more fallen trees, and she noticed their gray color and wondered if they had petrified to stone over the years. After ten minutes at a good pace, Avalon stopped to look back for Kensington, but he was right on top of her and he yelled, "Go!" so he would not run her over. Avalon turned and took to the path again, realizing in her quick look that Kensington was wearing a large pack on his back. She marveled at his stamina. She ducked over and under branches in places, and the adrenaline carried her across the ravine. She could see the rope net on the opposite wall getting larger as she approached.

Avalon heard a horn blow in the distance startling her. She worried that this was the horn of the Runners, but then Kensington yelled, "Good man!" His voice echoed off the side of the ravine as the men on the top pointed at their king. "You go straight up, King Avalon. Do not wait, just start climbing."

Avalon could see that there were about fifteen men standing on the large rock ledge tying packs off to ropes that had been lowered from the men above. Davev was with them and he didn't turn to face Avalon as she approached. He was pointing to men and calling them out in pairs, presumably who would go up the obstacle after the king. Avalon noticed some of the men looking at the ground in front of them. She could not see where their eyes landed for the branches and debris between them, but it didn't matter. As instructed by Kensington, she didn't hesitate when she reached the net. She planted her feet on the last rock, pulled the bag of keeley dust closed in her pants pocket, and tucked her waist pocket over Jackie.

"Hold on, Jackie," she said with a small pat on the outside of the pocket. Then she heaved her feet over her head and somersaulted onto the net. When she steadied herself, she patted her pocket to make sure Jackie was still safe. She started pulling herself up the net and the rope moved little under her weight so Avalon made steady progress. It was draining on her arms by half way, the angled forward position of the net making Avalon feel like she was trying to walk across the ground on her hands and feet. Her calloused hands were no match for the rope, and she stopped for a moment letting her knees hold her upright as she rubbed her hands on her sleeves. That's when Avalon saw what the soldiers on the rocks had been looking at.

Forty feet below her, two soldiers lay still in the dirt. One of them had his legs covered in sand eels, and the other had his arms and part of his face covered. Avalon's jaw dropped open as she watched the gray eels slowly gain more skin. Before she could think, Avalon was climbing back down the net.

"Your Highness," Kensington called from the bottom. "Once you are at the top these men can join you." Avalon disregarded his wish and made it to the bottom of the net within a minute. She swung down and took to the rocks, her hand in her pocket to remove the keeley dust as soon as she was afoot. "King Avalon, I'm begging you," Kensington whispered from behind her, but Avalon was already on the move. He followed her around the branches to the two fallen soldiers. She stopped five feet away and saw the men lying motionless. Their eyes were content, and Avalon realized that the sand eels had paralyzed their bodies and had numbed their minds with their poison. Her hands were shaking as she pulled the bag from her pocket and reached in, taking a step closer and then tossing the keeley dust on one soldier's face. The sand eels released their suction and began to melt away into the dirt. The sand eels on the second soldier's legs must have sensed danger and they had already begun their slow slither off his pants, but Avalon quickly sprinkled the keeley dust destroying them before they could hide in the sand.

The men didn't move, and Avalon wondered if they were still alive. Kensington was on the rock opposite Avalon, and he crouched down, placing his palm on each man's chest in turn. "They are alive," he told Avalon who looked at the dust that clung to her open hand. She pulled the bag closed and tucked it back in her pants pocket, wiping the rest of the dust away on her pants. Kensington looked at Avalon. "Please, King Avalon, none of us will feel safe until you are out of this hole in the ground. We will take care of these men." Kensington sounded grave and Avalon nodded.

"Pull them to the rock shelf and see if they come to," she said and then turned away from Kensington. As she climbed the net, she watched Kensington and Davev pull the two soldiers to the safety of the rocks. They lay motionless, and Avalon remembered her time on that rock while her legs had slowly regained feeling. She saw two more soldiers don small packs and jump from the stone ledge, and she knew they were coming to the safety of the rope net. She looked up and saw that she was almost out.

Avalon climbed above the top of the ravine, lay down on the net, and then somersaulted forward and hung for a moment before dropping to the ground. The men were near her in case she needed help, and they greeted her with a bow, but Avalon stepped back from the edge and took a moment to herself. The two soldiers lying helpless were her responsibility, but there was nothing more that she could do for them.

The men on top of the ravine were focused on pulling the packs up without touching the side of the ravine, and they had devised a way by using a massive branch broken off and shaped like a fork. Some men sat on the branch and other men heaved the rope through the fork in the branch that hung out over the side of the ravine and pulled the packs up. When the two packs were at the top, Jakon lay down and leaned out over the ravine, untied the packs and handed them over to the men behind him. He threw the rope back over the edge and yelled, "Send Woodpecker up first."

Glad that the men's attention was absorbed elsewhere, Avalon sat down on a fallen tree and pulled her small canteen from her belt. She took a sip and placed a teaspoon of water in her palm. When she was sure the men were too busy to notice, Avalon put her palm by her pocket and made a clicking noise with her tongue, prompting Jackie to scramble out and lick from the small pool. When he'd had his fill he retreated to the safety of Avalon's pocket.

Woodpecker was the man with the sand eels on his face. Jakon pulled him over the edge and placed him gently on the ground and left him there, all the men returning their attention to pulling the other injured man up. When all of the men were safely out of the ravine and Kensington had made it up the net, they all gathered around their two fallen comrades.

"Lay them in the shade on some blankets," Kensington said, pointing at two soldiers. "You two will stay here and tend to the men and guard this side of the ravine. Our Guide will tell you where you can find water. You can safely hunt these woods, just stay out of the ravine." The two men nodded and accepted one pack, the rest of the men taking a well-deserved break. They had moved the two injured men to the edge of the trees and made them comfortable in quick time. It was then that Kensington approached and bowed to Avalon.

"King Avalon," he said in a soft but stern tone so that none of the other men could hear. It was then that Avalon noticed that all of the men had gathered far away from her in small circles, and they were whispering amongst themselves. "Please, do as I ask, sire. You know where we are going and why, and these men do not. If you are lost, we are all lost." Avalon was about to argue that the Guide was the only one who knew the way to the window when she realized that Kensington was talking on a deeper level. "You could have been injured down there."

"Your men would have died," she protested. "My men."

"And they knew what they were getting into when they joined the King's Guard. It would be any of these men's honor to die for their king," he whispered, and Avalon thought of Walthan's sacrifice. He had died for her, but she could not believe that had been his intention.

"Look at them, Your Highness. You told them that they were heading into a wood that was not haunted, and yet you have shown them witchcraft with your powder."

"It's not my powder. I got it from the Guides a year ago."

"That doesn't matter. They have never seen anything like it. Those sand eels, I have to say, I thought Taggerty was pulling my leg when he told me about them." Kensington shook his head with a grim look on his face. "I never imagined..." He turned and walked away, leaving Avalon to consider his words. Was the keeley dust magical? It could have been salt that she had poured on the sand eels as one would pour on a slug causing it to shrivel up. Then Avalon felt Jackie moving in her pocket and she remembered how Kensington had shied away from the tiny lizard. These men, these brute soldiers might react the same if they saw Jackie because he was an anomaly.

"What is this?" Kensington called from the edge of the ravine. Avalon stood and tried to see what Kensington was upset about. She saw a deep five-foot gash cut in the side of the ravine. Davev walked to where Kensington stood and Avalon strained to hear.

"That was me, sir. When I saw the men fall in the ravine, I did not think, I reacted. The rope took my weight, but the rock here is like sand, and my quick descent ripped away at the ground."

"We went over this time and again," Kensington berated Davev. "The whole reasoning for the nets is so that we don't touch the side of the ravine and leave a track back to Fontanasia."

"Yes, sir," Davev said reddening. "I have no excuse, sir."

"Get the men ready," Kensington told him as he crouched down and ran his hand along the edge of the deep gouge. More stones fell away and he jerked his hand back. There was nothing to be done.

The Guide had been sitting just inside the trees, and he approached Avalon, his long black ponytail moving in the wind. "Do not be concerned about the keeley dust, King Avalon. These men will see the elbagrass glow blue in two days time. As they walk today, it will be good for them to decide if they will allow their minds to believe their eyes." He smiled at her, turning and taking his wisdom into the trees, and Avalon followed.

Hawker had led the Monarch and his soldiers through the tightly packed trees, waiting every twenty feet as they sawed down the shallow trunks at ground level so that the wagons could follow. He knew it was a foolish plan, but he didn't tell the Monarch that. He had two more nights before the full moon in Fontanasia, and the longer they took to reach the field, the less he would have to talk to the Monarch.

The massive soldiers sawed and snapped the trees, but the thicker the woods got, the harder it was for them to clear a path. The tall, skinny trunks had nowhere to fall. The men in the wagons were told to stand down, as it would take much more time than anticipated to get through. Hawker tried not to laugh at the Monarch's impatience and frustration as he growled at the men to quicken their pace, but they were going nowhere fast. Even once the trees were all cut, Hawker could see that the horses would have a hard time navigating the stubs of tree trunks left in the ground. The White Robes watched the slow progress in silence, and each impediment warmed Hawker's heart knowing that he would be able to manipulate the situation when the time was right.

It took the soldiers a full day to cut a path through to the elbagrass that was wide enough for the wagons. The grass was tall, but Hawker could see over the tops. He knew that the field would be blue on the other side for the next three nights. It would change as soon as the sun set, and he couldn't help but wonder if any of the Guides would come across to try to find him, but he doubted it. Hawker had realized that Avalon was completely ignorant of his own plan. If his nephew had figured it out, he would have brought an army to the window.

The sun was setting and Hawker told the Monarch that there was a short journey left. The Monarch could not see the city of Fontanasia that he had been promised, but there was nothing to do but trust his captive. Hawker suggested that the Monarch bring all of the men through the tree trunks tomorrow and stage them there for the attack. The Monarch agreed, and they all trekked back to the camp outside the tree line for the night. Hawker smiled as the lunky soldiers stumbled over the tree trunks, and he wondered if the Monarch would actually be so stupid as to try to bring the horses through.

Hawker slept on the ground and shivered in the measly blanket he'd been given. He was filthy and smelled rotten, but he didn't mind because it kept anyone interested in him from coming too close. He truly hated people, and he liked to have his space to observe everyone around him.

He could see here as in the castle that each White Robe was a leader in his own right, keeping his own guards near at all times. He could see that these smaller but smarter men had carved a semblance of society out for themselves. They were the weaker men, but they were also the leaders, organized enough to know how things should be done. In return, they commanded the larger, beast-men who protected the White Robes instead of snapping them in half like twigs. It was a well-balanced dance for survival.

Hawker woke with the sun as the makeshift camp came alive. He was pleasantly surprised when a plate of hot meat was delivered to him by one of the smaller servants. Hawker wanted to show restraint but he was starving, and he swallowed the meat down like a starving animal as he watched the servant return to one of the covered wagons. A White Robe leaned his head out the back of the wagon and looked at Hawker, offering one nod of acknowledgement. The glee that Hawker felt between the hot juices running into his stomach and the knowledge that he had taken the interest of one of the white robes so soon was exhilarating. Hawker barely noticed the cold as he ran his plan over in his mind.

The soldiers were assembled and the wagons hitched up but nothing went as planned. The Monarch was crazed with anger as he watched several horses go down only forty feet into the tree road, their ankles twisted and snapped on the tightly packed stumps. "Stop!" he yelled, calling the carriages to stop in their tracks. Hawker was amused to watch as the tattooed soldiers unhitch the horses and turned them back toward solid ground, more soldiers taking up the hitch where the horses should have been and pulling the carriages through. The White Robes would not walk to the field, and it was infuriating for the Monarch to watch and wait as their pampered egos were led through to safety.

After a day of work the carriages were lined up end to end in a crescent along the elbagrass to make room for the army of men that was finally pressing through the trees and over the stumps. There was little time before dark, and the Monarch's men erected his tent and built a makeshift platform with ladder out of the tree trunks they had cut down. It wasn't very sturdy, there was only room for one or two on top, but it gave the Monarch a vantage point to command his men from the top.

Hawker had been waiting for this moment. He had noticed some men wandering into the elbagrass to relieve themselves, and they had not returned. However, there were hundreds of soldiers, all brutes, and none seemed to be friendly with any other, so no one was missed. The Monarch had Hawker brought to his open-sided tent at dusk. There were torches placed in the ground lighting the area, and the Monarch stood in front of a patch of fresh dirt. He had marked their position with a black rock and handed Hawker a stick that had been simply snapped from a tree. Hawker looked at the long stick and held his smile. He couldn't believe that the Monarch was so plain. He was the leader. He should have commanded something more exotic, or he should have used the sheath from a sword at least. Perhaps he didn't want Hawker getting any ideas.

"We are here," the Monarch said, pointing to the rock at the edge of the dirt.

"Yes, I see," Hawker said, drawing a large circle next to the rock. "This is the field of grass there." Hawker pointed toward the field. He drew a very small rectangle in the center. "In the middle of this field is a pond of sorts. Tell your men to look at their reflection in the pond. Tell them to look into their own eyes, and then they will be in Fontanasia." Hawker smiled as he looked up too late. The Monarch was already swinging, and he punched Hawker full in the face. Hawker stumbled and fell over hard, drawing the attention of the White Robes who were starting to climb down from their wagons.

Hawker slowly pushed himself up onto his knees and felt his lip. His hand drew away blood, and he rose slowly trying to lick the blood clean. He staggered back to the

Monarch and held up his hands knowing that the Monarch would strike him again.

"You have trusted me this far. You need to attack tonight, right now. This is the way to Fontanasia." Hawker prepared to turn his body when the Monarch struck so the next blow wouldn't hurt as much, but the punch never came. He could see the anger and frustration on the Monarch's face, but the White Robes had gathered around the open tent and they watched intently. Hawker hadn't realized just how much persuasion that the White Robes held, but he should have guessed. No council members should be near a battle, and yet here they were out near the front line. Hawker felt the light sensation of assuredness that his plan would come to fruition.

"You say that we look into the water and once we see the reflection of our own eyes, we will be in Fontanasia, and you expect me to just accept this?" The Monarch's contemptuous tone had softened as his mind tried to work out the truth of this statement.

Hawker nodded. " Brick told you about this, did he not? After you talked to Prince Avalon and Walthan the warrior, how did they escape? Where could they have possibly gone? Did you even search for them?" Hawker was pushing his luck with the Monarch, but the White Robes were intrigued. The Monarch was clearly insulted, but he wanted to cut this conversation short instead of admitting that he had searched for months for the escaped prisoners to no end.

"We will move out now. Prepare!" The Monarch yelled, and hundreds of soldiers yelled back in a war cry. They assembled as quickly as they could in the area away from the wagons. The Monarch climbed the ladder to his small platform and tried to look out over the field of grass and see this pond, but it was dark and he could see little. He was forced to trust this Prince Hawker who had come from nowhere to turn over his own kingdom to the Runners. The

Monarch wouldn't have believed this was possible if he didn't rule over thugs in his own kingdom. He could see that Hawker was jealous that his nephew was the king, and he would stop at nothing to gain Fontanasia for himself. With a twisted smile, the Monarch pulled his sword over his head and let out a deafening echo of battle cry that was repeated by his men on the ground.

"You will form two columns," he yelled to them. "You will find the pond in the center of this field, and you will look into your reflection." Hawker was impressed that the Runners took the Monarch at his word. They watched him, heeded his words, and not one showed any sign of disbelief or disobedience. "Once you have seen your eyes in your reflection, be ready for battle. You will kill the enemy and then we will regroup to take their army." He paused and moved his head so his men could see him looking over them, and that seemed to Hawker to make them stand even taller. "Victory!" he yelled, and the men lined up in two columns four across. The soldiers with the most tattoos gathered their troops in packs of twenty, and Hawker could see a rag tag army take shape.

The first men marched into the elbagrass and less than ten steps in they began to stagger. They tripped and fell, slowing down the men behind them. They were dying quickly by the poison of the elbagrass, and the men behind them started to push back. It was too late for them as well, and they dropped where they stood. The next line of men began to understand and tried to turn and run, but even in the cold these men had a lot of exposed skin, and the poison ran through their large bodies in due time. The men at the edge of the grass frantically pushed back at the men who were looking up at their Monarch and trying to advance to their glory, but there was none to be had.

"Stop!" The Monarch yelled from his perch. "Move back!" he commanded, and all of the men who had been trying to press forward fell back, allowing the last few men who had touched the field of tall elbagrass to fall clear and crawl out to meet their death.

The Monarch descended the ladder in three giant steps and walked straight into Hawker who was waiting for his punishment. He did not cower though in front of the white robes. He was gaining footing, and he had information that the Monarch needed.

"There is witchcraft here," the Monarch growled.

"There is no witchcraft," Hawker said, every inch of him carrying his upbringing of royalty. He would make his stand here and now, and he would either die or rule Cormicks.

"Then you can lead my men to this pond," the Monarch said with a smile, his temper subsiding to the watchful eyes of the White Robes. Hawker had his head held high, his long, black hair falling all around his shoulders. He turned his head and took a moment to look at the counselors. He wanted them to weigh in. That would lessen the Monarch's influence and infuriate him, causing him to make mistakes.

One of the White Robes who had a small triangle tattooed on his forehead stepped forward and did the equivalent of siding with Hawker when he said, "But you are here. That is proof that there is a way across."

Hawker smiled at the triangle tattoo and they silently came to an understanding, but Hawker didn't want to offer too much. He feigned deference to the Monarch. "I am fully robed, and the grass could not poison me. Perhaps you should robe your soldiers." This was ironic because the soldiers wore leather pants and only the straps that held their weapons for shirts.

The Monarch looked at the White Robes and bellowed in Hawker's face, "I need no help from you!" He stepped from under the tent and called for a man in a gray robe who looked like a small servant. Hawker was intrigued when he heard the Monarch order, "She will call for the Anthracites. She will have them come here and lay in this field of grass from the edge to the pond within. We will use them as a bridge." Hawker looked around for the face of a woman so he would know who the lady was who could command the Anthracites. He watched as the man in the gray robe bowed and ran off toward the opening in the trees that led back toward Cormicks. The Monarch turned to his men with a cunning smile. "Rest men. You will know when we are ready to begin again!"

Chapter 15
Rock Bridge

*A*valon could tell that they were close because she saw the Guide looking to his left every ten steps. It wasn't close to dark yet, so she wasn't sure how the Guide would find the bright blue light that signified they had arrived. He stopped and she walked toward him, Kensington putting his hand up so all of the men would stop where they were. The Guide knelt and touched the ground, turning leaves over in his hand. He picked up a stick and sniffed it, and then he stood. He looked at Kensington who approached and waited for the Guide to speak.

"We are not the first ones here," he whispered. Avalon missed his meaning. Taggerty had been through at least a week earlier, and there had been Guides watching the window for months.

"What is it?" Kensington asked.

"Ready your soldiers. I don't know what we are going to be walking into."

Avalon felt the dread and weight of Fontanasia press upon her at that moment. If the Runners were here, they were done for. She had pulled fifty good men from the protection of her city. She felt like a fool. Avalon knelt down and saw a print in the ground where the Guide had been standing, but she had no idea what it meant. She stood and looked as deep into the forest as she could, but in this spot the trees had grown closer together and it was difficult to see very far. She turned back and saw the Guide and Kensington moving among the men, dividing them into small parties of four men each, and sending them into the wood in different areas. They spoke quietly, but Avalon could tell by their hand gestures that they were having the men move away into the woods to surround the elbagrass. She tucked a leaf in her pocket for Jackie and pulled the knife from her belt with her left hand, keeping her right hand open for her sword in case the time came to pull it on the enemy.

"You are with me," the Guide said as he walked by Avalon with Kensington falling in behind her. They walked slowly, stepping around each stick and branch on the ground. In seconds her men had melted into the woods, and it was just the three of them now. There was only the sound of distant birds chirping and playing in the leaf cover above their heads, and Avalon tried to hold her breath to conceal the sound of her heartbeat. She felt that her exhales were loud, but she knew that she was the only one who could hear her breathing.

Kensington stepped out next to her as they crept behind the Guide, his sword already drawn. The walk that had once taken her less than ten minutes now took twenty, and Avalon's muscles strained at the slow going. She wanted to rush in, but that would be foolish, so she allowed the slow torture of time to move ahead. They stopped when the clearing was in front of them, and Avalon did not recognize the place in the daytime with the elbagrass looking like plain, tall green reeds. She had a moment of panic realizing that she had not told her men that the tall grass was poisonous, and just when she was going to speak up, the Guide looked at her and shook his head. It was as though he had read her mind, and that startled her.

There was open space between where the trees ended and the grass started, and there were no men visible at all. They watched and listened as the wind blew through the grass. They saw one of the Guides then coming around the outside of the elbagrass. He was looking in their direction, and her Guide stood up, so Avalon and Kensington stood too. The Guide looking at them smiled mischievously and then Jackie started moving around in Avalon's pocket.

"Hold," they heard from behind, and Avalon almost jumped out of her skin. They turned slowly to see Taggerty standing behind them, sword in hand with Chylyn next to him. Avalon was relieved that they were safe, but she was immediately angered by the sly smile on Taggerty's face. "Bring the others!" he called out to the Guide who was in the clearing. "They are our men."

Taggerty sheathed his sword and bowed to Avalon before being embraced by Kensington. "You sly devil. You scared the wits out of me!" Kensington patted Taggerty so hard on the back that he almost lost his breath. Chylyn rolled his eyes and stepped into the clearing, following the other Guide. Avalon followed him and soon saw three of the parties of her men being brought forward, their hands bound with rope. They were gladly cut free but stood still, waiting to see where the rest of the men were.

Taggerty stepped into the clearing and approached Avalon. Bowing his head, he said softly, "Your Highness, do I have your leave to command the men?"

Avalon gulped back her breath, remembering at that moment that Taggerty knew that she was a girl. "You have my permission, but you should speak with Kensington. They are his men now."

Taggerty smiled and turned swiftly. He patted Kensington on the back. "Where are the rest of your men?" he asked cheerfully.

"We shall retrieve them together," Kensington said, and they walked away ready to make a full circle around the large field to ferret out the other soldiers. "Come out, we are clear!" Avalon heard Kensington yell. Men began to straggle back along the edge of the trees, keeping noticeably away from the edge of the grass.

While Avalon waited, she watched the two Guides intently. They were discussing something serious near the edge of the grass, motioning several times back to the woods and then into the field. She approached them, and to her relief they did not stop talking.

"He was here. We were looking to make sure no one came through the window. We were looking the wrong way."

"Who was here?" Avalon interrupted.

Chylyn cleared his throat. "King Avalon, one of our men was killed one moon ago. We found him the morning after the grass was blue. He had been stabbed in the back by a branch that had been sharpened to a point." Chills ran up Avalon's spine, and a premonition that blackened her heart set upon her. Even without the presence of a dream to tell her, she knew what he would say next. "The track I saw in the wood, it was Prince Hawker's track."

"You cannot know that!" Avalon told him.

"And yet it is his track," Chylyn said simply. "I did not know for certain at the time, but Taggerty confirmed it when he arrived. Prince Hawker has passed through the window."

Avalon felt sick to her stomach and she needed to sit down. "We should move away from the grass while the field is poisonous," she said, turning to walk away. Avalon moved a few steps into the woods and took a seat, glad to be off her wobbly legs. It was Hawker, back from banishment, back from the dead. It was her uncle and her father's killer, and Avalon wished again that she had killed him when she had the chance.

Kensington and Taggerty returned with a lively group of soldiers that they had pulled from the woods. She watched as Taggerty took a moment to greet each of them, and she was impressed by his easy rapport. He knew them not only by name but also asked about wives and siblings and parents. Avalon never had the chance to meet and get close to that many people, but she had also spent the better part of eight years wedging a gap between her and even relatives who had the right to know her. Taggerty had been talking to the men, but his eyes had been scanning the area, and when he saw Avalon sitting in the wood alone, he elbowed Kensington who immediately rallied the men on task. She had let Jackie out of her pocket to inspect the ground and didn't notice as Jakon approaching a short time later.

"Your Highness, your tent is ready," he said with a bow. Avalon was surprised because she didn't see the white material obvious in the clearing.

"Show me," she said, and when Jakon turned to lead the way, she snatched Jackie up in her hand. He walked her around the clearing and back into the woods where her tent was set up and ready. She walked past Jakon and through the flap and came face to face with Taggerty.

He bowed deeply and said, "King Avalon, I am glad that you traveled safely." Then he stood and his salty green eyes stopped her heart. He held his hand out and she took a seat at the small table. Jackie had been squirming in her hands since he had heard Taggerty's voice, and she reached her hand out to show him the lizard. Taggerty smiled wide and stepped to the table. He touched the back of Avalon's fingers and Jackie hurried up his arm. He was slow to remove his fingers from hers, and Avalon felt a surge of energy as he rubbed past her fingertips.

Avalon had a lot of questions for Taggerty, but they were personal questions and she was here on the business of Fontanasia, and all other matters would have to wait. He had been onto her secret for a full year and he had told no one, and that alone would answer her main question. He had followed her, as a girl, just as Walthan had. Without question, without recourse, he was loyal to her.

"Hawker came through," she said, and Taggerty's expression darkened. He took Jackie from his shoulder and put him on the table. "It was a month ago, before I arrived. He killed one man and we believe that he made it through the window, but we didn't see him or anyone else two weeks ago when they would have been able to come back through from Cormicks." Taggerty bit his lip, and for all of his bravado, Avalon had never seen him truly nervous.

"This is not your fault," she told Taggerty. "I shoulder the blame for not ending this matter when I had the chance."

"You could not have known..."

"I should have guessed," she interrupted. "He sat in the dungeon for months all the time plotting. You don't know who he was, Taggerty."

They were quiet for a full minute, looking at each other and then looking away. Avalon picked at her fingers. There were hours of conversation that she wanted to have with Taggerty, but in the woods with fifty men near was not the place to start.

"I fear my Uncle Hawker is near unstoppable." Avalon felt defeated and she leaned forward and put her hands over her face. Months of repair were starting to come unraveled, and Avalon wanted to give up her secret and go back home and curl up in a ball forever. She sighed but didn't cry, and she heard Taggerty take a step closer. They remained silent for minutes, the sound of their breathing the only noise in the tent. Avalon clenched her teeth and tried to find the courage to move. She and no one else was the king. She had been bred for this moment. And besides, she didn't know what would happen if she couldn't move forward, but she was certain that Zaria and everyone in Fontanasia would pay for her weakness if she didn't.

Avalon stood up quickly and dropped her hands, and she was startled to see Taggerty a foot from where she was standing. He didn't move away though, just stood still and looked down into Avalon's eyes. She felt a pang in her heart. She tried not to go there, but she couldn't help but wonder if there was a future for her and Taggerty. She felt her cheeks turning pink, but she didn't look away.

"I liked the preparations you made for this journey. The rope nets for the men to climb on, that was a good idea. It must have been difficult to carry all that rope." They were standing so close, and Avalon's voice was near a whisper.

"It was," Taggerty said, rubbing his shoulder involuntarily. "It isn't perfect, we will still leave some tracks, but not as many as we would have climbing up and down the walls. It will be harder for the enemy to follow if they ever come."

"If Hawker is through the window, they will come someday," Avalon said, knowing it was true. She hoped that the Anthracites killed him before he ever had the chance to get to the castle and talk to the Monarch. Her skin crawled thinking of the Monarch and the white robed men. They were sniveling leaders with their faithful dog-man servants who would kill on command. Avalon shuddered.

"The Guides have prepared your watch towers and we are trying to make plans for other defenses. Would you like to see them before it is dark?" Taggerty hesitated a moment and then he took a step back from Avalon and held his arm out toward the exit. "Your Highness," he said with a smile that made Avalon want to crumble into bits. She cleared her throat and told Jackie to stay in the tent and then led Taggerty out. When they were outside the tent, she had to stop and wait for him to show her where the watchtowers were. It reminded Avalon of Taggerty showing her the way through the Fingers to the castle. The thought of that day had irritated her for most of a year, but now she looked back with fondness.

Her tent was set back from the elbagrass, and they stepped through the trees toward the clearing. Taggerty stopped near the edge and looked up, Avalon's eyes following his through the thick leaves. She stared, and after a while she could see a wood flat up in the branches.

"Come out here and I can show you a little better," Taggerty told her. When they walked into the clearing, Taggerty pointed off in the distance to a large tree along the edge. Avalon could see that the top branches of the tree facing the field had been cut away and there were men looking over the field. "They are standing on a platform and they can see far into the field," he told her. "We have six of these so far. You can't see the pond from there, but close I think." Avalon wanted to climb to the closest platform to see for herself, but that would have to wait.

Kensington joined them under the tree. "What now?" she asked her two most trusted advisors.

"We have two weeks until the window opens on the Cormicks side," Kensington said. "We will rest tonight. The men are about to get their first look at the elbagrass under a full moon and it will be quite an experience for them." Avalon remembered seeing the bright blue ocean of tall grass swaying lazily under a soft breeze. It was mesmerizing, and she was sure the men would have a lot to talk about tonight.

"It is dusk. Should I say something to the men to prepare them?" Avalon asked.

"That might be a good idea if you didn't tell any of them what to expect before leaving Fontanasia," Taggerty said.

"I'm not so sure," Kensington disagreed. He looked around to make sure no one was close enough to hear. "They serve you, King Avalon, but this is a small group and we will be together for at least a month. I don't want them getting too comfortable around their king or they might forget their duty."

"Maybe," Taggerty said, not convinced.

Kensington took a half step closer. "King Avalon, you told the men that the wood was not haunted, and they would have followed you in even if it was. Then they saw the sand eels that you melted with the magic dust you possess." Kensington and Taggerty exchanged a meaningful look. "And if I am to believe Taggerty, they are now about to see a poisonous field of grass glow blue in the moonlight."

"Don't forget the alleya leaf that will grow full in one night, and in the dark," Taggerty added. "Where are you going with this?"

"I will assign the men their posts and then advise them on what they are going to see. King Avalon will quietly inspect the posts tonight. You have seen this before. We have not. This is all new to us, but your family has been keeping this secret for over two hundred years. You are our leader. The king should not explain anything to anyone." Kensington looked at Avalon expectantly, and she could see that he was right, but she agreed to his advice mostly because she didn't relish making a speech in front of the men again. She had been standing on a pulpit in front of people her whole life, but not at such close quarters.

Avalon could appreciate Kensington's plan for another reason. He was right to separate her from the men, and using the mysticism this trip had brought might make Avalon seem older and more knowledgeable than she was. She was the youngest king of Fontanasia and this was a chance for her to look more seasoned. She thought of Julius Creighton wearing robes and walking slowly like an old man to make others think he was old and wise. Avalon could use quiet reserve to set her apart in the same way.

"I will return to my tent for dinner and I won't emerge until after dark."

"Very good," Kensington said with a short bow.

"I will escort you, King Avalon," Taggerty said. In a moment of dark uncertainty for her people, Avalon felt the warmth of joy in her heart.

Taggerty and Kensington joined Avalon for a small bite to eat that evening. There were only two chairs so Taggerty sat on the cot and played with Jackie, flicking small nuts at the lizard and watching him scramble to block them from falling off the cot before eating them. After some time Jackie was full and he curled up on Taggerty's knee.

"I don't know how you can enjoy that animal," Kensington said to Taggerty.

"Do you mean to offend the king?" Taggerty jibed.

"I do not," Kensington said. "King Avalon has asked me to speak freely as his brother, and I am glad to oblige."

Avalon smiled at Kensington. "Are you still suspicious of Jackie because he is the only red lizard you have ever seen?"

"No, sire. It's just that it's like playing with an insect."

Taggerty laughed. "The leader of the King's Guard is afraid of insects? Avalon, you must rethink your choice." They all shared a laugh before a voice outside the tent called for Kensington.

"Please excuse me," Kensington said as he stood and bowed before leaving. Once the tent flap closed, Avalon was all too aware that she was alone with Taggerty. They sat in silence, and she wondered if he was waiting for her to speak first, but Taggerty had never been that formal with her when they were alone and she knew if he wanted to speak, he would. This was his opportunity to question her, but he did not. Avalon wanted to ask him so many things, but she had no idea where to start, and she realized that the thin walls of this tent might not keep her secret. Perhaps Taggerty had noticed the same thing.

He stood and Avalon jumped a little in her chair. She was not nervous when they were all together, but alone she felt anxious. She didn't know what to say. She only allowed herself to sit and look at the table, her senses straining to figure out what he was doing without looking directly at him. She heard his footsteps short and shuffling behind her, but he didn't come around to the front of the table. Avalon wondered if he was dancing and she finally turned her head. She was surprised to see Taggerty's wrist guards and coat on her cot and his sleeves rolled up. He was sliding his hands over his chest.

"What are you doing?" She asked trying not to laugh at his spasms.

"It's Jackie. He's inside my shirt!" Avalon stood and squinted in the dimming light, noticing a small bulge moving back and forth. She laughed and made a clicking sound with her tongue and then Jackie reappeared on Taggerty's bare arm, drawing Avalon's attention to Taggerty's round tattoo. Taggerty reached his arm out to Avalon and she scooped Jackie up and tucked him into her pocket. Avalon's eyes never left Taggerty's tattoo though, and so he did not drop his arm and the black ink on his wrist hung between them. She had seen it once before.

"I forgot," Avalon said.

"That is sad," Taggerty replied. "I have shared my history with one person and they have forgotten." Avalon felt her cheeks burn instantly and she kept her eyes on the tattoo. She had not forgotten that Taggerty had the mark of the Guides. She had remembered their conversation time and again. She would never forget that he had been prophesied by the Guides to be the future of the King and that he had worked his whole life to be a part of the King's Guard.

"I can forgive a king instantly though. You have much larger matters to concern your mind." Avalon froze in place. She wanted to laugh because she knew how much time she had concerned herself with Taggerty.

"I should be ashamed of myself if I could not remember such a respected thing about one of my closest friends."

"Then we are friends," Taggerty said, regret obvious in his tone.

Avalon gulped down the nerves that had frozen in her throat. "Did it hurt?" was all she could say, returning her attention to his tattoo.

Taggerty didn't reply. Instead, he reached down to Avalon's side and pulled her hand up to his arm, placing her palm on the back of his wrist. Avalon's heart was pounding and she chanced looking up into Taggerty's eyes. He was smiling, standing tall and confident. She moved her fingers over the black circle pattern and felt the low bumps in his skin. It was much deeper than a tattoo on the surface but more of a scar coloring his skin. Avalon wondered if he had been branded and then tattooed, but she did not want to break the magic of the moment with words. She heard Taggerty breathe in deeply as her fingers touched every bit of the marking. The candlelight was not enough for her to get a good look at the pattern, and she longed to ask him a million questions, but it would have to wait.

Avalon heard some men outside the tent and she instinctively pushed Taggerty's arm away, sorry that the moment was lost. Taggerty pulled his sleeves down and donned his coat, his ever-present metal wrist guards taking their place to cover his tattoo. "It's dark," he said with a tight smile. "The men should be getting their first look at the elbagrass. Should we go see how they are taking the change?" She nodded and led him from the tent. They needed to spend some time alone getting to know each other, but Avalon found the silent understanding between them acceptable for now.

The pounding that Hawker felt underneath his feet shook the trees, and his heart sped up in response to the fear that was building. He was excited beyond belief as he heard the bone-scraping sound of rock upon rock approaching. It was the Anthracites, he knew. He wished that it were earlier in the evening so he could better see the giant black figures as they crushed their way through the trees and stopped at the edge of the elbagrass. Hawker was in awe as their black masses blotted out the stars in the sky. It was as though death had approached and taken everyone's breath away. The only movement was the soldiers trying to move out of the way between the trees and elbagrass, and they pushed at each other in panic. Servants of the Monarch scrambled about and put out the small cooking fires they had built. Hawker was frozen in awe as the huge leg-like figures passed by in one massive stride.

"That's right," the Monarch said evenly. "Lay yourselves down so that we may pass over you." He was talking in an even tone as though he was trying to lull small children into taking a nap. Hawker watched as the black figures moved into the elbagrass, and in eight steps the first fell over with a thundering crash. The second moved into the field and there was a groaning crunch as he fell, leaving the third Anthracite to fall forward at the edge of the grass. There was a thundering roar followed by a gust of wind and dust that blew everyone back several steps. Hawker felt tears in his eyes but it wasn't from the dust. The sheer size and unimaginable destructive ability of the Anthracites that he had read about had not prepared him to experience them in the flesh, and he was awe struck.

"Go!" the Monarch yelled, waking everyone from their stupor and whipping the soldiers into action. Hawker watched as the soldiers climbed up the rocks that made up the Anthracites. He wanted to move closer to touch the giants, but he couldn't leave the Monarch and the White Robes. Hawker hadn't anticipated this move by the Monarch, and he knew that his prey was smarter than he had given him credit for. He guessed that the Monarch would be taking him over the Anthracites and back to Fontanasia, and he would get a better look at the rock giants at that time.

Long minutes passed as the soldiers climbed up and over and then ran out of sight. If they were afraid of the Anthracites, they didn't show it. They were ready to taste the blood of their enemy, and their minds were focused on the brutality of battle that they anticipated. The Monarch called down for Hawker to join him on the platform, and Hawker doubted that they would both fit on top, but he wanted to see as much as he could, so he climbed up slowly. The platform was surprisingly steady and when he reached the top, he was able to keep one foot on the top step and put one foot on the platform. He was very tall, and even at this disadvantage, his height was equal to that of the Monarch. Hawker made sure to keep hold of both railings knowing the Monarch might push him off on a whim. That is what Hawker would have done.

Hawker squinted in the darkness, and he was able to start to discern between the different shades of gray and black. The Anthracites were the pure black road lying across the field, with the gray figures of men walking across. Hawker thought he could see in the distance men jumping off into nowhere.

"Where did my men go?" the Monarch's face showed amazement.

"I told you, they are in Fontanasia now. You can't see it, but believe me, it is there." More men dropped from the side of the Anthracites and were gone. The Monarch turned and looked into Hawker's eyes, and the lanky prince simply smiled back.

Chapter 16
Inferno

Taggerty led Avalon and Kensington slowly around the field in the space between the grass and the tree line. Avalon had thought of the elbagrass almost every day since she had first seen it, but her memory did not do it justice. The breeze swayed through the field, and the tall reeds of grass reached over her head and shined bright blue in the white moonlight.

She looked at Kensington and could tell that he was trying to hide his astonishment at the change. Just as he had said before, it was magic that she had led him to. As they passed by pairs of soldiers, Avalon saw the look of sheer amazement in their eyes before they bowed and Avalon nodded back. She could make out some soldiers on the platforms above and longed to climb up and take a look over the field. Taggerty stopped to talk to Chylyn, and trying not to focus outright on Taggerty, Avalon struck up a conversation with Kensington. "How many men do we have here?" she asked.

"Not including you and I, there are forty-three soldiers and eight of the Guides. We will get a better look at the area we are to guard tomorrow, and we can assign men on a rotation from there."

"So there was one thing you and Taggerty didn't figure out in advance," Avalon said as a joke, but Kensington didn't see her smile and he took her word seriously.

"Yes, Your Highness. I beg your pardon. We wanted to see the area and devise a plan upon arriving. I'm sure Taggerty has already put a plan together if you would like to implement it right away."

"No, Kensington. I was joking. Let the soldiers take in the view. We will have time to ready ourselves before the window opens on the other side in two weeks."

"Right," Kensington said as he let out a sigh. Avalon was surprised at his formality with her, but with the men's eyes on him as he walked with the king, he must have felt a large amount of responsibility.

"Wait!" Avalon heard Chylyn say to Taggerty as he held his hand up and turned his head toward the elbagrass. Everyone else's head followed and they all stared at the blue reeds moving in the wind. "They are here," the Guide said. "Ready the men!" He turned and ran to the nearest tree that held a platform and climbed hand and foot up the side of the tree until he found the lowest branch. From there he was gone.

Avalon felt terrified as she recalled their reconnaissance in Cormicks and how Chylyn had known that the enemy was near when no one else had. She could dream the future. Perhaps the Guides could know the next two minutes when they were upon them. "Do they have some sort of secret power?" Avalon asked Taggerty.

"No, but they have spent their lives honing their senses. If he says we have trouble, then trouble is upon us. King Avalon, we need to get you to safety."

Avalon could already hear the wisp of arrows overhead as her men started to fire from the tree platforms into the elbagrass. She wished she could see what they saw, and she wanted to climb up the tree. It was as though Kensington had read her mind, and he grabbed her arm. "King Avalon, I will report to you what I see. We can better coordinate our defenses if you are on the ground to command the men." He didn't wait for an answer, taking a rope and using it around the bottom trunk of the tree and walking it up with his arms as his feet took small steps until he reached the branches. Avalon wondered if she had the strength to pull herself up as Kensington had, but she was not willing to try and fail in front of her men.

"Ready the ground!" a soldier yelled from the trees off to her left, and Avalon heard more arrows in flight as Jakon and Davev ran by her toward the danger. Avalon turned to make chase at the same time a Runner came careening out of the elbagrass. She saw his massive chest and the disturbing tattoos on his face and tried to dive out of the way. His beastly frame almost collided with Avalon, but Taggerty had drawn his sword and he cut the man across the stomach. His legs coupled with Avalon's and she tumbled to the ground, the air knocked from her lungs as they smashed together.

"Davev!" Taggerty yelled, calling the soldier back. "Are you all right?" Taggerty asked Avalon as he pushed the huge man off her. He leaned down and grabbed Avalon's arm. He was talking to her but looking into the elbagrass, anger and concern playing on his face.

"Yes," Avalon answered. She sucked in air and knew that she would have several bruises but she felt no real injury. When she looked down she saw blood splattered across her clothing and it frightened her. The Runner that had just died half on top of her was as big as Jakon. Avalon recognized the huge beast-like figure of the Monarch's personal soldiers, and she shuddered.

"King Avalon!" Davev yelled as he approached and saw the blood. Jakon was on his heels and they both watched as Avalon let Taggerty pull her up.

"The king is not hurt," Taggerty said. "Guard this location," he commanded, and then he pulled Avalon into the woods.

"Where are we going?" Avalon asked.

"We will wait for Kensington to report. It won't take long. Stay close." Avalon drew her sword and kept right on Taggerty's heels, the blue light from the elbagrass making moving in the woods at night a simple task this close to the field. They crouched down and she could see Jakon and Davev spread out fifteen feet as they waited for more soldiers to come out of the field. In less than two minutes, Avalon saw Kensington slide down the bottom of the tree. Taggerty whistled as he ran toward Kensington and Avalon followed without a word.

"They are coming from the middle, but we can't see where from. They don't seem to have a plan, and none of them seem to be following anyone else. We are cutting them down where we can see them, but some are getting through. I'm worried that with this large expanse of terrain, our small numbers won't contain them for long."

"How are our men?" Avalon asked.

Kensington drew his sword and stood on the other side of Avalon to watch the field. "They are holding their own where they can see the enemy emerging from the grass. It's the ones who come out where we don't have a man that concerns me. They could flank our men or worse, make for Fontanasia."

"But how are they coming over?" Avalon asked. "We have the window. The grass on their side is poisonous right now." Kensington shrugged knowing the least about their situation with the window and how the magic worked.

Taggerty ran over to the soldier he had killed. He knelt down and pulled off the man's boot, smelling the black soot that was stuck to the boots and the pants. Avalon and Kensington followed and Jakon and Davev closed ranks around them, facing the field in a ready stance. "They are using the Anthracites as a bridge," Taggerty said, looking up at Avalon. "This is bad, Your Highness. They will be coming in force with nothing to stop them."

Avalon looked up into the tall, blue grass and clenched her teeth. There had to be a way to stop the flow of soldiers. There was a whole night of darkness before daylight would make the field of grass poisonous again, but hundreds or perhaps thousands of men could cross over in that time. Avalon heard the clash of metal swords, and she heard the wisp of arrows being loosed above her from the tree stands into the field. She looked down at the boot that Taggerty held in his hand, and she had her answer. "Burn it," she said, and her throat ran dry.

Taggerty looked at the boot with a question on his face. "Burn the boot?" he asked.

Perhaps the thought of Hawker had made her think of fire, she wasn't sure. Avalon took the boot and rubbed it on the ground so the black soot made a black, chalk line. She took a striker from her pocket and the sparks lit the black powder on fire. It flared and crackled just as she had seen it do in the dungeon of Cormicks.

"Set fire to the elbagrass. Burn it all," she said heavily, disgusted with her solution but carrying in her decision the life of every person in Fontanasia.

"We can't burn it. It's our only protection, the only barrier between Cormicks and us. There has to be another way," Taggerty said.

"The protection this field brings has been compromised. It's an open gate that needs to be closed. All that matters is tonight."

"The king is right," Kensington said. "They will have to turn back from the flames."

Taggerty nodded. "Jakon, Davev, tell the archers on the far side to light their arrows and torch the field. I will be going through here, so make sure they don't hit me." Both men nodded and took off in opposite directions to skirt the edge of the field and alert the men on the platforms on both sides at the same time.

"You aren't going through," Avalon said.

"Who knows what Hawker looks like better than me?" he answered, his daring smile ready on his face. He drew his knife and pulled three alleya leaves from their low stems at the bottom of the elbagrass and chewed the bitter foliage down.

Avalon's eyebrows perked up. No one knew what her Uncle Hawker looked like better than her, but Taggerty stopped her before she could start.

"Not a chance, Your Grace," Taggerty said before she could make her move into the field. Avalon let out a sigh and looked at Kensington. He had spent two months with Hawker and knew what he looked like, but as much as Avalon didn't want to chance losing Taggerty, she couldn't send Kensington into harms way. Her sister would never recover if she lost him.

"A torch," Taggerty said, and Kensington scrambled to the base of the tree where there were several waiting to be used.

"Don't do this," Avalon begged. "The fire will stop them."

"I need to get rid of the Anthracites. I'll be right back." His smile danced in the flame of the torch that Kensington handed him, and Taggerty turned and plunged into the elbagrass.

"Wait!" Avalon yelled, her high-pitched voice not disguised by her fake king voice, but he was gone, and Kensington was holding Avalon's arm so that she wouldn't follow. Avalon watched the torch over the tops of the grass. There she could see it stop and then start again, getting smaller as Taggerty pressed on through the grass away from her. Large patches of fire popped up and she knew he was stopping to light the grass around him on fire.

"King Avalon," Kensington beckoned. He had been watching the torch too, watching his friend sacrifice his life for Fontanasia.

Avalon grit her teeth, but for once she did not ask herself what her father would do. She thought of Walthan dying in the elbagrass. She thought of his dead eyes next to the pond that was letting her enemy in right now. She had to set it ablaze.

"King Hall?" Kensington asked with urgency, and Avalon stopped trying to pull against him.

"Burn it all," Avalon whispered.

"Yes, Your Highness." Kensington turned away from her, and Avalon thought of running after Taggerty the moment Kensington left with her order, but he didn't leave her side.

"You," he barked to the nearest guard. "Set the grass on fire. Burn it all. Tell these towers to send flaming arrows, but aim clear of where you see that torch in the field. Go now!"

Avalon was grateful that it was Kensington calling out the orders. He was a natural. She was also grateful that he hadn't left her. She was the king, not an impulsive girl, and she belonged to her people. She watched the first of the fiery flaming arrows fly over the bright blue grass. She saw the blue light that glowed over the field turn yellow. She watched the beautiful sea of grass burn, and she would never forgive herself for any of it.

Hawker stood on the ground and watched as the Monarch descended the ladder behind him. He was coming down to gloat to the White Robes. He was in his glory, still calling out to encourage his men as they climbed up the Anthracites and ran off into the darkness. The White Robes all smiled, their eyes squinting up in an evil satisfaction, but Hawker could see that some of them were still testing the waters between Hawker and the Monarch and watching what each would do. Hawker was pleased at this because even though it looked like the Monarch would succeed in getting across to Fontanasia, their reaction showed Hawker that some of the counselors were still willing to accept a new leader.

A horrible screeching noise rang out and it reminded Hawker of when he had set a cat's tail on fire, but this screeching was deafening. Everyone instinctively covered their ears and looked toward the field, but no one could see far enough in to know what was going on. There were blood-curdling screams heard between the piercing screeches as the flow of soldiers that was going up and over the Anthracites turned, and men began jumping from the Anthracites in retreat. The Monarch ran to the bottom of the Anthracite bridge and tried yelling at his soldiers to turn back, but they were leaping for their lives and running toward the trees. Hawker had followed the Monarch and he could see the gray shadows of men pushing and shoving each other from the huge rock figures, some men spilling off into the deadly elbagrass. He didn't know what was happening, but he did know this was his chance. He walked back to the covered tent where the White Robes waited.

Hawker had been the willing prisoner since he had walked into Cormicks, but after tonight he knew he would be ruler or he would be dead. Instead of leaning to one side as he had practiced his entire life, Hawker stood to his full height and squared his shoulders. He looked directly at each White Robe in turn, and he looked at the tattooed beasts who guarded each of these counselors. They were brutes, but Hawker knew they would only do what their masters commanded, and he was not in danger of any of these men unless he could not win the throne.

There was a third loud screech and the Anthracites began their slow crackling rise into the sky. Hawker could see balls of fire falling as soldiers who had somehow caught fire were thrown from the Anthracites. Hundreds of men who could not make it back to safety fell and were either trampled or poisoned as the three black monsters stomped from the deadly field. The top of the Anthracite that came last was snapping and crackling with fire, and it free-fell onto a large boulder that sat at the edge of the field, crushing all of the men in his path. The crackling piece of rock broke free from the beast and crashed into the trees starting some of the brush on fire. The light from the small fires showed the outline of the Anthracite as it rose from the ground again with a screeching that made Hawker cover his ears. The black powder that fell away crackled into nothing and the Anthracite stormed off shaking the ground as it went.

Most of the noise went with the Anthracites, and now the screams of individual men could be heard as they lay dying from their wounds. The Monarch watched in despair as the flow of returning men came to a stop. He waited and watched as men stumbled from the grass and fell over dead from the poison. A few soldiers returned from the field, somehow smart enough to walk over the dead bodies of their fallen comrades to make it back alive.

Hawker looked again at each of the White Robes and nodded his head slowly. None of them said a word, and he knew that they would watch in silence as he challenged their leader. The Monarch screamed at the top of his lungs and clenched his fists, turning from the destruction and walking to the edge of the covered tent to face his advisors.

"You are defeated?" Hawker asked slyly.

"I am just getting started," the Monarch yelled back at Hawker. He turned and climbed the ladder up onto the edge of his platform to survey the damage in the grass. His men were dead and dying, the Anthracites had retreated, and he had no idea really what was happening. Where had his men disappeared to, and where had the fire come from? Was there a city under this field?

On the ground under the platform, Hawker spoke up. "I sent you the warrior Brick. I sent you the head of young Prince Avalon. I gave you the door to Fontanasia, and all you had to do was go through and conquer." Hawker paused for effect, and his nose twitched. "You are disgraced!"

The Monarch was down the ladder before Hawker was finished talking. He took three long steps and lifted his massive arm to wring Hawker's neck. Hawker hadn't taken his eyes off of the White Robes, but his hand slid under his worn black robe and he pulled the small knife that was hidden in the design of his belt buckle. He twisted at the last moment and his long arm turned the knife into the Monarch's chest just as the Monarch reached for Hawker's neck. There was a cracking sound as the knife broke through the Monarch's sternum. The force of the blow pushed the air from the Monarch's lungs, and as the knife pierced his heart, he slipped down to the ground. Hawker casually ripped off the Monarch's sword belt. He watched the Monarch drop to his feet, blood pooling from his chest.

The Anthracites and dying soldiers had thrown the Runners into disarray. The Monarch's death had happened so quickly that the Monarch's guards hadn't fully reacted. By the time they stepped in, the White Robes had signaled their man-dogs to protect Hawker. Huge men rushed in from all sides and then stopped in front of each other as the

Monarch let out a last gurgling breath. Hawker kicked the Monarch's body away and looked at the men around him. Then, he opened his arms as though welcoming them to his home.

"I am your humble servant," Hawker said to the White Robes, their round, bald faces looking at him and then to each other. There was silence while the small men calculated their future, the beasts ready to fight at a second's notice. Finally, one of the oldest White Robes stepped forward.

"Your name is Hawker. It comes from Hawkerness, the long defeated city of your people."

"My people," Hawker spat in contempt, and then he smiled. "You are my people," he concluded for them. He turned his heels slowly into the dirt to ready himself in case they had their men attack, but no one moved. The old man nodded slowly, turning to the other men who, with raised eyebrows, were racing the possible odds and outcomes through their minds.

"What is your purpose, Prince Hawker?" the White Robe with the triangle tattoo asked.

Hawker's eyes twitched for a moment and rolled back into his head as he looked up at the black moon above. "I am not a prince, I am your king. You may address me as King Hawker. I have slain your Monarch, and in that act I so take his place. This is your tradition, is it not?" This was his moment. This was the crux of his plan, and on this cold night Hawker felt the heat of his blood streaming through his veins.

The old man raised an eyebrow to Hawker, and then without turning away, he looked back at the other men. "We are content in our positions, are we not?" he asked. Each man nodded in turn and signaled their guards to stand down. In one motion, all of the White Robes bowed their heads to Hawker, and their guards took a few steps back and knelt. Hawker took a deep breath in, and for the first time in his life, his heart filled with great pleasure.

Chapter 17
Ashes

Two weeks later just after dusk, Taggerty walked out of the ashes. Avalon and Kensington heard excited voices in the distance and ran from the tent to see Jakon and Davev patting Taggerty on the back. His Uncle Chylyn had descended from the tree platform and showed no restraint as he outright hugged Taggerty.

Avalon wanted to burst into tears and run to hug Taggerty herself, and that thought stopped her in her tracks. Aside from the ashes that clung to his boots, he looked no worse for his ordeal. He actually looked healthy and ready for anything, like he had been out for a stroll and happened upon their camp. He was wearing a long blue robe over his clothes, and Avalon could see the bulges of multiple weapons. He was smiling and patting the backs of his friends as more men gathered around him. Kensington looked at Avalon and back at Taggerty, and Avalon saw a look of curious caution cross his face.

"King Avalon, please return to your tent. I will have Taggerty clean up and then come and report his findings."

"That will be fine," Avalon croaked as she took one last look at Taggerty. She turned and walked as fast as she could to her tent, hitting her knees as soon as the flap was closed, and crying as quietly as she could as the despair ran out of her and joy took its place. She had not lost Taggerty forever, and it was more than her heart could bear. She was ready to tell him, from her own lips, that she was in love with him. She was ready to step down from the throne and live in exile if it meant that she could be with him. Avalon felt small feet moving on her back, and she knew that Jackie had climbed on top of her. She sat up slowly and allowed Jackie to scamper over her shoulder and down into her waist pocket.

"Your Highness, it is Taggerty," she heard and then the tent flap moved.

"Enter," she called in reaction. He wasn't supposed to just barge in, he was supposed to wait for his king to answer. Avalon leapt to her feet, and in five short strides Taggerty was in her tent and standing within arms reach. He stopped and bowed deeply.

"King Avalon," Taggerty said softly. "I did not mean to distress you."

Avalon's hands made it up to her red cheeks. She was devastated that he was seeing her like this, and she prayed that Kensington was not close behind him. Avalon's eyes were swollen from crying, and salt water still swam on her cheeks and in her mouth. She sighed heavily and regained control, crossing to the small basin of water afforded her each day. She bent forward and submerged her face for a moment, letting the cool water calm her nerves. Once she had wiped her face clean, she crossed to the table and placed Jackie on it, leaving him to scamper to the nearest bowl of food.

"Please," she said, offering Taggerty a chair at the table.

"I already ate," he said. "But thank you," he followed as an afterthought. His shoulders were slumped forward and he was leaning toward her as though he would reach out and take Avalon in a hug, but he remained frozen like a statue. Avalon stayed where she was too, staring at Taggerty, her heart full of joy that he was alive. She remained silent for a moment not wanting to break the spell between them, but reality was pushing down on them with force, and she took a seat at the table.

"Tell me what you saw," Avalon croaked, keeping control of her emotions.

Taggerty looked down at his hands. "I set fire to men," he whispered. Then he cleared his throat and said, "I set fire to Runners at the window as they were crossing over, and that was the end of the battle for us and them." His forehead moved between crumpled concentration and relaxed calm, and Avalon knew that Taggerty was remembering the vision of the men he had killed. She remembered the mouse's tail as it ran and screeched, and she couldn't imagine the sight of a man on fire. She gave him a minute to work it out in his head and he continued when he was ready.

"The Runners who retreated into the pond didn't know to eat the alleya leaf, so they were dead already." He was talking in a calm voice, laying out the facts, trying to separate himself from them. "I waited as long as I could, and when the grass around me started to burn, I had to cross over. The Anthracites had caught fire and were already gone taking the soldiers with them. There were so many soldiers dead in the grass as I walked. They must have fallen off the Anthracites. It was like a road of bodies straight out of the field to the enemy. I got as close as I dared, but I was safe. No one was looking toward the field anymore, and if they were, they didn't really expect to find anything alive in there."

Avalon sat forward, her elbows on her knees. She closed her eyes and looked down at the ground trying to imagine everything Taggerty was telling her. She could hardly imagine the carnage Taggerty had witnessed.

"I heard Hawker, King Avalon. He was there, and he killed the Monarch." Avalon could not feel bad about that. The Monarch had plagued her thoughts for a year, and she had no use for him. Still, the Monarch didn't know how to find Fontanasia without Hawker, and she knew that Hawker would be a cunning adversary. She wondered how she could defend herself against someone who knew everything about Fontanasia. She felt a small victory in setting fire to the field even if it slowed Hawker down for only a little while.

"I saw small men in white robes with Hawker, and they looked like some sort of council. They all pledged themselves to his rule without contest. It was very strange." Avalon looked up at Taggerty and he seemed to be trying to find answers in the air. He shook his head to clear his mind. He had walked from the ash field so confidently, but Avalon could now see the strain in his eyes and weariness on his face.

"After Hawker announced that they would return to Cormicks so he could begin his reign as king, I moved out of the grass. Staying alive and safe was easy. They left the area the next day and I didn't see anyone after that. There was food and clothing left behind, and I collected as much as I could. They left their dead lying as they were, hundreds of men, and it's going to take a long time to erase that memory from my mind." Avalon was sure that Taggerty would never forget.

"Did you see anyone that you recognized?" Avalon asked. She still felt certain that Hawker had to have more help than just Brick and the old librarian.

"No one," Taggerty answered.

"And you are sure?" Avalon asked again.

"I saw all of the counselor's faces, and I did not see anyone I recognized. Their guards are very large and tattooed all over, and no one I know comes close to their physiques except maybe Jakon."

Avalon nodded and leaned back in her chair. She felt certain that if there was anyone working with Hawker, they would be with him now, but she remembered the White Robes and the guards, and Taggerty would easily be able to tell the difference. She could see Hawker in her mind, sniveling, nose twitching, playing the king for all he was worth. Avalon could not fathom that he was a warrior in any way. He was a bookworm and quiet on the outside. He seemed to truly love Zaria and Avalon, and he was a liar. She felt a familiar ache in her throat, but there were no longer tears attached to the regret she felt. She clenched her teeth and turned her attention to Jackie who was sound asleep on the table in the empty bowl where Avalon had placed three grapes for him.

"You must leave this place," Taggerty said. "I could not bear if anything happened to you." Avalon looked up at Taggerty and saw so much concern in his eyes that it warmed her heart. Zaria had told the truth, and he was doing more than protecting his king. Taggerty truly had feelings for her.

"As much as I like to argue with you," Avalon said with a feigned smile that left her face just as quickly, "you are right. I need to get back to Fontanasia and make an army of the people."

Taggerty nodded slowly. "You can leave me some of the men and take the rest back. They will have to help train and ready the city."

"Leave you?" Avalon asked as she jumped to her feet. "You are coming back with me."

"I am staying here. I need to plan for Hawker. The Guides will send some men back to work with us. Kensington can work with Gamon and the other men in preparing the city." Avalon was shaking her head, but she knew that it was a good plan. She had to bring Kensington back to Fontanasia to marry Zaria in a matter of weeks, and Kensington needed to return for that if nothing else.

Avalon would not speak the words. She pursed her lips and nodded. Taggerty stepped closer and bowed low. She wanted to reach out and put her hands in his tight curly black hair. She wanted to lift his face and pull him close to kiss his lips. She wanted so many things, but she stood frozen.

Taggerty looked into her eyes and tried to smile, but he had seen too much, and he was too tired to put forth his typical charm and wit. He knelt fast in front of her and Avalon sucked in her breath. Taggerty took her hand and pulled it toward his mouth, kissing the king's ring, but then taking a moment to kiss the back of her hand, the way she had seen Kensington kiss Zaria's hand. She let out a long breath and then the warmth of his hand and his lips were gone, and Taggerty left without another word.

In the end, Avalon was forced to leave Taggerty with thirty soldiers and some of the Guide who had been at the window for a long time. They would set up what defenses they could and keep a constant watch over the field of gray ash. Avalon was scared to leave anyone so close to danger, but she was more afraid for her sister and Myra, and the people of her city. If Hawker could build an army and return, he would take them straight into battle at the walls of Fontanasia. As much as she despaired leaving Taggerty, she knew that he was right. This was all much bigger than just their lives.

She also said goodbye to Jackie, her faithful pet. Taggerty refused to take Jackie at first, and Avalon had given orders that no one should pass through the window again, but she wanted Taggerty to keep the tiny red lizard for her. They both knew that on the other side of the window Jackie would morph into a beast larger than two horses, and she wanted him in a place where he might help if needed. Taggerty agreed but said he would bring Jackie back to the castle next month when he would return for Kensington and Zaria's wedding.

As she walked back through the forest with Kensington at her side, all Avalon could think about was how to stop Hawker before he got started. Taggerty had said that hundreds of Runners had died, and she hoped this meant Hawker would have to take months out to train more soldiers. It was still not enough time because Kensington would also need time to train the people of Fontanasia. The soldiers already walked atop the outer walls of the city, but they needed to start using the Fingers that Walthan had devised. They would have to understand how to keep the enemy out of the city, and needed a plan of action in case they broke through.

Avalon had left her tent behind and when she wanted privacy now, she took her leave of Kensington and wandered off on her own. She was less nervous around the men. She didn't know what would happen if she were exposed, but she could see a studied solemnity on the other's faces and they weren't paying close attention to their king. They were thinking about the enemy that they hadn't known existed and of the bright blue field of grass burning in the night, and they were thinking of their families just as Avalon had been.

When they reached the ravine, they greeted the four soldiers they had left behind and they were met with grave looks at the small party returning. Kensington pulled the men together and explained the danger, and they volunteered to stay and guard the ravine with orders to cut the rope bridge at all cost if the enemy was seen. Jakon had remained with Taggerty, and Davev was ordered by Kensington to command this new post. Where he had felt shunned when forced to leave his cousin in danger at the window, Davev was happy with the new order. He would protect the path to Fontanasia at any cost.

Avalon pulled Davev aside and handed him the pouch of keeley dust. The Guides watched as she instructed Davev of what the dust would do to the sand eels. She didn't have to say much, he had already seen on the way over.

"That was a gift to Taggerty, and he made it a gift to the king. He would not like to see you taking chances," Chylyn told her.

Avalon nodded but she disagreed. "Taggerty would want to make sure that the last man across this ravine makes it back to Fontanasia to warn us of the enemy's approach." Chylyn nodded slowly and Avalon knew he was still concerned for her.

"Then we will rest our legs and eat before crossing. We will need to be nimble to get across safely." He smiled and shared some berries with Avalon. When the time came, she patted her pocket remembering that Jackie wasn't there, and then she mounted the rope net to climb down into the ravine.

Although Avalon and all the other men had heavy hearts their minds were focused on the sand eels at the bottom of the ravine, and they crossed with no problems. Avalon climbed the net on the other side focusing all her strength on her arms and legs. They rested on the side of the ravine filling their canteens and having a small bite to eat. Kensington left two more soldiers with the two that were here already, and one of the Guide remained as well. He knew that the two who had seen the elbagrass would have plenty of time to share their story with the two that had not, and he left them with short orders to make sure the enemy did not get across.

Avalon tried to strike up a conversation with the Guides as they traveled back through the woods. She had walked them away from the soldiers and had spoken discreetly because she did not want the soldiers to know that Hawker was still alive. She wanted to know what the Guides thought of Hawker being the king of Cormicks. Avalon was looking for advice and she felt that she had left her best advisor behind.

"You should not be worried about a battle that has not taken place yet," Chylyn told her. "You need to take one step at a time. What will you tell the people of Fontanasia when you return with only half of their sons? Will you tell them the truth?"

This statement hit Avalon hard. She didn't know what she would tell her people. In the end Avalon decided to wait until after Zaria and Kensington's marriage to make any announcement. She decided that she would speak to any of the families that came to her asking about their husbands or sons who were still away, and when they reached the edge of the forest, she spoke with the small group of soldiers before they made that last half days journey back to Fontanasia.

"You are loyal to me but you are also loyal to your families and to each other. I will not ask you to lie, but I will ask you to keep your tongues. We all have a lot to think about, and we need to band together so that we are ready if this enemy approaches us." Avalon saw Kensington and several of the other soldiers nodding their heads in agreement. They all carried a look of great concern. Their lives had changed forever whether or not the enemy ever got to their gates, just as Avalon's life had changed the moment she had seen Cormicks. There was a world beyond their world. They had lived all these years in ignorance, and they were each trying to reconcile that in their own way. Avalon was sure that these men would be silent until she could figure out how to tell the people. They were probably wondering if anyone would believe the story. If they had not seen it with their own eyes, they would not have believed it.

They returned to the castle late on purpose so that there would not be many people out to watch their return. Avalon rode on horseback up the center of the Fingers as she had every day of her sword training. She grit her teeth as she looked at her city. There was no room left in her life for trivial things.

She was not surprised to see Julius Creighton waiting for her as they rode into the compound where the King's Guard lived. She could see Creighton's eyes pass over her and the remaining men and she knew he was counting, and she knew what his half smile meant when he squinted and nodded at her. Creighton waited for her near the passageway to the castle.

"Come," she said to Creighton as he walked slowly behind her. Avalon led Counselor Creighton up to her study. Her journey was making her short-tempered, and Avalon longed to go to her chambers and spend some time alone. She hadn't realized how much of a toll her nerves had taken protecting her secret on this journey. She had spent a month in full view of her soldiers, and even in her tent she had felt on display. She was exhausted.

Avalon sat behind the table used for writing and offered Creighton a seat opposite her. "You have been waiting for my return. Tell me, what could not keep one more night? Is Counselor Nelson well?" Avalon asked.

"He is healing and will recover to a great percentage of his original capacity." Creighton sounded as though he was bartering for a horse and he seemed impatient, so Avalon gave him leave to speak.

"What is it?" she asked.

"I have very little to report, King Avalon. I was hoping that you could tell me about your trip. You have returned with only half of the men you left with."

"Less than half," Avalon retorted. In less than ten minutes of her return, he was making her feel defensive again because she felt compelled to answer him. "They are all alive save one Guide who was killed before we arrived at the window."

Creighton stood and reached into his robe pulling at a long tube and Avalon jumped up in defense. Her chair slid back and hit the wall behind her. She placed one hand on the hilt of her sword.

"Still slow to trust? It is not a sword, King Avalon. It's the map," Creighton said calmly as he slowly pulled out the rolled up canvas. "I thought it ironic that you brought me here instead of your suite, but this map is meant to be in this room. It's where your father kept it."

Avalon let go of her sword and reached for the canvas. She felt its weight in her hands and walked around the small table to the larger worktable that her father used. She rolled out the map and then she let out a sigh. She looked at the ravine and noticed "The way down" printed on the map. She saw the field of blue, running her finger over the area and thinking of Taggerty and the two-dozen men she had left behind.

"It's Hawker, he has given us up to the Monarch."

"You saw Prince Hawker?" Creighton asked. Avalon had never admitted that Hawker was alive, but Creighton had hinted as much, and she could not deny it anymore.

"I didn't see him. He killed the Guide and crossed over to Cormicks," Avalon admitted. "Taggerty saw him. He is now King Hawker of Cormicks, and I fear that he will come for Fontanasia in due time." Avalon suddenly hit the table with her fist. She had just helped to stop an invasion, but she still felt defeated. "Counselor Creighton, I need you to treat me as your equal," she demanded.

"King Avalon, I would not presume to act as the equal to a king." He was using his typical verbal tap dance to change the meaning of the conversation, but he only offered a halfhearted smile.

"Julius," Avalon prompted. "You are most likely the smartest man in Fontanasia, and if you are to be a counselor, then I expect the best counsel that you have every time I ask something of you. In fact, don't wait to tell me anything that you think I need to know. I would like to think that there is no change coming to Fontanasia and that we can all go on as we always have, but some time next month or next year or in the next ten years, we both know that Hawker is coming for us, and I expect to be prepared."

Creighton moved back to the chair taking on the weight of the situation. Avalon had seen him play a slightly hunched weak man, but she had never seen him overcome as he was now. "I have a thousand questions, King Avalon," he said in a soft voice.

Avalon sighed heavily. "And I have a thousand more."

Chapter 18
Zaria's Day

Avalon waited in the hall outside of the king's suite. Zaria was inside with her bridesmaids undertaking their final preparations for the wedding ceremony, and Avalon wanted no part. She was here to escort Zaria to the chapel and to give her over to Kensington.

The door opened and four of Avalon's cousins came out. When they saw the king, they each bowed and Avalon smiled at them in turn. She knew them from childhood, but the distance she had kept from everyone in her family had taken its toll. They were courteous strangers and none stopped to talk to Avalon, but she didn't mind.

Avalon stepped to the door and pushed it open enough to see Zaria. She was in a white gown that was more flowing than any of her other ball dresses had been. She was wearing a special tiara in her hair, and Avalon wondered where she had gotten it when she noticed Myra sitting in a chair dabbing her eyes. Avalon stepped in and closed the door behind her.

"Well that's a dress you definitely don't have to set aside for me," Avalon said quietly. Zaria turned and smiled at her younger sister. "You are more beautiful than ever," Avalon said with genuine reverence. "I wish father could see you." They shared a moment of reflection.

"Do you like my hair?" Zaria asked running her hands over the jeweled piece that held her hair up.

"It's wonderful," Avalon said, admiring the tight bun pulled up in curls and again appreciating her own close-cropped cut.

Myra stood and took Zaria's hand. She held her other hand out to Avalon and they stood in a circle sharing the moment. "Myra, you look very nice today," Avalon reflected aloud. This was only the third time Avalon had seen Myra George out of her daily servant's uniform.

"Thank you, King Avalon. I hope you don't mind," Myra said. "That head piece was your mother's on the day she was married, and I just thought..."

"It's perfect," Avalon said with a smile. "Are you ready?" she asked Zaria.

"I am more ready than you know," Zaria answered. Myra gave Zaria and Avalon a gentle squeeze of the hand and then stepped back to dab her eyes again. Avalon cleared her throat and smiled in an effort to keep herself from shedding any tears. She knew her role today was that of a king and not a sister. She would give Zaria away in all the pomp and circumstance that she deserved. She had decided to look forward instead of back now. She had been king for over a year, and it was time for her to stop mourning her father. She would never stop regretting his death, but she needed to carry on where he had left off.

Avalon turned toward the door and held her arm out, but Zaria didn't take it. "I would like you to wear these gloves," Zaria said to Avalon and handed over a pair of blue leather gloves that looked new, but Avalon could tell that they were old. "But before you put them on, I would like you to return Jackie to his box."

"But you like him!" Avalon protested with a smile.

"There will be no pets at my wedding," Zaria countered with a smile of her own. Avalon conceded and walked to her room where she deposited Jackie on the nightstand next to the carved box. He scrambled around for a minute and then settled in his tiny bedding.

Avalon pulled on the large blue gloves, her own hands swimming inside the finger holes. She knew these were her father's gloves. Perhaps he wore them at his wedding and Myra had found them with the tiara. Avalon decided not to ask right now. She needed a happy and confident face and bringing up the past would not help. She took a deep breath in and escorted Zaria to the chapel, Myra straightening the train of the dress several paces behind. When they reached the outer doors, the King's Guard took their posts and the bridesmaids approached Zaria with glowing smiles. An attendant rushed away, and a moment later Avalon heard music playing.

"It's not too late to change your mind," Avalon said with a smile. Zaria looked down at Avalon and shook her head. "Good," Avalon said taking her arm again. "I have come to like Kensington very much." They entered the chapel at the front and Avalon saw that the small room was packed full of her extended family. Weddings were for family only, with friends attending the reception afterwards, and Avalon recognized some strange faces near the front. She knew that they must have belonged to Kensington's family, and she would meet them all in time.

Avalon was very surprised to see that seated just behind immediate family on both sides of the chapel were her counselors and their wives. Each of the counselors sat tall in their seats, and Avalon made eye contact with each of them as she walked Zaria in. She could tell that to a man, they were all pleased to have been invited to the ceremony.

Avalon gave a short nod in their direction and made a note to ask Zaria about that later.

All eyes were on Zaria as she moved next to Kensington. He was dressed like a prince, shined and sharp for the occasion. Kensington was all smiles and Avalon could see that he blushed a little when he took Zaria's hand. Zaria let out a small giggle and Avalon's heart filled with joy for her sister.

Avalon stole a moment to look at Taggerty. He was also dressed like a prince standing next to Kensington. Avalon swallowed hard. She wished deep down in her heart that she could find a future with Taggerty and gave up the wish just as quickly. Today she was grateful that her sister had found the love of her life. Kensington knelt and Avalon said, "Rise, my brother, and take your bride." Kensington rose and took Zaria's hand and they faced the people in the chapel. The vicar stepped forward and looked up at the couple.

"Do you have words to share?" he asked.

"We do," Kensington said. He turned to Zaria and grasped both of her hands. "Princess Zaria," he started, "my Zaria, you are the only love of my life. I pledge myself to you and to Fontanasia."

Zaria smiled and her beauty took the breath from everyone in the chapel. She seemed to be made for this moment. "Kensington, you are the love of my life. I pledge myself to you and to our families, that we may extend our love to all of those around us."

The vicar gave Kensington a sapling. "May you grow together as one, and may your love for each other never die."

Kensington leaned forward and kissed Zaria, a couple now married for life, and everyone in the chapel clapped and cheered. Princesses had been married into other families for centuries, but Avalon knew that she had no idea what the future would bring. She did not want to lose her sister to Kensington's family. Instead, she wanted to bring Kensington into her family. Before they could move away to greet their families, their cousin did as Avalon had asked of him the previous night. When the king nodded at him, the middle aged man stood and held up his hand.

"The King has something to say," he called and the small crowd settled in silence.

Avalon stepped toward the newly married couple and tried to ignore the tears hanging in Zaria's eyes. "Kensington, Zaria is now part of your family, as you are part of mine. We are brothers now." Avalon took a ring from her pocket. It was a large gold ring with the Hall crest engraved on the front. "You will take this and wear it. You represent the Hall family now." Kensington's mouth was open. He did not expect this, and he was awestruck.

"Avalon," Zaria muttered in surprise, touched by the gesture. Avalon smiled at her sister as Zaria placed the ring on Kensington's finger. The crowd in the chapel erupted in applause as Kensington bowed to the king.

They moved from the chapel to the Hall of Kings. The decor was magical and the celebration lasted half the night. Avalon danced with Zaria twice and even asked two of her cousins to dance to appease Zaria and to avoid being recommended to any of the young ladies who were watching the king with plotting eyes. Taggerty didn't approach Avalon until some of the guests were starting to leave. She had been watching him that evening, seeing who he talked to, feeling the slight ruffle of jealousy when one of the young ladies flirted with him. But Taggerty had remained uncharacteristically aloof this evening, and although she would hardly admit it to herself, Avalon knew why.

"King Avalon," he said with a slight bow. There was a coolness in his tone, and all of the emotion on their last meeting in the tent by the field of ashes was gone. She was glad he was reserved though. It was the only way she could keep her head in front of all of these guests.

"Taggerty, you made it back just in time for the wedding. You did not spare a minute," she said, knowing that he had returned late last night when he'd sent Kensington to deliver Jackie to her suite.

"I had just enough time to prepare for today."

When Avalon was certain no one was close enough to hear, she asked, "What news?"

"We have seen no one these weeks, so it is the best news possible."

Avalon nodded in agreement. Their true reality seemed too incredible to be comprehensible at such a lavish party.

"And better news. The elbagrass has regrown in full." Taggerty watched Avalon's eyes opened wide as she looked at him in humored disbelief. "It's true. On the first full moon, it grew back in one night, all of it. The wind and the rain has washed away some of the ash, and I think in a few more months it will look the same as the field that we saw for the first time last year.

Avalon was relieved to feel some protection from Hawker. They would be at full alert each night the grass glowed blue on either side of the window, but they had back the protection of the poison for every other night.

"Thank you," she said, swallowing back her tears.

Not able to spend the real time that she longed to spend with Taggerty in front of all of these people, she left him standing there and returned to her room. Mixed with joy for her sister and Kensington, and relief for the protection that the elbagrass provided, Avalon lie back on her bed and fell asleep fully dressed.

Avalon awoke and sat straight up. The room was pitch black, and she had been dreaming. A tingle of energy ran up her spine. The dream had seemed so real. The kiss had seemed so real.

"Taggerty?" she asked the darkness, but he wasn't here. It had been a dream after all. She touched her lips and tried to remember every detail, and then she smiled in relief. Avalon hardly ever dreamed in her sleep, but when she did, her dreams always came true. She trembled with anticipation and let out a long breath. She knew that within a week, Taggerty would finally kiss her.

Thanks for reading! If you loved the book and have a moment to spare, I would really appreciate a short review as this helps new readers find my books.

For the final book in the Avalon Hall trilogy, *Queen's Call*, please go to anitarenaghan.com where you can find more titles and join the email list to receive a free ebook.